SO-AET-522

FOOLS' GOLD

By the same author

Order of Darkness
Changeling
Stormbringers

The Cousins' War
The Lady of the Rivers
The White Queen
The Red Queen
The Kingmaker's Daughter

History
The Women of the Cousins' War:
The Duchess, the Queen, and the King's Mother

The Tudor Court Novels
The Constant Princess
The Other Boleyn Girl
The Boleyn Inheritance
The Queen's Fool
The Virgin's Lover
The Other Queen

Historical Novels
The Wise Woman
Fallen Skies
A Respectable Trade
Earthly Joys
Virgin Earth

The Wideacre Trilogy
Wideacre
The Favored Child
Meridon

ORDER OF DARKNESS

BOOK THREE
FOOLS' GOLD

PHILIPPA GREGORY

SIMON PULSE
New York   London   Toronto   Sydney   New Delhi

SIMON PULSE
An imprint of Simon & Schuster Children's Publishing Division
1230 Avenue of the Americas, New York, NY 10020
First Simon Pulse hardcover edition February 2014
Text copyright © 2014 by Philippa Gregory
First published in 2014 in Great Britain by Simon & Schuster UK Ltd.
Interior illustrations copyright © 2014 by Fred van Deelen
Jacket photograph copyright © 2014 by Steve Gardner, PixelWorks Studios
Jacket and title page art of dragon copyright © 2013 by Pale Horse Design
Jacket design by Regina Flath
All rights reserved, including the right of reproduction in whole or in part in any form.
SIMON PULSE and colophon are registered trademarks of Simon & Schuster, Inc.
For information about special discounts for bulk purchases, please contact
Simon & Schuster Special Sales at 1-866-506-1949 or business@simonandschuster.com.
The Simon & Schuster Speakers Bureau can bring authors to your live event.
For more information or to book an event contact the Simon & Schuster Speakers Bureau
at 1-866-248-3049 or visit our website at www.simonspeakers.com.
The text of this book was set in Plantin.
Manufactured in the United States of America
10 9 8 7 6 5 4 3 2 1
Full CIP data is available from the Library of Congress.
ISBN 978-1-4424-7690-5
ISBN 978-1-4424-7692-9 (eBook)

FOOLS' GOLD

RAVENNA, SPRING 1454

The four horse riders halted before the mighty closed gates of the city of Ravenna, the snow swirling around their hunched shoulders, while the manservant Freize rode up to the wooden doors and, using his cudgel, hammered loudly and shouted: "Open up!"

"You won't forget what to say," Luca reminded him quickly.

Inside, they could hear the bolts being slowly slid open.

"I should hope I can—though naturally truthful—tell a lie or two when required," Freize said with quiet pride, while Brother Peter shook his head that he should be so reduced as to depend on Freize's ready dishonesty.

The gateway pierced the great wall that encircled the ancient city. The defenses were newly rebuilt; the city had just been occupied by its conquerors: the Venetians, who were spreading their unique form of government—a republic—through all the neighboring cities, fueled by gold, driven by trade. Slowly the little sally-port door opened and a guard in the bright livery of the victors presented arms and waited for the travelers to request admission.

Freize launched himself into a mouthful of lies with ill-concealed relish. "My lord," he said, gesturing to Luca. "A young and wealthy nobleman from the west of Italy. His brother: a priest." He pointed to Brother Peter, who was indeed a priest but was serving as Luca's clerk and had never met him before they were partnered on this series of missions. "His sister is the fair young lady." Freize gestured to the beautiful girl who was Lady Isolde of Lucretili, no relation at all to the handsome young man but traveling with him for safety. "And her companion the dark young lady is riding with her." Freize was nearest to the truth with this, for Ishraq had been Isolde's friend and companion from childhood; now they were exiled together from their home, looking for a way to return. "While I am—"

"Servant?" the guard interrupted.

"Factotum," Freize said, rolling the word around his mouth with quiet pride. "I am their general factotum."

"Going where?" the guard demanded, putting out his hand for a letter that would describe them. Unblushingly, Freize produced the document sealed by Milord, the commander of their secret papal Order, which confirmed the lie that they were a wealthy young family going to Venice.

"To Venice," Freize said. "And home again. God willing," he added piously.

"Purpose of visit?"

"Trade. My young master is interested in shipping and gold."

The guard raised his eyebrows and shouted a command to the men inside the town. The great gate swung open as he stood deferentially to one side, bowing low as the party rode grandly inward.

"Why do we tell lies here?" Ishraq asked Freize very quietly, bringing up the rear as servants should. "Why not wait till we get to Venice?"

"Too late there," he said. "If Luca is going to pass for a wealthy young merchant in Venice, someone might ask after his journey. Someone may see us here at the inn. We can say we came from Ravenna. If they bother to enquire, they can confirm here that we are a wealthy family and hope that they won't trouble to look beyond, all the way from Pescara."

"But if they do trace us back, beyond Pescara, to the village of Piccolo, then they'll learn that Luca is an inquirer, working for the Pope himself, and you are his friend, and Brother Peter his clerk, and Isolde and I are no relation at all but just young women traveling with you for safety on our way to Isolde's kinsman."

Freize scowled. "If we had known that Luca's master would have wanted him to travel disguised, we could have started this whole journey with new clothes, spending money like lords. But since he only condescended to inform us at Piccolo, we have to take the risk. I will buy us some rich elegant capes and hats here in Ravenna and we'll have to get the rest of our clothes in Venice."

The guard pointed the way they should go, toward the best inn of the town, and they found it easily, a big building against the wall of the great castle, on the little hill above the market square. Freize jumped down from his horse and left him standing as he opened the door and bellowed for service for his master, then he came back out and held the horses while Luca, Lady Isolde and Brother Peter swept into the inn and ordered two private bedrooms and a private dining room, as befitted their great rank. Freize helped Ishraq down from her horse, and she went quickly after her mistress as Freize led all the horses and the pack donkey round to the stable yard.

As they settled into their rooms they could hear the bells of the churches chiming for Vespers all over the city, the air loud with their clamor, birds whirling into the sky from the many towers. Isolde went to the window, rubbed the frost away from the panes, and watched Brother Peter and Luca leave the inn and head toward the church through the occasional swirls of light snow.

"Aren't you going to church?" Ishraq asked, surprised, as Isolde was usually very devout.

"Tomorrow morning," Isolde said. "I couldn't concentrate tonight."

Ishraq did not need to ask her friend why she was so distracted. She only watched her gaze follow the young man as he strode down the cobbled street.

When the men came back from Mass they all dined together in the private room, Freize bringing up food from the kitchen. When he had spread all the plates: the pie, the pitadine—a sort of pancake with rich savory toppings—the venison haunch, the roast ham, the braised chicken and the sweetbreads on the table, he stood by the door, the very picture of a deferential servant.

"Freize: eat with us," Luca commanded.

"I'm supposed to be your general factotum," Freize repeated the grand word. "Or servant."

"No one can see," Isolde pointed out. "And it feels odd when you don't sit down. I'd like you to eat with us, Freize."

There was no need for her to repeat the invitation. Freize pulled up a chair, took a plate and started to serve himself generously.

"Besides, this way you'll get two dinners," Ishraq pointed out to him with a little smile. "One now, and one in the kitchen later."

"A working man needs to keep up his strength," Freize said cheerfully, buttering a thick slice of bread and sinking his white teeth into it. "What's Ravenna like?"

"Old," Luca remarked. "The little that I have seen of it so far. A great city, wonderful churches, as beautiful as Rome in some parts. But before we leave tomorrow I want to go to the tomb of Galla Placidia."

"Who's that?" Isolde asked him.

"She was a very great lady in ancient times, and she prepared herself a great tomb that the priest at church told me to go and see. He says it is very beautiful inside, with mosaics from floor to ceiling."

"I should like to see that!" Ishraq remarked and then flushed, anxious that Isolde would think that she was trying to get into Luca's company.

As soon as Isolde saw her friend's embarrassment she blushed too and said quickly: "Oh but you must go! Go with Luca while I pack our bags for the journey. Why don't the two of you go in the morning?"

Brother Peter looked from one red-cheeked girl to another as if they were troubling beings from another world altogether. "What on earth is the matter with you now?" he asked wearily.

"If you are to pass as my sister and Ishraq as your servant then you had both better come and see the tomb," Luca said, quite blind to the girls' embarrassment. "And surely Ishraq should always accompany you, Isolde, when you are walking around a strange city. You should always have a lady-in-waiting."

"And in any case, we can't go halfway across Christendom with you two carrying on like this," Freize said gently.

"Why, what's the matter?" Luca looked from one to another, noticing their confusion for the first time. "What's going on?"

There was an awkward silence. "We had a disagreement," Isolde said awkwardly. "Before we left Piccolo. Actually, I was in the wrong."

"You two quarrel?" Luca exclaimed. "But I've never known you to quarrel. What's it all about?"

Freize, who knew that they had quarreled over Luca, stepped into the silence. "Lasses," he said generally to the table. "Often upset about one thing or another. Highly strung. Like the little donkey. Think they know their own mind even when it's not quite right."

"Oh don't be ridiculous!" Ishraq said crossly. She turned to Isolde. "I should want everything to be as it was between us, and anything else will work itself out."

Isolde, her eyes on the table, nodded her fair head. "I am sorry," she said, her voice low. "I was utterly wrong."

"That's all right then," Freize said with the air of a man having brought about a diplomatic compromise in a difficult situation. "Glad I settled it. No need to thank me."

"You had better pray for patience," Brother Peter said crossly to the two girls. "God knows that I have to." He rose from the table and went solemnly out of the room. As the door closed behind him the four young people exchanged rueful smiles.

"But what was the matter?" Luca persisted.

Freize shook his head at him, indicating he should be silent. "Best left alone," he advised. "Like the little donkey when it has finally settled itself down."

"Anyway, it's over," Isolde ruled, "and we should go to bed as well."

As soon as she rose to her feet Luca held open the door for her and followed her out into the hall. "You're not upset with me, about anything?" he asked her quietly.

She shook her head. "I was quite at fault with Ishraq. She told me that she had held you in her arms for comfort, when you were grieving, and I was angry with her."

"Why would you be angry?" he asked, though his heart hammered in his chest, hoping that he had guessed her answer.

She raised her face and looked at him honestly, her dark blue eyes meeting his hazel ones. "Alas, I was jealous," she said simply. He saw her little, rueful, smile. "Jealous like a fool," she confessed.

"You were jealous that she held me in her arms?" he said very low.

"Yes."

"Because you and I have never held each other close?"

"Well, we cannot," she reasoned. "You are promised to the priesthood and I was born a lady. I can't go around kissing people. Not like Ishraq. She's free to behave as she wants."

"But you do want me to hold you?" He stepped closer and whispered the question against her blonde hair, so that she could feel the warmth of his breath.

She could not say the word, she merely leaned her head toward him.

Very gently, very softly, as if he was afraid of startling her, Luca put one arm around her slim waist and the other round her shoulders and drew her close. Isolde rested her head on his shoulder and closed her eyes to savor the intense pleasure that rushed through her as she felt the length of his lithe body against her and the strength in his arms as they tightened around her.

"Did she tell you I kissed her forehead?" Luca whispered in her ear, delighting in the touch and the rose-water scent of this young woman he had desired since the moment that he had first seen her.

She raised her head. "She did."

"Were you jealous of that too?"

There was a gleam of mischief in his eyes, and she saw it at once and smiled back at him. "Unfortunately, I was."

"Shall I kiss you as I kissed her? Would that make it fair?"

In answer she closed her eyes and raised her face to him. Luca longed to kiss her warm mouth but instead, obedient to his offer, he gently kissed her forehead, and had the satisfaction of feeling her sway, just slightly, in his arms, as if she too wanted for more.

In a moment she opened her dark blue eyes.

"Shall I kiss you on the lips?" Luca asked her.

It was a step too far. He sensed her flinch, and she leaned back so she could see his warmly smiling face.

"I think you should not," she said, but, in contradiction, her arms were still around his waist and she did not let him go. His arms held her close and she did not step back.

Slowly, he leaned forward, slowly her eyes closed, and she raised her mouth to his. Behind them the door opened and Freize came out with the dishes from dinner. He checked himself when he saw the two of them, enwrapped in the darkened hall. "'Scuse me," he said cheerfully, and went past them to the kitchen.

Luca rapidly released Isolde, who put her hands to her hot cheeks. "I should go to bed," she said quietly. "Forgive me."

"But you're not angry with Ishraq, nor upset with yourself anymore?" he confirmed.

She went to the stairs, but he could see that she was laughing. "I scolded Ishraq like a fishwife!" she confessed. "I accused her of loose behavior for allowing your kiss. And now here am I!"

"She'll forgive you," he said. "And you will be happy again."

She went up the stairs and turned back and smiled at him. He caught his breath at the luminous loveliness of her face. "I am happy now," she said. "I think I have never been as happy in my life as I am now."

In the morning, as Freize went out to buy new and beautiful capes and hats for their sea voyage to Venice, Brother Peter and Luca—holding to their pretense of being merchant brothers—and Isolde and Ishraq—as their sister and her companion—went to walk in the town of Ravenna.

It was a small city, tightly enclosed within the encircling walls, the great castle dominating the jumble of shabby roofs around the castle hill. The morning was bright and sunny, the early frost melting from the red-tiled roofs. Rising to the blue sky, at every street corner, were the tall bell towers of great churches. A shallow canal flowed into the very center of the town, where a market sold everything on the stone-built quay. The city had been the capital of the ancient kingdom, and the great stone roads running north and south and east and west across the whole of Italy crossed at the very heart of the old city.

The two girls hesitated beside the great church that towered over the area, admiring the rose-colored brick. "The church is what takes your eye, but the tomb I want to see is just here," Luca said, and led the way to a modest little building set to one side.

"This little place?" Isolde ducked under the low opening; Ishraq followed her, Brother Peter behind her. The building was in the shape of a cross, and they entered by the north door. For a moment they paused at the entrance of the tiny church and then as Isolde crossed herself, and bent her knee, Luca exclaimed at the explosion of color inside the modest building.

Every part of the arched interior was glistening, almost as if it had been freshly painted. The walls, the floor, even the curved ceilings were rich with bright mosaics. Isolde gazed around her in amazed delight; Ishraq could not take her eyes from the roof above their heads, which was deep-sea blue, studded with hundreds of golden stars. It was like a silk scarf sweeping over their heads and down into the arches on all four sides.

"It's beautiful!" Ishraq exclaimed, thinking how similar it was to the rich designs of the Arab world. "What is it? A private chapel?"

"It's not a church at all, it's a mausoleum," Brother Peter told her. "Built by a great Christian lady hundreds of years ago for her own burial."

"Look," Isolde said, turning back to the door where they had entered. A spacious mosaic over the doorway showed a warmly colored scene of the Good Shepherd, leaning on his crook, crowned with a golden halo and surrounded by his sheep. "How could they do this hundreds of years ago? The tenderness of the picture? See how he touches the sheep?"

"And that is the story of a Christian risking his life for the gospels," Brother Peter said piously, pointing to the opposite wall where a man was depicted running past the flames of an open fire, with a cross over his shoulder and an open book in his hand. "See the gospels in the library?"

"I see," Ishraq said demurely. In this exquisite and holy

place she did not want to tease Brother Peter about his devotion, or to express her own skepticism. She had been raised in the Christian household of Isolde's father, the Lord of Lucretili, but her mother had taught her to read the Koran. Her later education encouraged her to examine everything, and she would always be a young woman of questions rather than of faith. She looked around the glittering interior and then found her attention caught by a wash of color on some white mosaic tiles. Someone had glazed the open windows of the mausoleum, and one of the pieces of glass had been broken. The morning sunlight, shining over the chipped surface, threw colored rays on the white tiles and even on Ishraq's white headscarf.

"Look." Ishraq nudged Isolde. "Even the sunlight is colored in here."

Her words caught Luca's attention, and he turned and saw the brilliant spread of colors. He was dazzled by the rainbow shining around Ishraq's head. "Give me your scarf," he said suddenly.

Without a word, her eyes on his face, she unwrapped it, and her dark thick hair tumbled down around her shoulders. Luca handed one end to her and kept the other. They spread it out to catch the light from the window. At once the white silk glowed with the colors of the rainbow. Together, as if doing a strange dance, they walked toward the window and saw the colors become more diffuse and blurred as the stripes grew wider, and then they walked away again and saw that the brightly colored beam narrowed and became more distinct.

"The broken glass seems to be turning the sunlight into many colors," Luca said wonderingly. He turned back to the mosaic that he had been examining. "And look," he said to her. "The mosaic is a rainbow too."

Above his head was a soaring wall going up to the vault above them, decorated exquisitely in all the colors of the rainbow and overlaid with a pattern. Luca, his hands holding out Ishraq's scarf, nodded from the rainbow mosaic to the rainbow on the scarf. "It's the same colors," he said. "A thousand years ago, they made a rainbow in these very colors, appearing in this order."

"What are you doing?" Isolde asked, looking at the two of them. "What are you looking at?"

"It makes you think that a rainbow must always form the same colors," Ishraq answered her when Luca was silent, looking from the scarf to the mosaic wall. "Does it? Is it always the colors as they have shown here? In this mosaic? Don't look at the pattern, look at the colors!"

"Yes!" Luca exclaimed. "How strange that they should have noticed this, so many hundreds of years ago! How wonderful that they should have recorded the colors." He paused in thought. "So, is every rainbow the same? Has it been the same for hundreds of years? And if the chip of glass can make a rainbow in here, what makes a rainbow in the sky? What makes the sky suddenly shine with colors?"

Nobody answered him, nobody had an answer. Nobody but Luca would ask such a question; he had been expelled from his monastery for asking questions that verged on heresy, and even now, though he was employed by the Order of Darkness to inquire into all questions of this world and the next, he had to stay within the tight confines of the Church.

"Why would it matter?" Isolde asked, looking at the rapt expressions of her two friends. "Why would such a thing matter to you?"

Luca shrugged his shoulders as if he was returning to the real world. "Oh, just curiosity, I suppose," he said. "Just as we didn't know the cause of the great wave in Piccolo, we don't know what makes thunder, we don't know what makes rainbows. There is so much that we don't know. And while we don't know the answer, people think that these strange tricks of nature are carried out by witchcraft or devils or spirits. They frighten themselves into accusing their neighbors, and then it is my job to discover the truth of it. But I can't give them a simple explanation, for I don't have a simple explanation. But here—since whoever made these mosaics knew the colors of the rainbow—maybe they knew what caused them too."

"But why are you interested?" Isolde pursued. "Does it matter what color the sunset was last night?"

"Yes," Ishraq said unexpectedly. "It does matter. For the world is filled with mysteries, and only if we ask and study and go on discovering will we ever understand anything."

"There is nothing to understand, for it has already been explained," Brother Peter ruled, speaking with all the authority of the Church. "God set a rainbow in the sky as his promise to Man after the Flood. *I will set my bow in the clouds, and it shall be the sign of a covenant between me, and between the earth. And when I shall cover the sky with clouds, my bow shall appear in the clouds.*" He looked gravely at the young women. "That is all you need to know."

He turned his hard stare to Luca. "You are an inquirer of a holy Order," he reminded the younger man. "It is your duty and your task to inquire. But beware that you do not ask about things outside your mission. You are commanded by our lord and by the Holy Father to discover if the end of days is coming. You are not commanded to ask about every-thing. Some questions are heretical. Some things are not to be explored."

There was a silence as Luca absorbed the reproof from the older man.

"I can't stop myself thinking," Luca replied quietly. "Perhaps God has given me curiosity."

"Nobody wants to stop you thinking," Brother Peter said as he opened the low door to the mausoleum. "But Milord will have made it clear, when he hired you, that you are to think only inside the limits of the Church. Some things are not known—like the change of a man into were-wolf, like the cause of the terrible Flood—and it is right that you hold an inquiry into them. But God has told us the meaning of the rainbow in His Holy Word, we don't need your thoughts on it."

Luca bowed his head but could not stop himself from glancing sideways at Ishraq.

"Well, I shall go on thinking, whether your Church needs it or not," she declared. "And the Arab scholars will go on thinking, and the ancient people were clearly thinking too, and the Arab scholars will translate their books."

"But we are obedient sons of the Church," Brother Peter ruled. "And actually, what you think—as a young woman and an infidel—does not matter to anyone."

He turned and led the way out, and they obediently followed him. Isolde lingered in the doorway. "It's so beautiful," she said. "As if it were a freshly painted fresco, the colors so rich."

There was a little pause before Luca came out, and she

saw he was putting something in the pocket of his breeches, under the fold of his cape.

"What d'you have there?" Isolde whispered to him as Brother Peter led the way back to the inn.

"The chipped piece of glass," he said. "I want to see if we can make a rainbow with it, anywhere."

Gravely, she looked at him. "But isn't it God's work to make a rainbow? As Brother Peter just said?"

"It's our work," Ishraq corrected her. "For we are in this world to understand it. And like Luca, I want to see if we can make a rainbow. And if he is not allowed to do it, then I will try. For my God, unlike yours, has no objection to me asking questions."

Freize was waiting for them back at the inn, and they mounted up and rode the little way out of Ravenna alongside the silted-up canal to the port of Classe. The ferry-boat was waiting for them at the stone harbor wall; other merchant ships and the famous Venice galleys were tied up alongside.

"But do you have the courage to get on board?" Ishraq teased Freize, who had not been on board a ship since he had been swept away by a terrible storm.

"If Rufino my horse can do it, then I can do it," Freize

answered. "And he is a horse of rare courage and knowing-ness."

Ishraq looked doubtfully at the big skewbald cob, who looked more doltish than knowing. "He is?"

"You need to look beyond ordinary appearances," Freize counseled her. "You look at the horse and you see a big clumsy lump of a thing, but I know that he has courage and fine feelings."

"Fine feelings?" Ishraq was smiling. "Has he really?"

"Just as you look at me and you see a handsome down-to-earth straightforward sort of ordinary man. But I have hidden depths and surprising skills."

"You do?"

"I do," Freize confirmed. "And one of those skills is get-ting horses on board a boat. You may sit on the quayside and admire me."

"Thank you," Ishraq said, and sat on one of the stone seats that led into the harbor wall as he led all five horses and the little donkey to the wooden gangway that stretched from boat to quay.

The horses were nervous and pulled away and jibbed, but Freize was soothing and calm with them. Ishraq would not feed his joyous vanity by applauding, but she thought there was something very touching about the way the square-shouldered young man and the big horses exchanged glances, caresses and little noises, almost as if they were talking to each other, until the animals were reassured and followed him up the gangway to their stalls on the boat.

There were no other travelers taking the ship that day, and so when the horses were safely loaded, the four travelers took hunks of bread and pots of small ale for breakfast and followed Freize on board as the master of the ship cast off and set sail.

It took all day and all night to sail to Venice, going before a bitterly cold wind. The girls slept for some of the time in the little cabin below the deck, but in the early hours of the morning they came out and went to the front of the ship, where the men were standing, wrapped against the cold, waiting for the sky to lighten. Ishraq's attention was taken by a small sleek craft coming toward them on a collision course, moving fast in the dark water, a black silhouette against the dark waves.

"Hi! Boatman!" she called over her shoulder to the captain of the boat who was at the rudder in the stern of the boat. "D'you see that galley? It's heading straight for us!"

"Drop the sail!" the man bellowed at his son, who scurried forward and slackened the ropes and dropped the mainsail.

"Here! I'll help," Freize said, going back to haul the sail down. "What's he doing, coming at us so fast?"

The two girls, Brother Peter and Luca watched as the galley, speeding toward them, powered by rowers hauling on their oars to the beat of a drum, came closer and closer.

"A galley should give way to a vessel with sails," Brother Peter remarked uneasily. "What are they doing? They look as if they want to ram us!"

"It's an attack!" Luca suddenly decided. "It can't be an accident! Who are they?"

Brother Peter, squinting into the half darkness, exclaimed: "I can't see the standard. They're showing no light. Whose boat is it?"

"Freize!" Luca shouted, turning to the deck and grabbing a boat hook as the only weapon on hand. "Beware boarders!"

"Get the sail back up!" Brother Peter shouted.

"We can't outsail them," Ishraq warned.

A galley with a well-trained rowing crew could travel much faster than a lumbering ship. Ishraq looked around for a weapon, for somewhere that they could hide. But it was a little boat with only the stalls for the horses on deck, and a small cabin below.

Freize joined them, his club in his hand. He pulled a knife out of his boot and handed it to Ishraq for her defense. His face was grim.

"Would this be the Ottoman lord come back for us?" he asked Luca.

"It's not an Ottoman pirate," Luca said, staring at the oars biting into the waves as the galley came swiftly closer. "It's too small a craft."

"Then someone else is very eager to speak with us," Freize said miserably. "And it looks like we can't avoid the pleasure."

Slowly, as their little caravel came to a halt and wallowed in the water, the galley changed course and drew up alongside them. Two of the rowers got to their feet and threw grappling hooks upward at once, gripping the rail of the boat. Isolde resisted the temptation to throw them off as the rowers in the mysterious galley hauled on the ropes and drew in close.

Summoning their courage, Luca and Isolde looked down into the galley at the rowers, who were free, not chained, and at the man who stood in the stern.

"Who are you? And what do you want with us?" Luca demanded.

The commander at the back of the boat had drawn his cutlass. The cold light glinted on the hammered blade. He looked up at them both, businesslike. "I am commanded by the Lord of Lucretili to take that woman into my keeping," he said, pointing at Isolde. "She is the runaway sister to the great lord, and he has commanded her to come home."

"Your brother!" Ishraq exclaimed under her breath.

"I'm not her," Isolde said at once in the strong accent of a woman from the south. "I don't know who you are talking about."

The man narrowed his eyes. "We have followed your trail, my lady," he said. "From the convent where the lord your brother entrusted you to the good sisters, to when you fell in with these men of God, to the fishing village, to here. You were charged with witchcraft . . ."

"She was cleared!" Luca interrupted. "I am an inquirer for the Church, commanded by the Pope himself to discover the reasons for strange happenings in this world and to see the signs for the end of days. I examined her, and I sent my report to the lord of my Order. I have cleared her of any wrongdoing. She's not wanted by the law of the land nor of the Church."

The man shrugged. "She can be innocent of everything, but she's still the Lord of Lucretili's sister," he said flatly. "She's still his possession. If he wants her back, then no one can deny his rights to her."

"What does he want her for?" Ishraq asked, joining the two of them at the rail of the little ship. "For he was quick enough to get her out of the house when her father died, and quick enough to make an accusation that would have seen her burned to death. Why does he want her back now?"

"You too," the man said shortly. "The slave, Ishraq. I am

commanded to take you back too." He turned to Luca. "You have to give that one to me because she is a runaway slave and the lord is her master. And the lady has to be given to me because she is the Lord of Lucretili's sister and as much a part of his property as his chair or his horse."

"I am a free woman," Ishraq spat. "And so is she."

He shrugged as if the words were meaningless. "You're an infidel and she is his sister. She was at the disposal of her father and then, on his death, her brother. He inherited her like the cows in his fields. She's his property just like a heifer."

He turned his attention to Brother Peter. "If you prevent her coming with me, then you have stolen Lord Lucretili's property, his slave and his sister, and I will have you charged as a thief. If you keep her, you are guilty of kidnap."

Freize sighed. "Difficult," he remarked into the silence. "Because legally, you know, he's right. A woman does belong to her father or brother or husband."

"I don't belong to my brother anymore," Isolde suddenly asserted. She slipped her hand in Luca's arm and gripped his elbow. "We are married. This man is my keeper. I am his."

He looked from her determined face to Luca's set jaw. "Really? Is this so, Inquirer?"

"Yes," Luca said shortly.

"But you are a man of the Church? Tasked to inquire into the end of days and report to your Order?"

"I have broken my vows to the Church and taken this woman as my wife."

Brother Peter choked but said nothing.

"Wedded and bedded?"

"Yes," Luca said, gripping Isolde's hand.

There was a moment, and then the man shook his head. He smiled disbelievingly, looking up at them both. "What? You bedded her? Took her with lust, had her beneath you, made her cry out in joy? You two kissed with tongues and you caressed her breasts? You held her waist in your hands, and she gladly took you into her body?"

Isolde's face was blazing red with shame. Ishraq looked furious.

"Yes," Luca said unblinking. "We did all that."

"Kiss her."

"You can't . . ." Isolde began, but Luca turned to her and put a finger beneath her chin to raise her face, and then he kissed her slowly and deeply, as if he could not bear to move his mouth away from hers. Despite her embarrassment Isolde could not stop herself, her head tipped back, her arms came around his shoulders, they held each other, her hand on the nape of his neck, her fingers reaching into his hair.

Luca raised his head. "There," he said, a little breathlessly, when he finally let her go. "As you see. I do not hesitate to kiss my bride. We are husband and wife, she is my chattel now. Her brother has lost all his rights over her. She belongs to me."

Freize nodded sagely. "A wife must go with her husband. His rights come first."

Brother Peter's face was frozen with horror at the lies spilling out of Luca's mouth, but he said nothing.

The Lucretili man turned to him. "Am I supposed to believe this? What about you, Priest? Are you going to tell me you are married to the other one? Are you going to kiss her to prove it?"

"No," Brother Peter said shortly. "I live inside my vows."

"But these two are truly husband and wife? In the sight of God?"

Brother Peter opened his mouth. A little swell rocked the boat, and he put his hand on the rail to steady himself.

"You are their witness before God," the man reminded him. "I conjure you, in His name, to tell me the truth."

Brother Peter gulped.

"On your oath as a priest," the man reminded him. "The truth, in the sight of God."

Brother Peter turned to Isolde as she stood, her arm still around Luca's waist. "I am sorry," he said, his voice very low. "Very sorry. But I can't lie on God's name. I cannot do it."

She nodded. "I understand," she said quietly, and moved away from Luca as he let her go.

"He doesn't have to say anything," Ishraq spoke up. "I will bear witness."

The man shrugged. "Your word means nothing. You are an infidel and a slave and a woman. Your words are like birdsong in the morning. Too loud, and completely meaningless. Now"—he turned his attention briskly to Luca—"send both of the women over the side of the ship or I will order my men to board your craft, and we will take them by force."

Luca looked down; there were about a dozen men in the galley, fully armed. He glanced at Freize, who stoically hefted his cudgel. Clearly, they could fight, but the odds were heavily against them. They were certain to lose.

The commander turned to the boatman, who was grimly listening at the stern of the boat. "You are carrying stolen goods: these two women belong to the Lord of Lucretili. If I have to, I will board your ship to take them, and there may be damage to your ship or danger to you. Or you can give them up to me and there will be no trouble."

"I took them in good faith as passengers," the boatman shouted back. "If they are yours, they can go with you. I'm not responsible for them."

"There's no point fighting," Isolde said very low to Luca.

"It's hopeless. Don't try anything. I'll give myself up."

Before he could protest, she called down to the man in the galley below: "Do you give your word that you will take us safely to my brother?"

He nodded. "I am commanded not to harm you in any way."

She made up her mind. "Get our things," she said over her shoulder to Ishraq, who quickly went to the cabin and came out with their two saddlebags, tucking Freize's knife out of sight, into the rope at her belt.

"And what is to happen to me?" Isolde demanded. She beckoned Ishraq to go with her as she went to the prow of the boat. The commander gestured to Luca and Freize that they should haul his boat alongside, so that the young women could climb down over the rail and into the waiting ship.

"Your brother believes that you are trying to get to the Count of Wallachia for his help. He thinks you will try to get an army to come against him and claim your home. So he's going to marry you to a French count who will take you away and keep you in his castle."

"And what about me?" Ishraq asked as Luca, Freize and Brother Peter each took a grappling iron and, pulling on the ropes, walked the galley to the prow of the boat.

"You, I have to sell to the Ottomans as a slave, in Venice," the man said. "I am sorry. Those are my orders."

Luca, whose father and mother had been captured by an Ottoman slaving galley when he was just a boy, went white and gripped the rail for support. "We can't allow this," he said to Freize. "I can't allow it. We can't let this happen."

But Freize was watching Isolde, who had suddenly halted at the news that Ishraq would not be with her. "No. She comes with me," she said. "We are never separated."

The man shook his head. "My orders are clear. She is to be sold to the Ottomans."

"Be ready," Freize whispered to Luca. "I don't think she'll stand for that."

Isolde had reached the front of the ship. Stowed at her feet was an ax kept for emergencies—if a sail came down in a storm or if fishing nets had to be cut free. She did not even glance at it as she stepped up on the tightly knotted anchor rope, so that she could look down over the rail at the man who had come for her. "Sir, I have money," she pleaded. "Whatever my brother is paying you I will match, if you will just go back to him and say that you could not find us. Your men too can have a fee if you will just go away."

He spread his hands. "My lady, I am your brother's loyal servant. I have promised to take you back to him and sell her into slavery. Come down, or I will come and get you both, and your friends will suffer."

She bit her lip. "Please. Take me, and leave my friend. You can tell the lord my brother that you could not find her."

Wordlessly, he shook his head. "Come," he said bluntly. "Both of you. At once."

"I don't want any fighting," she said desperately. "I don't want anyone hurt for me."

"Then come now," he said simply. "For we will take you one way or another. I am ordered to take you dead or alive."

Freize saw her shoulders set with her resolve, but all she said was: "Very well. I'll throw my things down first."

The commander nodded and put a hand on the grappling iron's rope and drew his galley closer to their gently bobbing ship. Isolde leaned over the rail, holding the heavy saddlebag. "Come closer," she said. "I don't want to lose my things."

He laughed at the acquisitive nature of all women—that Isolde should be such a fool as to be still thinking of dresses while being kidnapped!—and hauled the galley in even closer. The moment that it was directly under the prow of the ship, Isolde dropped the saddlebag down to him. He caught it in his arms, and staggered back slightly at the weight of it, and at the same time she snatched up the hatchet and, with three or four quick, frenzied blows, hacked through the rope, which held the heavy ship's anchor against the side of the boat.

Solid hammered iron, it plunged downward, monstrously heavy, and crashed straight through the galley's light wood deck, and straight through the bottom of the galley, smashing an enormous hole and breaking the sides of the craft so the water rushed in from the bottom and from the sides.

In a second Ishraq had jumped to be at her side and had thrown her knife straight into the man's face. He took the blade in his mouth and screamed as blood gushed out. Luca, Freize and Brother Peter took the grappling irons and flung them onto the heads of the rowers below them as water poured into the galley and the waves engulfed the ship.

"Hoist the sail!" Luca yelled, but already the boatman and his lad were hauling on the ropes, and the sail bellied, flapped and then filled with the light wind, and the ship started to move away from the sinking galley. Some of the rowers were in the water already, thrashing about and shouting for help.

"Go back!" Isolde shouted. "We can't leave them to drown."

"We can," Ishraq said fiercely. "They would have killed us."

There were some wooden battens at the front of the boat. Isolde ran to them and started to haul on them. Freize went to help her, lifted them to the rail and pushed them into the water to serve as life rafts. "Someone will pick them up," he assured her. "There are ships up and down this coast all the time and it will soon be light."

Her eyes were filled with tears, she was white with distress. "That man! The knife in his face!"

"He would have sold me into slavery!" Ishraq shouted at her angrily. "He was taking you back to your brother! What did you want to happen?"

"You could have killed him!"

"I don't care! I won't care! You're a fool to worry about him."

Isolde turned, shaking, to Brother Peter. "It is a sin, isn't it, to kill a man, whatever the circumstances?"

"It is," he allowed. "But Ishraq was defending herself . . ."

"I don't care!" Ishraq repeated. "I think you are mad to even think about him. He was your enemy. He was going to take you back to your brother. He was going to sell me into slavery. He would have killed us both. Of course I would defend myself. But if I had wanted to kill him, I would have put the knife through his eye, and he would be dead now, instead of just missing his teeth."

Isolde looked back. Some of the crew had clambered back aboard the wreckage of their boat. The commander, his face still red with blood, was hanging on to the battens that she and Freize had thrown over the side.

"The main thing is that you saved yourself and Ishraq,"

Luca said to her. "And they'll have to report back to your brother, so you should be safe for a while. Ishraq was wonderful, and so were you. Don't regret being brave, Isolde. You saved all of us."

She laughed shakily. "I don't know how I thought of it!"

Ishraq hugged her tightly. "You were brilliant," she said warmly. "I had no idea what you were doing. It was perfect."

"It just came to me. When they said they would take you."

"You would have gone with them rather than fight?"

Isolde nodded. "But I couldn't let you be taken. Not into slavery."

"It was the right thing to do," Luca ruled, glancing at Brother Peter, who nodded in agreement.

"A just cause," he said thoughtfully.

"And your knife throw!" Luca turned to Ishraq. "Where did you ever learn to throw like that?"

"My mother was determined I should know how to defend myself." Ishraq smiled. "She taught me how to throw a knife, and Isolde's father, the Lord of Lucretili, sent me to the masters in Spain to learn fighting skills. I learned it at the same time as my archery—and other things."

"We should give thanks for our escape," Brother Peter said, holding the crucifix that he always wore on a rope at his waist. "You two did very well. You were very quick, and very brave." He turned to Isolde. "I am sorry I could not lie for you."

She nodded. "I understand, of course."

"And you will need to confess, Brother Luca," Brother Peter said gently to the younger man. "As soon as we get to Venice. You denied your oath to the Church, you told a string of untruths and"—he broke off—"you kissed her."

"It was just to make the lie convincing," Isolde defended Luca.

"He was tremendously convincing," Freize said admiringly, with a wink at Ishraq. "You would almost have thought that he wanted to kiss her. I almost thought that he enjoyed kissing her. Thought that she kissed him back. Completely fooled me."

"Well, I shall give thanks for our safety," the older man said, and went a little way from them and got down on his knees to pray. Freize went down the ship to speak to the boatman at the rudder. Ishraq turned away.

"It was not just to make the lie convincing," Luca admitted very quietly to Isolde. "I felt . . ." He broke off. He did not have words for how he had felt when she had been pressed against him and his mouth had been on hers.

She said nothing, she just looked at him. He was fascinated by the ribbon that tied her cape at her throat. He could see it fluttering slightly with the rapid pulse at her neck.

"It can never happen again," Luca said. "I am going to complete my novitiate and make my vows as a priest, and you are a lady of great wealth and position. If you can raise your army and it wins back your castle and your lands, you will marry a great lord, perhaps a prince."

She nodded, her eyes never leaving his face.

"For a moment back then, I wished it was true, and that we had married," Luca confessed with a shy laugh. "Wedded and bedded, as the man said. But I know that's impossible."

"It is impossible," she agreed. "It is quite impossible."

Some hours after, the sky slowly grew bright, and the five travelers got up from where they had been sitting at the back of the boat and went to the prow to look east, where the rising sun was turning the wispy clouds pink and gold with the dawn light. From the back of the boat the boatman called to them that they were entering the Lagoon of Venice, God be praised that they were safe at last after such a night, and at once they felt the movement of the ship quiet as the waves stilled. This inland sea, sheltered by the ring of outer islands, was as calm as a gently moving lake, so shallow in some parts that they could see the nets that fishermen had pinned just beneath the surface of the water, but deep channels wound around the islands, sometimes marked by a single rough post thrust into the lagoon bed.

Ishraq and Isolde gripped each other's hands as their little ship found its way through a dozen, a hundred, little islands, some no bigger than a single house and a garden, with a wherry or a small sailing boat bobbing at the quay. Some of the smaller islands were little forests and mudflats, occupied only by wading birds; some looked like solitary farms with one farmhouse and outbuildings with roofs thatched with reeds, the fields taking up all the space on the island. The bigger islands were bustling with people, ships loading and unloading at the stone quays, the chimneys of low houses bursting with dark smoke, and they could glimpse the red shine of furnaces inside the sheds.

"Glassworks," the boatman explained. "They're not allowed to make glass in the city because of the danger of fire. They're terrified of fire, the Venetians. They have nowhere to run."

As they drew closer to the city, the islands became more built up, bordered by stone quays, some with stone steps down to the water, the bigger ones with paved streets and some with little bridges linking them, one to another. Every house was surrounded by a garden, sometimes an orchard, every big house stood behind high stone walls, so that the travelers could just see the tops of the leafless wintry trees and hear the birdsong from the gardens.

"This is the Grand Canal now," the boatman said as the

boat went slowly up the wide, sinuous stretch of water. "Like the main road, like the biggest high street of the city. The biggest high street in the world."

The bigger houses were built directly onto the canal, some of them with great front doors that opened straight onto the water; some of them had a gate at the front of the house to allow a boat to float directly into the house as if the river were a welcome guest.

As Isolde watched, one of these water doors opened and a gondola came out, sleek as a black fish, with the brightly dressed gondolier standing in the stern and rowing with his single oar as a gentleman sat in the middle of the boat, a black cape around his shoulders and an embroidered hat on his head, his face hidden by a beautifully decorated mask that revealed only his smiling mouth.

"Oh! Look!" she exclaimed. "What a beautiful little boat, and see how it came out of the house?"

"Called a gondola," the boatman explained. "The Venetians have them like land dwellers have a litter or a cart to get about. Every big house has a water gate so that their gondola can come and go."

Isolde could not take her eyes from the beautiful craft, and the gentleman nodded his head and raised a gloved hand to her as he swept by.

"Carnival," Brother Peter said quietly as he saw the

magnificently colored waistcoat under the gentleman's dark cape and the brilliantly colored mask that covered his face. "We could not have come to the city at a worse time."

"What's so bad about the carnival?" Ishraq asked curiously, looking after the black gondola and the handsome masked man.

"It is twenty days of indulgence and sin before Lent," Brother Peter replied. "*Carnevale*, as they call it, is a byword for the worst behavior. If we were inquiring into sin, we would have nothing to do but to point at every passerby. The city is famous for vice. We will have to stay indoors as much as possible and avoid the endless drinking and promenading and dancing. And worse."

"But what a grand house!" Isolde exclaimed. "Like a palace! Did you see inside? The stone stairs coming down to his own private quay? And the torches inside the building?"

"Look!" Ishraq pointed ahead of them. There were more houses directly on the water's edge, most of them standing on little islands completely surrounded by water, the islands connected by thin, arching wooden bridges. On the left side the travelers could see the spires of churches beyond the waterfront houses, and at every second or third house they could see a narrow dark canal winding its way deeper into the heart of the city, and smaller canals branching from it, each one crowded with gondolas and working boats, every quay busy with people, half of them dressed in fantastic costumes, the women tottering on impossibly high shoes, some of them so tall that they had a maidservant to walk beside them for support.

"What are they wearing on their feet? They're like stilts!" Ishraq exclaimed.

"They are called chopines," Brother Peter said. "They keep the ladies' gowns and feet clear of the water when the streets are flooded." He looked consideringly at the women, who could not stand unsupported but looked magnificent, tall as giantesses, in their beautiful billowing long gowns. "The Holy Church approves of them," he said.

"I would have thought you would have called them a ridiculous vanity?" Ishraq asked curiously.

"Since they prevent dancing, and women cannot walk about on their own while wearing them, they are a great discouragement to sin," Brother Peter replied. "That's a great advantage."

"It is as everyone said, the city is built on the water," Isolde said wonderingly. "The houses stand side by side like boats moored closely in a port."

"I've never seen anything like it. How will the horses get about?" Freize asked.

"The boatman will take them a little out of the city, after he has set us down," Brother Peter told him. "When we need them, we'll take a boat to get to them. There are no horses in Venice; everyone goes everywhere by boat."

"The goods for market?" Freize asked.

"Come in by boat and are loaded and unloaded at the quayside."

"The inns?"

"Take travelers who leave and arrive by boat. They have no stable yards."

"The priests who attend the churches?"

"Come and go by boat. Every church has its own stone quayside."

"Aha, and so how do they get the stone for building?" Freize demanded, as if he was finally about to catch Brother Peter in a travelers' tale.

"They have great barges that bring in the stone," Brother Peter replied. "Everything comes by boat, I tell you. They even have great barges that bring in the drinking water."

This was too much for Freize. "Now I know you are deceiving me," he said. "The one thing this city does not lack is water! They must be born with webbed feet, these Venetians."

"They are a strange and unique people," Brother Peter conceded. "They govern themselves without a king, they have no roads, no highways, they are the wealthiest city in Christendom, they live on the sea and by the sea. They are expanding constantly, and their only god is trade; but they have built the most beautiful churches on every canal and decorated them with the most inspiring holy pictures. Every church is a treasure house of sacred art. Yet they act as if they are as far from God as they are from the mainland and there is no way to get to Him but a voyage."

Now they were approaching the heart of the city. The broad canal on either side was walled with white Istrian stone to make a continuous quay, occasionally pierced by a tributary canal winding deeper inside the city. Many of the smaller inner canals were crossed by little wooden bridges; a few were crossed by steeply stepped bridges of white stone. The ferry was losing the cold breeze, and so the boatman took down the sails and set to row; he took an oar on one side, and his lad heaved on the other. They wound their way through the constant river traffic of gondolas going swiftly through the water with loud warning cries from the gondolier in the stern of "Gondola! Gondola! Gondola!"

The canal was crowded with fishing ships, the flat-bottomed barges for carrying heavy goods, the ferryboats heaving with poorer people, and crisscrossing through the traffic, going from one side to the other, were public gondolas for hire. To the two young women who had been raised in a small country castle, it was impossibly busy and glamorous; they looked from right to left and could not believe what they were seeing. Every gondola carried passengers, heavily cloaked with their faces hidden by carnival masks. The women wore masks adorned with dyed plumes of feathers, the eyeholes slit like the eyes of a cat, a brightly colored hood covering their hair, a bejeweled fan hiding their smiling lips. Even more intriguing were the gondolas where the little cabin in the middle of the slim ship had the doors resolutely shut on hidden lovers, and the gondolier was rowing slowly, impassive in the stern. Sometimes a second gondola followed the first with musicians playing lingering love songs, for the entertainment of the secret couple.

"Sin, everywhere," Brother Peter said, averting his gaze.

"There's only one bridge across the Grand Canal," the boatman told them. "Everywhere else you have to take a boat to cross. It's a good city to be a ferryman. And this is it, the only bridge: the Rialto."

It was a high wooden bridge, many feet above the canal, arching up so high that even masted ships could pass easily beneath it, rising up from both sides of the canal, almost like a pinnacle, crowded with people, laden with little stalls and shops. There was a constant stream of pedestrians walking up the stairs on one side and down the other, pausing to shop, stopping to buy, leaning on the high parapet to watch the ships go underneath, arguing the prices, changing their money. The whole bridge was a shimmer of color and noise.

The square of San Giacomo, just beside the bridge, was lined with the tall houses of the merchants. All the nations of Christendom, and many of the infidel, were shown by their own flag and the national costume of the men doing business at the windows and doorways. Next to them stood the great houses of the Venetian banking families, the front doors standing open for business, absurdly costumed people coming and going, trading and buying in all seriousness, though dressed as if they were strolling players, with great plumed hats on their heads and bright jeweled masks on their faces.

In the square itself the bankers and gold merchants had their tables laid out all around the colonnade, one to every arch, and were trading in coin, promises and precious metals. When money was changing hands, the masks were laid aside as each client wanted to look his banker in the eye. Among them were Ottoman traders, their brightly colored turbans and gorgeous robes as beautiful as any costume. Venice had all but captured the trade of the Ottoman Empire and the wealth of the East flowed into Europe across the Venice traders' tables. There was no other route to the East, there was no easy navigable way to Russia. Venice was at the very center of world trade, and the riches of east and west, north and south poured into it from every side.

"The Rialto," Luca reminded Freize. "This is where

that infidel, Radu Bey, said that there was a priest, Father Pietro, who ransoms Christian slaves from the galleys of the Ottomans. This is it, this is the bridge, this is where he said. Perhaps Father Pietro is here now, perhaps I will be able to ransom my father and mother."

"We'll come out as soon as we are settled in our house," Freize promised him. "But, Sparrow, you will remember that the Ottoman gentleman, Radu Bey, seems to be the sworn enemy of the lord who commands your Order, and he, himself, did not exactly inspire me with trust."

Luca laughed. "I know. You do right to warn me. But, Freize, you know I would take advice from the devil himself if I thought I could get my father and mother back home. Just to see them again! Just to know they were alive."

Freize put his hand on his friend's shoulder. "I know," he said. "And they will have missed you too—they have missed your growing up. If we can find them and buy them out of slavery, it will be a great thing. I am just saying—don't get your hopes up too high. They were captured by the Ottoman slavers, and it was an Ottoman general who told us that we might buy them back. Just because he was well-read and spoke fair to you does not make him a friend."

"Ishraq liked him too, and she's a good judge of character," Luca objected.

A shadow crossed Freize's honest face. "Ishraq liked him

better than she liked the lord of your Order," he told Luca. "I wouldn't trust her judgment with the foreign lord myself. I don't know what game he was playing with her when he spoke to her in Arabic that only she could understand. Come to that, I don't know what game she was playing when she swore to me that he said nothing."

"And here is your palazzo," the boatman remarked. "Ca' de Longhi, just west of Piazza San Marco, very nice."

"A palace?" Isolde exclaimed. "We have hired a palace?"

"All the grand houses on the canal are palaces, though they are all called Casa—only the doge's house is called a palace," the boatman explained. "And the reason for that is that they are each and every one of them the most beautiful palaces ever built in the world."

"And do princes live here?" Ishraq asked. "In all these palaces?"

"Better than princes." He smiled at her. "Richer than princes, and greater than kings. The merchants of Venice live here, and you will find no greater power in this city or in all of Italy!"

He steered toward the little quayside at the side of the house, leaned hard on the rudder and brought the boat alongside with a gentle bump. He looked up at the beautiful frescoes on either side of the great water door, and all around the house, and then at Luca with a new level of respect. "You are welcome, Your Grace," he said, suddenly adjusting his view of the handsome young merchant who must surely command the fortune of a prince if he could afford such a palace to rent.

Freize saw the calculating look and nudged the boatman gently. "We'll pay double for the trouble and danger," he said shortly. "And you'll oblige us by keeping the story of the galley to yourself."

"Of course, sir," the boatman said, accepting a heavy purse of coins. He jumped nimbly onto the broad steps, tied the boat fore and aft and put out his hand to help the ladies on shore.

Glancing at each other, very conscious that they were playing a part, Ishraq and Isolde, Luca and Brother Peter stepped onto the stone pavement before their house. The door for pedestrians was at the side of the house, overlooking the smaller tributary canal. It stood open and the housekeeper bobbed a curtsy and led the way into the cool shaded hall.

First, as always, before they did anything else, Brother Peter, Luca and Isolde had to go to church and give thanks for their safe arrival. Ishraq and Freize, as an infidel and a servant, were excused.

"Go to the Rialto," Luca ordered Freize. "See if they have heard of Father Pietro. I will come myself to speak with him later."

Luca, Brother Peter and Isolde, with her hood pulled modestly forward, left the house by the little door onto the paved way beside the narrow canal and turned to their right to walk through the narrow alley to Piazza San Marco, where the great church bells echoed out, ringing for Terce, sending the pigeons soaring up into the cold blue sky, and the gorgeously costumed Venetians posed and paraded up to the very doors of the church itself.

Ishraq and Freize closed the side door on their companions and stood for a moment in the quiet hall.

"May I show you the rooms?" the housekeeper asked them, and led them up a wide flight of marble stairs to the first floor of the building, where a large reception room overlooked the canal with huge double-height windows leading to a little balcony. The grand room was warm, a small fire burned in the grate and the sunshine poured in through the window. Leading off were three smaller rooms.

The housekeeper led them up again to the same layout of rooms on the upper floor. "We'll take the top floor," Ishraq said. "You can have the first."

"And above you are the kitchens and the servants' rooms," the housekeeper said, gesturing to the smaller stairs that went on up.

"Kitchens in the attic?" Freize asked.

"To keep the house safe in case of fire," she said. "We Venetians are so afraid of fire, and we have no space to put the kitchens at a distance from the house on the ground floor. All the space on the ground floor is the courtyard and the garden, and at the front of the house, the quay and the water gate."

"And are you the cook?" Freize asked, thinking that he would be glad of a good lunch when the others came back from church.

She nodded.

"We'll go and run our errands and perhaps return to a large lunch?" Freize hinted. "For we had a long cold night with nothing but some bread and a few eggs, and I, for one, would be glad to try the Venetian specialities and your cooking."

She smiled. "I shall have it ready for you. Will you take the gondola?"

Freize and Ishraq exchanged a delighted grin. "Can we?" Ishraq asked.

"Of course," she replied. "It's the only way to get around this city." She led the way down the marble stairs to the ground floor, to the waterside front of the house, and their own private quay, where their gondola rocked at its moorings. The housekeeper waved them down the final flight of stairs and indicated the manservant who came out of a doorway, wiping his mouth and adjusting his bright feathered cap.

"Giuseppe," she said by way of introduction. "He will take you wherever you want to go, and wait and bring you home."

The man pulled the boat close to the quay and held out his hand to help Ishraq aboard. Freize stepped heavily after her, and Ishraq cried out and then laughed as the boat rocked.

"This is going to take some getting used to," Freize said. "I am missing Rufino already; how ever will he manage without me?" He turned to the gondolier, Giuseppe. "Can you take us to the Rialto?"

"Of course," the boatman said, and loosened the tasseled tie that held the gondola prow against the wall of the house. He stepped onto the platform in the stern, and with one skillful push of the single oar, thrust them out of the house and into the teeming water traffic of the Grand Canal.

Freize and Ishraq sat in the middle of the boat and looked around as their boat nosed through the crowded canal. Hucksters and merchants were on little ships, coming close to every craft and offering their wares, wherries and rowing boats for hire were threading their way through the traffic, great barges carrying beams and stone took the center of the canal and rowed to the beat of the drum. Freize and Ishraq— the fair, square-faced young man and the brown-skinned, dark-haired girl in their expensive private gondola—drew glances as the gondolier drew up at the Rialto Bridge with a flourish, leaped ashore and offered his hand to Ishraq.

She drew her hood over her head and her veil across her face as she stepped on the shore. She noticed that there were serving women, and workingwomen, beggars and store-keepers, and women in gaudy yellow with heavily painted faces, tottering along on absurdly tall shoes; but there were no gentlewomen or noblewomen on the wide stone square before the bridge, and at all the windows of the trading houses there were severe-looking men in dark suits who seemed to disapprove of a young woman in the square among the businessmen.

"Where d'you think Father Pietro might be?" Freize asked, staring around him.

The square was so filled with people, so noisy and so bustling, that Ishraq could only shake her head in wonderment. Someone was charming a snake for a handful of onlookers, the basket rocking from one side to another as he played his pipe, the straw lid starting to lift, only a dark eye showing, and a questing forked tongue. A row of merchants had their table under the shelter of the broad colonnade and were changing money from one foreign currency to another, the beads on the abacus rattling like castanets as the men calculated the value. Beside the river, a belated fisherman was landing his catch and selling it fresh to a couple of servants. The huge fish market had opened at dawn and already sold out a few hours later. There was a constant swirl of men coming and going from the great trading houses that surrounded the square on all sides. Errand boys with baskets on their heads and under their arms dashed about their business, shoppers crowded the little stores on either side of the high Rialto bridge, traders shouted their wares from the rocking boats at the quayside; every nationality was there, buying, selling, arguing, making money, from the dark-suited

German bankers to the gloriously robed traders from the Ottoman Empire, and even beyond.

"We'll have to ask someone," Ishraq said, quite dazzled by this, the busiest trading center in the world. "He could be next to us, and we wouldn't know it. He could be two steps away, and we would hardly spot him. I've never been in such a crowd, I've never seen so many people all at once. Not even in Spain!"

"Like Hell," Freize said matter-of-factly. "Bound to be crowded."

Ishraq laughed and turned away from the river to look for someone, a priest or a monk or a friar she could ask, when she saw a gambler.

The girl had laid out her game on the stone floor of the square, covering one of the white marble slabs with sand, to make a little area where the play could take place. The crowd had gathered around her, three deep. It was the ancient game of cups and ball. Ishraq had seen it played in Spain, and had been told it came from ancient Egypt; she had even seen it at Lucretili Castle when she was a little girl and a troubadour had taken her pocket money off her with the simple trick.

It was three downturned cups with a little ball hidden underneath one of them. The game player moved the cups at dazzling speed, then sat back and invited the onlookers to put down their coins before the cup where they had last seen the ball.

It was the simplest game in the world since everyone knew where the ball was, everyone had watched as the cup was moved. Then the player lifted the cups and *voilà!* The ball was not under the one that the crowd had picked. The player lifted another cup and it was under the second one. The player picked up the pennies of the bet, showed the empty cups, showed the little ball—but in this case it was a most beautiful translucent glass marble—put the ball under the cup again, bade the onlookers to watch carefully and moved the cups around, two or three times, at first very slowly and then a dozen moves, very fast.

What attracted Ishraq to this game was the game player. She was a girl of about eighteen years old, dressed in a brown gown with a modest hood; her pale intent face was downturned to her work, but when she looked up she had dark eyes and a bright smile. She sat back on her heels when she had moved the cups and looked up at the crowd around her with an air of absolute trustworthiness. "My lords, ladies, gentlemen . . ." she said sweetly. "Will you bet?"

Nobody looking at her could think for one moment that she had managed some sleight of hand. Not while they were all watching, not in broad daylight. The ball must be where she put it first: under the cup on the right, which she had slid to the left, swirled to the center, back to the right, then there had been some moving of the other cups as a rather obvious diversion, before she had finally moved it again to the center.

"It's in the middle," Freize whispered in Ishraq's ear.

"I'll bet you that it isn't," Ishraq said. "I was following it, but I lost it."

"I watched it all the while! It's plumb in the middle!" Freize fumbled with coins and put down a *piccoli*—a silver penny.

The girl waited for a moment until everyone had put down their bets, most of them, like Freize, favoring the central cup. Then she upturned the cup and showed it: empty. She scooped up all the coins that the gamblers had put down on the stone before the empty cup, and put them in the pocket of her apron, and then showed them the empty cup on the left and then finally the glass marble beneath the right-hand cup. Nobody had guessed correctly. With a merry smile that encouraged them to try their luck again, she smoothed the sand with her hand, placed the marble under the left-hand cup and swirled the cups around once more.

Ishraq was not watching the cups this time, but observing an older man who was moving among the crowd, standing close to the group of gamblers. He looked like a betting man himself, his gaze was bright and avid, his hat pulled low over his face, his smile pleasant. But he was watching the crowd, not the fast-moving hands of the girl.

"That's the shill," Ishraq said to Freize.

"The what?"

"The shill—her partner. He might distract the crowd at the exact moment that she makes the switch, so that they don't see where the ball has gone. But I think she's too good for that. She doesn't need anyone to distract the gamblers, so all he has to do is watch the crowd and prepare for trouble. Certainly, he'll take the money when she has finished and walk her home."

Freize hardly glanced up, he was so fixed on the game. "This time, I'm certain, I know where the marble is."

Ishraq laughed and cuffed his bent head. "You will lose your money," she predicted. "This girl is very good. She has very quick hands and excellent poise. She looks at her calmest when her hands are going fastest. And she smiles like an honest child."

Freize pushed Ishraq's hand away, confident of his own skill. He put down a second *piccoli* before the cup on the left and was rewarded with a little gleam from the girl in the brown gown. She lifted the cups. The marble was under the right-hand cup.

"Well, I—" Freize exclaimed.

Ishraq's dark eyes smiled at him over her veil. "How

much money do you have?" she asked. "For they will happily take it all day, if you are fool enough to put it down."

"I saw it, I am sure!" Freize exclaimed. "I was completely sure! It was like magic!"

The girl in brown glanced up and winked at him.

"It's a clever game, and you are a clever player," Freize said to her. "Do you ever lose?"

"Of course," she replied with a slight Parisian accent. "But mostly, I win. It's a simple game, good for amusement and for a few pence."

"More than a few pence," Ishraq observed to herself, looking at the pile of small silver coins that the girl scooped up.

"Will you try your luck again?" the girl invited Freize.

"I will!" Freize declared. "But I cannot bet my lucky penny."

With great care he took a penny from the breast pocket of his jacket, kissed it and put it back. The girl laughed at him, her brown eyes twinkling.

"I hope it works for you this time," she said. "For it has not done much for you so far."

"It will," he promised her. "And this time I shan't take my eyes off you!"

She smiled and showed him the three empty cups. Freize squatted down so that he was opposite her and nodded as she put the marble on the ground and then the central cup on top of it. Watching carefully, he saw she slid it to the right and then round to the extreme left, she hopped another cup around it, and then she took it back out to the left again. There was a dizzying swirl of cups as she slid one and then another and then she was still.

"Which one?" she challenged him.

Freize tipped all the small coins from his purse into his hand and put them down before the cup on the left. All the men around him, who had been watching, put their coins down too.

With a little laugh the young woman lifted the left-hand cup. It was empty. She lifted the middle cup, and there was the shining marble stone.

Freize laughed and shook his head. "It's a good game and you outwitted me completely," he admitted.

"It's a cheat!" someone said in a hard voice behind him. "I have put down the best part of a silver lira and watched for half an hour and I can't see how it's done."

"That's what makes it a good game," Freize said to him, smiling. "If you could see how it was done, it would be a trick for children. But she's a bonny lass with the quickest hands I've ever seen. I couldn't see how it was done and I practically had my nose in the cups."

"It's a cheat, and she should be thrown out of the city as a trickster," the man said harshly. He looked like a sulky fool in his masquing costume of bright blue, with a dancing cap on his head and a dangling bell that tinkled as he thrust his face forward. "And you're probably part of the gang."

"The gang?" Freize repeated slowly. "What gang would this be?"

"The gang who are using her to cheat good citizens out of their hard-earned money!"

Freize looked past the angry man to his friends. "Best get him home?" he suggested mildly. "Nobody likes a bad loser."

"I should report her to the doge!" the man insisted, getting louder, his bell jingling as he nodded his head. "I have friends in the palace—I know several of the Council of Forty. I can write a denouncement and put it in the box as easily as the next good citizen. The city depends on honest traders! We don't like cheats in Venice!"

Freize rose to his feet and let the man see his height, his broad shoulders and his honest friendly face. Ishraq noticed the girl gather her money into a purse and tuck it under her robe, and the swift glance that passed between her and her accomplice in the crowd. Quietly, her partner moved so that he was between her and the disgruntled gambler. For a girl working as a gambler in the streets, she looked surprisingly apprehensive at this minor trouble. Ishraq would have expected her to be accustomed to brawls.

"It's really nothing to do with us," Ishraq suggested quietly, putting a hand on the back of Freize's jacket. "And we don't want to draw attention to ourselves. Why don't we just go now?"

"I want my money back!" the man said loudly, tossing the hem of his cape over his shoulder and stripping off his blue gauntlets as if he was readying himself for a fight. "I want it now."

The shill stepped forward so that he was beside the girl, who bent down to smooth the sand out and kept her head low, almost crouching down, as Freize spoke to the angry man in blue.

"Now you wait a moment," Freize said, completely ignoring Ishraq's warning. "Did you bet that the pretty stone was under the cup?"

"Yes!" the man said. "Over and over."

"And were you wrong?"

"Yes! Over and over!"

"And did you put your money down?"

"Six times!"

"Six times," Freize marveled. "Then I have good advice for a man as clever as you. Don't waste your time here: go to the university!"

Completely distracted, the man hesitated and then asked: "Why? What d'you mean?"

Everyone waited for Freize's answer, the shill standing protectively over the girl as she looked curiously upward.

"At the university, at Padua, they take students who study for years. And here, in one morning, you have taken six tries to discover that her hands are quicker than your eyes. See how slow you are to observe the obvious! Think how long you could study at Padua! It could be the occupation of a lifetime. You could become a philosopher."

There was a roar of laughter from the man's friends, and they slapped him on the back and called him "Philosopher!" and jostled him away. Ishraq watched them go and turned back to see the young woman was laying out the game again. The little quarrel had attracted more attention, and this time there were more bets, on all three cups, so that she was forced to pay out to some players. She took some silver and handed over two quarter gold nobles and then packed up her cups and her ball and swept the white sand into the crevices of the paving stones to indicate that play was ended for the day.

"Thank you," she said briefly to Freize, and she fastened her little satchel.

"Thank you for the game," Freize said. "I am new in town and it is a pleasure to see a pretty girl at her work. What's your name, sweetheart?"

"Jacinta," she said. "This is my father, Drago Nacari."

"A pleasure to meet you both," Freize said, pulling off his hat and smiling down at her as she rose to her feet and handed the heavy purse of money to her father.

"Have you heard of a priest called Father Pietro?" Ishraq asked her, recalling Freize to their task.

She nodded. "Everyone knows him. He sits over there, at the corner of the bridge; he has a little desk and a great list of many, many names of people enslaved, poor souls. He comes after Sext. You will find him here after the clock has struck one." She gave them a little bow and walked away from them. Her father tipped his hat to them both and walked with her. Freize looked after her.

"I think I am in love," he said.

"I think you are hopelessly fickle," Ishraq said. "You swore a lifetime of service to Isolde, you insisted on a kiss from me, you flirted with the innkeeper's wife in Piccolo and now you are chasing after a girl who has done nothing but take money off you."

"But her hands!" Freize exclaimed. "So fast! So light! Think, if you married her, of the cakes she would make! She must make fantastic pastries with hands as quick and light as that."

Ishraq giggled at the thought of Freize lusting after a young woman because he thought she would make a good pastry cook. "Shall we wait for Father Pietro?"

Freize nodded, looking round. "While we're waiting, we could change some coins. I have a handful of coins that I took from Milord's funds. Luca has to study the gold coins here; the lord of his Order commanded him to look at the gold nobles. Shall we try that man, see if he has any English nobles?"

They walked over to a long trestle table. Behind it, on a row of stools, sat the money changers. Each man had a small chalkboard beside him, and constantly wrote and rewrote the exchange rate of the coins he had to offer. One man was busier than all the others; he had a queue of men waiting to do business with him. As they watched, he altered his sign to read:

Two Venetian Ducats for One Gold Noble of England.

Ishraq nudged Freize. "He has them," she said quietly. "That moneylender. He has English gold nobles, and at a better rate than all the others."

Freize stepped up to the man who was dressed all in black, except for a bright round yellow badge that he wore on his chest, his dark hair plaited away from his clean-shaven face, a small black cap, the *kippah*, on the back of his head, his fingers busy with a small worn abacus, two locked boxes on the table before him, a young man standing for protection behind him.

"I'd like to change some money," Freize said politely.

"Good day," the man replied. "Today, I am only offering English gold, English gold nobles. Their value at the moment is of two Venetian ducats."

"Good day to you," Freize replied. "Is that good value? I am a stranger in the city."

"I am Israel, the Jew. I can promise that you will find no better price."

Freize took out his purse and emptied it onto the desk, then he went through all his pockets, of his breeches and his jacket, and even the band of his hat, producing coins from the most unexpected places, much like a conjuror.

"What are you doing?" Ishraq asked, amused.

"Can't be too careful," Freize said. "You steal my purse from me but—*ecce!*—half my fortune is in my hat."

The trader started to sort the copper from the silver, the bronze and the chips of metal, and weigh them.

"Do you have much English gold?" Freize said casually.

"I buy only gold of the best quality," the man replied. "And last year these English nobles started to become available in great numbers. They are excellent quality, the best gold that can be got. They are as good as gold: the coin is pure gold, there is nothing added and nothing taken away."

He started to weigh the coins against tiny weights, the smallest the size of a grain of wheat, in a precisely balanced scale. "I see you are a traveler," the man remarked. "For here are coins from Rome and from Ravenna, and from the west of Italy too."

"I'm in the service of a lord from the west of Italy."

Freize told the lie that he and Ishraq had agreed upon. It was coming more and more easily to him. "A young lord who wants to visit this city and try his hand at trade here. He has a share in a cargo in a ship that is coming in any day now."

"He could come nowhere more prosperous. I wish him good fortune," the man said quietly. "Tell him to come to me for fair dealing in gold. Now . . ." He paused and looked doubtfully at the scales. "I am sorry to have to tell you that some of your coins are not very good. Some of them have been clipped to make them into smaller coins, and some of them have been shaved and the value stolen from them."

Freize shrugged. "It's the luck of the road. I trust you to deal fairly with me. Oh!" he exclaimed. "I had forgotten." He leaned over the table and picked out one copper penny coin. "I should not have put this among the others," he said. "It's my lucky penny. I don't want to change it. I keep it for good fortune."

"Since when did you have a lucky penny?" Ishraq asked him. "I thought you were just telling that girl a story. What's so lucky about it?"

"I had it in my pocket when I was snatched by the sea, and when everything else was washed from my pocket I still had this one penny," Freize said. "And do you see? It was minted by the Pope himself, in the Vatican, in the year of my birth. It's practically an amulet. What could be luckier than that?"

The merchant bowed slightly and put the rest of the copper coins in his set of scales, balanced a weight against them and showed Freize the result. "That's your copper."

"No worse than I expected," Freize said cheerfully. "Try the silver."

"I can give you a half noble for it all," the trader said, weighing the handfuls of coins and chips of coins in his scales.

"I'll take it," Freize replied.

The man tipped the copper coins into a little sack, and the silver into one of the boxes at his side. He opened the other box and, before Ishraq could glimpse more than the gleam of gold, took out an English half noble and handed it over to Freize.

"You don't weigh it?" Ishraq asked the man. "You trust the weight of the English noble?"

He made a little bow to her. "This is why everyone wants the English noble coins. They are all, always, full weight."

Confidently, he tossed it into the scales and showed her the weight. "Fifty-four grains," he said. "A full noble is 108. They all are. Always. They are perfect coins."

"It looks like new!" Freize exclaimed. "As if it were fresh from the mint."

The man nodded. "As I said, they're very fine coins," he confirmed.

"But how can it be so shiny and fine?" Ishraq asked him. "Since it must have come all the way from England, from the royal mint in England?"

The man shrugged. "Actually, it came from the English royal mint in Calais," he said shortly. "You can tell by the signs on the coin if you look closely."

"They hardly look like coins at all," Freize said, accustomed to the worn and jagged currency that he usually carried, coins that had been snipped and clipped by people wanting to break them down into smaller currency, or worn smooth by years of use.

"Put it away before someone with less discernment takes it off you," the merchant recommended. "And before you make people think that there is something wrong with it." He glanced down the row of tables. Some of the traders were watching them. "We all exchange money here, the town depends on trade, like it depends on water. Nobody wants anyone looking at a coin and wondering about its value. A good *piccoli* buys you a loaf of bread and a fish for your dinner. Tell people that a *piccoli* is not really worth a penny, but only half a penny, and you'll only get a loaf and no fish. Faith in the currency is what makes trade in this town. We don't like people questioning our coins. Our coins are good, these nobles are exceptionally good, everyone else is trading them for more than two ducats. I shall put up my price again, tomorrow. You are lucky that I have these at this price today. Take it or leave it."

"Indeed I wasn't questioning it," Freize said pleasantly. "I was admiring it, I was so impressed by the quality. Thank you for your patience."

He bowed politely to the money changer, and then the two of them turned away and strolled toward the Rialto Bridge. "Let me see it," Ishraq said curiously. "What's the coin like?"

In answer, Freize handed it to her. It was as bright as newly minted, newly polished gold. There was a picture of a king in the prow of his ship on one side, and an eight-petaled heraldic rose on the other side. In English currency it was worth three shillings and four pence, a sixth of a pound; in Venice it could be exchanged today for a gold ducat, tomorrow it might be more or less.

"It looks like new," Freize remarked. "Whatever he says."

"But who would be minting fake English nobles in Venice?" Ishraq wondered aloud.

"And that's the very question that Milord has set Luca to answer," Freize agreed. "But I can't help but wonder why Milord is so interested. It's hardly a sign of the end of days. It's hardly a holy inquiry. Since Luca is appointed to the Order of Darkness to travel throughout Christendom and find the signs for the end of the world, why would he be ordered to discover the source of gold coins in Venice? I would have thought it was rather a worldly question for an Order that was established by the Pope to discover the date of the end of the world. What do they care about the value of English nobles?"

He saw, in her downturned face, the same skepticism about Milord that he felt. "Ah, you don't like him any more than I do," he said flatly.

"I don't know him," she said. "Who does know him? He has never let any of us see his face. He didn't tell us anything, beyond ordering us to come to Venice in disguise to find out about the coins. He commands Luca and Brother Peter as the commander of their Order, but he gives the rest of us no reason to trust him. He hates the Ottomans as if they were poison—well, I understand that—they have just conquered Constantinople and he thinks that if they reach Rome, then the world will end. But I don't see how to trust a man who lives his life as if he were always on the very edge of world disaster. His whole work, his whole life, is waiting for the end of the world. He's an angry man and a fearful man. I really don't like him."

"And so you let his enemy into our house," Freize said gently.

"I let him *out* of the house," she corrected him. "I heard the Ottoman Radu Bey on the stairs, I don't know how he got in. He said he had just been talking in secret to Milord and I let him out of the house. I didn't know that he had threatened Milord. I don't know that I even care if he did."

"Milord said that the intruder was an assassin. That he could have been stabbed as he slept."

"Milord says a lot of things," she replied. "But it was Radu Bey for sure who got into his room and pinned his own badge over Milord's heart as he slept. He could have killed him, but he did not. I can see that he and the Ottoman lord are enemies—they're on either side of the greatest war there is: the Jihad to one, the Crusade to the other—but that doesn't tell me which is the right side, which is the better man."

She had shocked him. "We're Christians!" he exclaimed. "We serve Luca, who serves the Church. The Crusade is a holy war against the infidel!"

"You are," she pointed out. "You four are. But I'm not. I want to make up my own mind. And I simply don't know enough about Luca's lord—or about the Ottoman lord either."

"We have to follow Luca's lord, we can't desert Luca," Freize pointed out. "I love him as a brother and your lady won't leave him unless she has to. And you?" He gave her a quick sideways smile. "You're head over heels in love with him, aren't you?"

She laughed. "I'm not head over heels for anyone," she said. "I keep my two feet on the ground. He makes my heart beat a little faster, I grant you that. But nothing in this world would send me head over heels, I like to be right side up."

"One day," Freize warned her solemnly. "One day you will find that you are head over heels in love with me. I pray that you don't leave it too late."

She laughed. "What a mistake that would be! Look at how you run after other women!"

"And on that day," Freize predicted without paying any attention to her laughter, "on that day, I will be kind to you. I will take you in my arms, I will allow you to adore me."

"I'll remember that!" she said.

"Remember this too," Freize said more seriously. "Luca is sworn to obey the lord of his Order. I have promised to follow and serve Luca. You are traveling with us. You can't support our enemies."

"And what of your friends?" she challenged him. "And Luca's mysterious errands for his lord? A servant of the Church coming to Venice in carnival time, ordered to speculate in gold and trade in a cargo? Is this holy work in your Church?"

The church bell of San Giacomo started to ring over their heads, and flocks of pigeons fluttered from their roosts in the church tower, interrupting them. "One o'clock," said Ishraq. "And here, I think, is Father Pietro."

The two of them watched as an elderly gray-haired man wearing the undyed wool robes of the Benedictine order came from the church, still crossing himself, his forehead damp with holy water, and walked across the crowded square. Traders, merchants and passersby greeted him by name as he threaded his way through the crowd, making the sign of the cross over a child who said hello, until he arrived at the foot of the Rialto Bridge, where a small stone pillar—usually used for hitching boats—served as his seat.

He took his place, and the servant who had followed him through the crowd set up a small table for writing, unfurled a long, rolled manuscript and presented the priest with a pen. Father Pietro looked around him, bowed his head briefly in prayer and then dipped his pen in the inkwell and waited, pen poised. Clearly, he was open for business, but before Ishraq or Freize could speak to him a little crowd had gathered around him, shouting out the names of missing relatives, or asking for information.

As Ishraq and Freize watched, the friar looked through his list, noted down new names, reported on ones he could find, and advised the supplicants. For one young man he had great news: his cousin had been located in the occupied lands in Greece, and the master was ready to sell. Much of Greece had been invaded by the Ottoman Empire, and the Greeks had to serve the Ottoman lords and pay an annual tribute. This man was laboring as a slave on a farm of one of the Ottoman conquerors. The lord had named his price and Father Pietro thought it was a fair one, though it was a *lira di grosso*—ten ducats, a year's pay for a laboring man.

"Where am I to get that sort of money?" the man demanded.

"Your church should make a collection for your kinsman," the friar advised. "And His Holiness the Pope makes a donation every year for the freeing of Christians. If you can raise some of the money, I can ask for the rest. Come back when you have at least half and we will convert it into the English gold. The slave owners only want to be paid in English gold nobles this year. Even the tribute from the occupied lands has to be in English nobles this year. But I will get you a fair rate from the money changers."

"God bless you! God bless you!" the young man said, and darted away into the crowd.

A few other people drew near and had a muttered consultation, and then Freize and Ishraq were before the friar's little table.

"Father Pietro?" Freize inquired.

"That is my name."

"I am glad to find you. I will bring my master to you, he is anxiously seeking his parents who were taken into slavery."

"I am sorry for him, and for them. I pray that God will guide them home," the man said gently.

"Can I bring him here to you, tomorrow?" Freize asked.

"Yes, my son. I am always here. It is my life's work to seek out the poor lambs stolen from the flock. What is the name of his father and mother?"

"Their family name was Vero and he has had news of his father. His father was Guilliam Vero, said to be a galley slave on a ship owned by . . ." Freize slapped his hand on his broad forehead.

"Bayeed," Ishraq prompted. "But we were told that was some years ago. We are not certain where he is now."

Father Pietro inclined his head. "I know of this Bayeed.

I will look through the lists I keep at home, and ask some newly released slaves tonight," he said. "Bayeed sold one of his slaves to me a little while ago. Perhaps that man will know of Guilliam Vero. I hope I will have some sort of answer for you tomorrow."

"Bayeed himself sold a galley slave to you?" Ishraq queried.

"He is a merchant," Father Pietro said calmly, as if nothing in the world could surprise him. "He trades in slaves like the merchants from England trade in cloth. Christian souls are a form of merchandise to him, like any other, God forgive him. He sold a slave to me for ten ducats—though he insisted on being paid in English gold—so we sent him eight English nobles—they were worth less then than they are now."

"Why don't they take their ransom in ducats?" Ishraq asked. "That's the currency of Venice, surely?"

"They always want either solid gold or a currency that they can trust. This year they want the English nobles because there are always 108 grains of gold in each coin. They know what they are getting when they get English gold. Some coins of other countries are made with very impure metal. You will find the *piccoli* here contain hardly any silver at all. They are almost all tin. Beware of forgeries." The priest turned his gentle gaze on Ishraq. "And you, child? What are you doing so far from home? Are you enslaved or free?"

"I'm free." Ishraq blushed behind her veil. "My mother came to this country of her own free will and I was born here."

"Your father is a Christian?"

"I don't know my father," she said, her voice muffled with embarrassment. "My mother never told me his name. But she said they were married. My father was a Christian and my mother was free."

"And what is your faith?"

"My mother taught me the Koran, and the Christian lord who brought us to his home read me the Bible. But now they are both dead. I practice no religion, I am afraid that I have no faith."

He gave a little gasp of dismay at her lack of godliness, and shook his head. "My child, I shall pray for you, and hope that you can find your way to the true faith. Would you come to me for instruction?"

"If you insist," Ishraq said awkwardly. "But I am sorry to say, Father, that I am not a good student of religion."

He smiled at her, as if her boldness amused him. "Because you are such a good student of other studies? What do you read, my learned daughter?"

She nodded, ignoring the gentle sarcasm. "I really am a student, Father. I am interested in the new scholarship," she said. "The learning of the Greeks that the Arab scholars are starting to translate, so that we can all learn from them."

"God bless you, my child," he said earnestly. "I will pray that God moves your heart to come to Him, and that you become content to learn through revelation, not through study. But don't you want to go to your home again?"

She hesitated for a moment. "I don't really know where I would call home now. The house where I was raised—the castle of Lucretili—has been claimed by a thief—my friend's brother—and I am sworn to help her get it back. I'd be glad to fight for it and see it returned to her. But even if we win, even if she goes home to live there—I won't be able to say that it is truly my home." She looked at him with her direct dark gaze. "Father, sometimes I fear that I don't belong anywhere. I have neither father nor mother nor home."

"Or perhaps you are free," he said quietly.

It was so novel a thought that she said nothing in reply.

He smiled. "To belong somewhere is always to owe something: a debt of loyalty, your work or your time, your love or your taxes. You are an unusual young woman if you do not belong to a man nor to a place. You are not commanded by a master or a father or a husband. That means you are free to choose where you live. That makes you free to choose how you live."

"I am . . ." Ishraq stammered. "It is true. I am free."

He raised a finger. "So make sure you choose rightly, my daughter. Make sure that you walk in the way of God. You are free to live freely inside His holy laws."

He turned to Freize with a gentle smile. "And are you, my son, in Christ?"

"Oh, I'm of no interest to anyone," Freize said cheerfully. "First a kitchen boy in a monastery, now a servant to a young master, never enough money, always hungry, always happy. Don't you worry about me."

"You attend church?" the father prompted.

"Yes, of course, Father," Freize agreed, feeling a tinge of guilt that though he regularly attended, he seldom listened.

"Then walk in God's holy ways," the father urged him. "And make sure that you give to the poor, not to gamblers."

Ishraq raised her eyebrows, surprised that the priest had seen them gambling with the cups-and-ball game. "Are they always there?" she asked.

"Every day, and God knows how many *piccoli* they collect from the foolish and the spendthrift," he said. "They are a trap for the unwary, and every day they leave here with a purse full of silver coins. Don't you waste your money on them again." He smiled and raised his hand over them both in a blessing. "And tell your master, I will see him tomorrow."

Isolde, Brother Peter and Luca were waiting for Ishraq and Freize when the gondola arrived back at the grand house. Isolde had unpacked the new clothes that had survived the journey from Ravenna and had looked all around their new grand quarters. She took Ishraq upstairs to their floor as Freize, in the men's quarters, told Luca that they had found Father Pietro.

"It's the most beautiful house I have ever seen," she confided in Ishraq. "Lucretili was grand, but this is beautiful. Every corner is like a painting. There is an inner courtyard, on the side of the house, with a roofed walkway on all the four sides, which leads to a pretty walled garden. When the weather is warmer we can walk round the courtyard and sit in the garden."

"Surely we'll walk on the quays and the piazza? And we'll take the gondola out?" asked Ishraq.

Isolde made a little face. "Apparently, the ladies of Venice don't go out much. Maria, the housekeeper, said so. We'll have to stay indoors. We can go out to church once a day, or perhaps to visit friends in their houses. But mostly ladies stay at home. Or visit other ladies in their homes."

"I can't be cooped up!" Ishraq protested.

"That's how they do things in Venice. If we want to pass as the sister and companion of a prosperous young merchant, we'll have to behave that way. It won't be for long—just till

Luca finds the source of the gold coins and sends a report to Milord."

"But that could be weeks, it could be months," Ishraq said, aghast.

"We can probably go out on the water in our own gondola," Isolde suggested. "As long as we are veiled, or sit in the cabin."

Ishraq looked blankly at her. "We are in one of the richest, most exciting cities in Christendom, and you're telling me that we're not allowed to walk around it on our own two feet?"

Isolde looked uncomfortable. "You can probably go out to the market with Freize or a chaperone," she said. "But I can't. I wasn't even allowed to listen to the lecture, even though it was held in the chapel beside the church."

"What lecture?" Ishraq was immediately interested.

"At the church there is a priest who studies all things. He is part of the university of Venice, and sometimes he goes to Padua to study there. He was giving a lecture after Sext, and Luca waited to hear him. Luca talked to him about the rainbow mosaic in the tomb of Galla Placidia."

"And what did you do?"

"Brother Peter brought me home. Brother Peter does not believe in women studying."

Ishraq made a little irritated gesture. "But was Luca impressed with the lecture?"

"Oh yes, he wants to go again. He wants to learn things while he is here. There is a great library inside the doge's palace, and a tradition of scholarship. They have manuscripts from all over the world and a printing workshop that is making books. Not hand-painting them and copying them with a pen and ink, but printing hundreds at a time with some sort of machine."

"A machine to make books?"

"Yes. It can print a page in a moment."

"But I suppose neither you nor I can listen to the lectures? Or go to see the books made? All this study is just for men? Though in the Arab world there are women scholars and women teachers?"

Isolde nodded her head. "Brother Peter says that women's heads do not have the strength for study."

"*Testa di cazzo,*" Ishraq said under her breath, and led the way downstairs.

They found Luca and Brother Peter in the dining room overlooking the Grand Canal. Luca had the shutter on the tall windows closed and had opened one of the laths a tiny crack so that a beam of light was shining onto the piece of glass he had taken from the chapel at Ravenna. He looked up as they came in: "I spoke to one of the scholars at San Marco," he remarked to Ishraq. "He says that before we even think about the rainbow we have to consider how things are seen."

Ishraq waited.

"He said that the Arab philosopher Al-Kindi believed that we see things because rays are sent out from our eyes and then bounce off things and come back to the eye."

"Al-Kindi?" she repeated.

"Have you heard of him?"

"When I was studying in Spain," she explained. "He translated Plato into Arabic."

"Could I read his work?" Luca rose up from the table and put down the piece of glass.

She nodded. "He's been translated into Latin, for certain."

"You would have to be sure it was not heretical writing," Brother Peter pointed out. "Coming as it does from the ancient Greeks who knew nothing of Christ, and through an infidel thinker."

"But everything has been translated from the Greek to the Arabic!" Luca exclaimed impatiently. "Not into Italian or French or English! And only now is it being translated into Latin."

Ishraq showed him a small smug smile. "It's just that the Arabs were studying the world and thinking about mathematics and philosophy when the Italians were—" She broke off. "I don't even know what they were doing," she said. "Was there even an Italy?"

"When?" Isolde asked, pulling out her chair and sitting at the table.

"About 900 AD," Ishraq answered her.

"There was the Byzantine Empire and the Muslim occupation, there wasn't really an Italy, I don't think."

Freize helped to carry the dishes down from the kitchen, but once the dining room door was shut, he dropped the pretense and sat down to table with them. Isolde, looking around the table, thought that they could very well pass as a loving happy family. The affection between the four young people was very clear, and Brother Peter was like a stern, slightly disapproving, older brother.

"They invented Gorgonzola cheese," Freize announced, carving a large ham and passing out slices.

"What?" Luca choked on a laugh, genuinely surprised.

"They invented Gorgonzola cheese, in the Po Valley," Freize said again. "I don't think the Italians were studying the meaning of the rainbow in the year 960. They were making cheese." He turned to Luca. "Don't you remember Giorgio in the monastery? Came from the Po Valley? Very proud of their history. Told us about Gorgonzola cheese. Said they'd been making it for five hundred years. Good thing too. Probably more use than rainbows." He served himself two great slices of ham and sat down and buttered some bread.

"You are a source of endless surprises," Luca told him.

"Glad to help," Freize said smugly. "And I have more. You'll be interested in this." Freize put down the bread, wiped his fingers on his breeches and brought the gold half noble coin out of his pocket. "I exchanged some of my smaller coins for this. A gold half noble from England. Isn't this one of the coins that Milord wanted you to investigate?"

Luca held out his hand and looked at the bright coin. "Yes—an English half noble. It's perfect," he said. "Not a mark on it."

He passed it to Brother Peter who studied it and then handed it on to Isolde. "Why is Milord so interested in these coins?" she asked.

Ishraq and Freize exchanged a hidden look as Isolde named the very question that was troubling them.

"He believes that someone may have opened a gold mine and is minting them in secret," Brother Peter said. "Such a man would be avoiding tax and avoiding the fines he should pay to the Church. Milord would want to see that the Church reclaimed those taxes. It would amount to a fortune. Or some criminal may be forging them."

"So do you think the coins are forged? Made to look like

English nobles but made from lesser metal?" Luca asked.

"The money changer said they were from the English mint in Calais," Freize explained. "But he was very stern with us when I asked him about them—he warned me not to ask questions. He didn't want anyone saying anything that might spoil the value of the coins."

"Is the value good?"

"They might be overvalued, if anything," Freize volunteered. "They were rising in price as we stood there. He said he would put up his exchange rate tomorrow. Apparently, everyone wants to trade in them—there were men queuing behind us. Everyone says they are solid gold, without any alloy. That's very unusual. Most coins are a mixture of precious metal and something lighter. Or good ones are shaved and clipped. But these seem to be perfect."

"There's only one way to be sure. We'll have to test them to see how much real gold is in each coin," said Luca.

"How shall we test it?" Isolde asked. "We can't ask the goldsmiths—as Freize said, they won't welcome questions about the quality of their coins."

Brother Peter looked slightly uncomfortable. He put his hand to the inner pocket of his jacket.

"You've got orders!" Freize said accusingly, eyeing the small scroll.

"Milord honored me . . ."

"More secret orders!" Freize exclaimed. "Where do we have to go now? Just when we are settled and have discovered *fegato alla veneziana*? When Luca is studying at the university and is going to see Father Pietro? Just when he might find his father? Don't say we have to leave! We haven't completed our mission, we've not even started! The girls haven't even bought their carnival clothes!"

"Peace! Peace! We don't have to move yet," Brother Peter said. "And if it was an order from Milord, then the fact that you have discovered a Venetian culinary speciality of liver and onions, and that the girls want new dresses, would not prevent us. This is vanity, Freize. And greed. No, Milord simply gave me instructions for our time in Venice. How we are to go to the Rialto when our ship comes in and claim our share of the cargo. How we are to sell it at a profit, a manifest of the cargo it is carrying. And here, a list of the tests we were to make on the gold coins, when we had them."

He looked at Ishraq. "The instructions are in Arabic," he said awkwardly. "This is infidel learning. I thought you might read them to Brother Luca, and he would test the gold."

Ishraq beamed at him in gleeful triumph. "You need my learning, Brother Peter?"

The older man gritted his teeth. "I do."

"You don't think that translating a recipe for testing gold will strain my poor woman's intelligence to breaking point?"

"I hope that you will survive it."

"You don't think that such knowledge should be kept to men, only to men?"

"Not on this occasion."

She turned to Luca. "Do you want me to translate the recipes for you? Will you test the gold?"

"Of course," Luca said. "We can use the spare room next to mine. We will have our own goldsmith's assay room!"

Only Freize caught the shadow that crossed Isolde's face at the thought of the two of them working all day together in the small room.

"And tomorrow I will go out and exchange some more coins for gold," Brother Peter said. "We will have to test a number of coins to be sure."

"And the lasses can buy new gowns," Freize said happily. "And masks, and hats. And I shall look through my boxes and see if I can't find some more coins to turn into English gold nobles. A man could make a small fortune in this town by doing nothing but buying at the right time."

Immediately after breakfast the following morning, Ishraq and Luca were side by side at a table in the spare room off the dining room, quiet with concentration. Luca was staring at half a dozen beautiful golden coins purchased by Brother Peter from the money changers. Ishraq had a scroll of manuscript before her. Carefully, she unrolled it, weighted the top and bottom so that it could not roll up and started to translate from the Arabic into Italian. "It says first you have to look, to see if it has been stamped or marked by the goldsmith or mint."

Luca squinted at the coins, one after another. "Yes," he said. "They're all marked as English nobles, minted by the English at Calais. They're all marked in exactly the same way. Identical."

He made a note on a piece of paper beside him and then carefully put the paper over the coin and gently rubbed a colored stick of sealing wax over it. The image on the coin showed through. "Now what?"

Ishraq tucked a curl of dark black hair behind her ear. "Check for discoloration, especially wear," she read. "If another metal is showing through the gold, then this is gold plate, a gold veneer laid over a cheaper metal."

Obediently, Luca turned over every coin and looked at the beautifully beveled edges of the whole coins. "They're perfect. All of them. Same color all the way round."

"Bite it," she said.

"What?"

She giggled, and he glanced at her and smiled too. "It's what it says here. Gold is soft, bite it, hold it in your mouth for the count of one hundred, and then look at it. If it is gold, your teeth should mark it."

"You bite it," Luca replied.

"I'm the translator," she said modestly. "You're the assayer. I am a mere woman. In your faith I think it is me who tells you to bite the apple. Besides, I'm not cracking my teeth on it. You're the one that wants to know: you bite it."

"God Himself tells us your sex bit the apple first," Luca pointed out. "So we'll both bite one," he decided, and handed her a half noble and kept a whole coin for himself.

Solemnly, they both put the coins at the side of their mouths, bit down, held the coins, counted to one hundred and then looked at the result.

"I'm amazed!" she said.

"I can see my teeth marks!" he agreed.

"Gold, then."

"Write it down," Luca instructed her. "What's the next test?"

"We have to scratch it with an earthenware plate."

Luca went to the door, opened it and yelled down the stairs. "Freize! Bring me a bowl from the kitchen!"

"Hush!" Freize said, laboring up the stairs. "Lady Isolde has half of Venice in her room above us, fitting her with gowns, creating headdresses for her and Ishraq."

"I need a bowl from the kitchen!"

"Pewter?" Freize asked, preparing to go on, up the narrow stairs to the attic.

"No! No! Earthenware!"

"Earthenware he says," Freize complained to himself. They could hear his footsteps going the long way up to the kitchen and then coming back down. "Earthenware, as you asked," he said, peering curiously into the room.

"And now go away," Luca said hard-heartedly, though it was clear that Freize was aching to join in. To Ishraq he said: "Now what?"

"You have to break it. We need a smashed piece of earthenware."

Luca slammed the bowl against the edge of the table, and it shattered into a hundred pieces.

"Oh fine, just break it!" came Freize's voice from behind the closed door. "Don't worry about it, for a moment. Shall I fetch another for your lordship?"

"And take a piece and scratch the gold with it," Ishraq translated. "A black scratch means the gold is not real but a gold scratch shows the metal is true."

Luca drew the earthenware shard across the face of the gold noble. "It's good," he said tersely. He pressed down hard and then looked again. "Definitely good."

"Now we have to saw it in half."

He raised his eyebrows at the thought of damaging the coin. "I'll saw one of the quarter nobles," he said. "I won't touch the full noble."

She shook her head. "Oh for heaven's sake! Saw one of each: a noble and a half noble and a quarter noble. Go on, Luca. It's not as if it's your money. Milord is paying for all of this."

"You have expensive ideas," he said. "If you had been brought up as a farmer's son like me, you would not willingly be sawing coins in half."

She laughed at him, and he did as she requested and

soon the coins lay halved on the bench before them.

"Are they the same color all the way through?"

Luca picked up a magnifying glass and scrutinized the coins. "Yes," he said. "There's no skin on any of them, nor any trace of a different color inside. They're yellow all the way through, like pure gold."

"So now it's the last test: we have to weigh the coins," she said. "Weigh them very accurately."

Luca paused. "All right. What weight should they be?"

"A full noble is one hundred and eight grains," Ishraq said, scowling at the manuscript, trying to understand the symbols. "It says that density is equal to mass divided by volume."

"Hang on a minute," Luca said. "Say that again."

"Density is equal to mass divided by volume," she repeated. "The test is to weigh pure gold and then weigh the test gold to find the mass. Then the second test is to put it in water and see how much the water level rises. That gives the volume."

"Mass," Luca repeated. "Volume." Ishraq thought that he looked for a moment like a troubadour when he sings a particularly beautiful song. The words, which made no sense to her, were like poetry to him. "Density."

"It says here that we are to take a piece of pure gold and then put it in a measured jug of water and see how much the water rises. Then we do the same with the same weight of our test gold. Gold which has been mixed with other lighter metals will move more water. Gold that is pure is more dense—it will displace less water." She broke off. "You know, I'm reading the words, but I feel like a fool. I don't understand what we are to do. Do you understand what is meant?"

Luca looked transported. "Density is equal to mass divided by volume," he said quietly. "I do see. I do see."

He did not bother to shout for Freize but ran up to the kitchen himself and came back down with a clear glass of water. "We'll have to go out to a goldsmith and buy some pure gold," he muttered.

"What for?"

"So that I know how dense pure gold is. So that I know how much the water rises. So that I can compare it with the coins."

"Oh! I see," Ishraq exclaimed, suddenly understanding. "I have a gold ring that I know is pure gold."

"It's hollow, it's in the shape of a ring," Luca said, thinking furiously aloud. "Doesn't matter. The central hole has no weight. We are weighing the gold of the ring, not measuring the area. Get it."

"It's Isolde's mother's ring," Ishraq explained. "I have carried it and her family jewels for her ever since we left home."

"Are you sure it is pure gold?"

She nodded. "The Lord of Lucretili would have given his lady nothing less," she said.

He did not even hear her; he was looking from the gold nobles to the water in the glass. Ishraq ran from the room, up the stairs to the girls' rooms and lifted her gown, to rip at the hem of her linen shift.

"What on earth are you doing?" Isolde asked. She was standing on a wooden chair, a dressmaker kneeling before her, hemming a gown. On one side a tirewoman was making a magnificent headdress, and there were carnival masks all around the room—silks, satins and velvets thrown everywhere in a jumble of richness and color.

"Getting your mother's gold ring," Ishraq said tersely, tearing at the delicate hem stitches. "For Luca to weigh against the gold nobles."

"Still?" Isolde said irritably. "You've been locked in all morning. And I heard you drop a plate."

"Smashed it," Ishraq said cheerfully, retrieving the ring and pulling down her dress again.

"Make sure he doesn't damage it," Isolde said disagreeably. "That ring is valuable."

Ishraq said nothing but raced back to Luca. He was pacing up and down, scowling in thought, he hardly noticed her come in until she put the ring into his hand.

At once he turned and put it on the delicate spice scales that Freize had brought them from the kitchen. He added the tiny weights—the smallest was half a grain of wheat. Isolde's mother's ring was just over 121 grains.

"Write it down," Luca ordered Ishraq. "The ring is pure gold, 121 and a half grains. Now. How much water does it move?"

Luca lifted it from the scale and put it into the water glass. At once the water rose within the glass. With a sharp piece of chalk Luca marked where the water level rose, and then hooked the ring out with a fork and held it over the water so that every drop fell back into the glass and the water level was the same as before.

"You are certain this is pure gold?" he asked quietly.

Ishraq was impressed with his concentration. "Certain," she whispered.

"Well, the noble should be 108 grains," Luca said. "And the noble plus half of one of the quarter nobles should be exactly 121 and a half grains. So the mass is the same. If it is less dense, then it has been mixed with tin or something lighter than gold, and the water will rise higher." Gently, without making a splash, he dropped the full coin into the glass of water and then dropped the sawed half of the quarter noble on top of it.

They both held their breath as the water level rose,

sticking to the side of the glass, but definitely rising up and up until it reached the mark set by the ring.

"The coins are pure gold," Luca said in quiet triumph. "Someone, somewhere, is either stealing English nobles fresh from the mint in Calais, or else they are mining the purest gold and forging their own."

The five of them were elated, as if they had found the gold mine itself.

"So what next?" Isolde asked. "How will we find the mint? How will we find the forgers?"

"Could we buy so much gold that the money changer cannot serve us from his own store?" Luca suggested. "Then we'll ask him where we can go to collect it. If he won't say, we'll have to watch him, see where he goes to get a chest of gold."

"We can take it in turns to watch . . ." Ishraq started.

Luca shook his head. "No, not you," he said. He glanced at Isolde and saw her nod in agreement. "I am sorry, Ishraq, but you can't. If we want to pass as a wealthy family, then you two have to behave like ladies. You can't come to the Rialto and spy on the gold merchants."

"Really, we can't," Isolde told her.

"I could go dressed as a common girl. Or dressed as a

boy! Isolde has bought a roomful of costumes and masks! It is carnival time, almost everyone is disguised."

"It's not worth the risk," Brother Peter ruled. "And besides, you should not be wandering the streets exposed to danger. It happens that we are here in the only time of year that women are allowed out of their homes at all. All the women in Venice will dress up in disguise, wear masks, and go out on the streets for the twenty days before Lent; the city is never more unruly than now. They are a most extreme people. This is an exception, a time of utter license; the rest of the year they only go out to visit privately in each other's houses, or to church."

"But as it's carnival, surely we can go out masked and disguised?" Ishraq insisted. "Even if it is only for these weeks?"

"Only if you want to be mistaken for the whores of the city," Brother Peter said crossly. "You would be advised not to go out at all. It is a time of great sin and debauchery. I would advise you to stay indoors. Indeed, I have to request that you stay indoors." He glanced at Luca for his agreement. "Since you are traveling with us and have agreed to enact the pretense that we are your guardians, I think it is right that you should give us the power to decide your comings and goings."

"Nobody has that power over me," Ishraq said quickly.

"I don't give it to you, I don't give it to anyone. I didn't leave home and then run away from the nunnery to be ordered about by you and Luca."

Luca flushed. "Nobody is ordering you," he said. "But if we are to keep up the pretense that we are here as a noble family, you will have to behave like the companion of a noblewoman. That's simply what you agreed to do, Ishraq."

"I'll go out masked," she promised herself.

"As long as someone goes with you," Luca compromised. "Apparently, the whole city goes quite mad for the days of carnival. But if Freize goes with you, or the housekeeper, you should be all right."

"So can I come with you to the Rialto this afternoon?" she asked. "To see Father Pietro? If I am masked?"

Luca shook his head. "This is my quest," he said. "I go alone.

Freize beamed. "I go alone too," he said. "I'll go alone with you."

The two young men left the house together; Ishraq and Isolde, at the upper-floor window, watched the black gondola nose into the middle of the Grand Canal and swiftly cut through the busy waterway.

"I'm going out," Ishraq said. "I'm going to get us boys' clothes so that we can walk around as we please."

Isolde brightened. "Do we dare?"

"Yes," Ishraq said firmly. "Of course we dare. We've come all the way across Italy. We're hardly going to be stuck indoors now because a couple of priests think that Venice is too sinful for us to see."

"I have ordered us both gowns from the seamstress."

"Yes, but I don't want gowns, I want costumes. I want disguises. I want boys' clothes so that we can go where we like. So no one knows who we are."

"Go, then," Isolde said excitedly. She put her hand into the pocket of her modest gray gown and pulled out a purse. "Here. Brother Peter gave me this, for alms for the poor and for candles at church, and for other things—who knows what—that he thought we might need: trinkets that ladies of a noble family might have. Go and get us breeches and capes and big masks!"

Ishraq laughed, pocketed the money and went from the room.

"And get me a big hat." Isolde slipped from the room and leaned over the marble staircase to call to her friend. "One that will hide my hair."

"And I'll trade with some of your mother's jewels!" Ishraq called softly up the stairs.

Isolde hesitated. "My mother's jewels? Which ones?"

"The rubies," Ishraq insisted. "This is our chance to make a fortune. We'll trade in the jewels and buy English gold nobles and watch them rise in price. When they've doubled in value we'll buy the rubies back and you'll still have them plus a fortune to hire your army to march on your brother."

"We could make so much money just by trading in the nobles?" Isolde asked, tempted at the thought.

"We might," Ishraq said. "Shall I do it? Shall I go to the money changer and buy gold nobles with your rubies?"

"Yes," Isolde said, taking a chance, tempted by the thought of a fortune easily made, which might win her back her inheritance. "Yes, take them."

At the Rialto the two young men found Father Pietro in his usual place, the bustle of the crowd all around him, someone juggling with daggers nearby, and a performing dog circling slowly and mournfully, a small ball balanced on his nose, his clown-faced owner passing the hat. They did not notice Ishraq, dressed as a boy, hat pulled low over her pinned-up hair, a black mask over her eyes, transacting her business with Israel, the money changer. They did not see her get into a hired gondola and quietly go away.

"This is my master," Freize introduced him, elbowing his way through the crowd to get to the priest. "This is Luca Vero."

"You are seeking your father," the Friar said gently. "And I am glad to tell you that I have news of him." He looked at Luca's sudden pallor. "Ah, my son. Are you ready to hear it?"

Luca bent his head and said a swift prayer. "Yes," he said. "Tell me at once."

"A slave that I ransomed from Bayeed last year told me that Guilliam Vero was serving on his ship then," Father Pietro said quietly. "He was alive and strong then, only last year. It may be that he is still slaving on the ship now."

"He might be alive?" Luca repeated as if he could not believe the news. "Now? This very day?"

"He might. I can send a message to Bayeed and ask if your father is alive and if Bayeed would accept a ransom for him."

Luca shook his head, to clear his whirling thoughts. "I can't think! I can't believe it!"

Freize put a gentle hand on his back. "Steady now," he said as if he were soothing a horse. "Steady."

"Yes. Of course," Luca said to the priest. "Please. Do it at once. When would we hear back?"

"If Bayeed were at Constantinople—" The priest corrected himself. "Istanbul as they call it now, God forgive them for taking our city, the Rome of the East, the home of God—well, if Bayeed was there it would take about two weeks to get a message to him. But you might be lucky. I heard he had come into Trieste. If that's true, then we might get a message to him within a few days. He may even be coming to Venice."

"Days?" Luca repeated. "He might be coming here?"

The priest put his hand gently over Luca's clenched fist. "Yes, my son. You might have an answer in days. If he is in port at Trieste, and my messenger can find him, and get a ship back to us with Bayeed's price."

Luca and Freize exchanged one amazed glance.

"Days," Luca repeated. "I might see my father within the week?"

"Usually, Bayeed will reply at once. But it won't be cheap. He will ask around a *lira di grosso* for a working slave—that's ten ducats." He paused. "That's about five nobles."

Luca nodded; he had mentally converted the currency in a moment, even while Father Pietro was speaking. He could not help but think of the fortune that he was carrying on this mission, but did not own: the wealth that Milord had entrusted to him, to pretend to be a trader in Venice, the gold coins that he had tested, the suspect coins made with real gold that he was ordered to buy, the share of the cargo of the ship that was even now, sails spread, coming across the seas from the east to bring a small fortune to him, the money he had been given to lay around to make the illusion of wealth. "I have that," he said quietly. "I have a fortune. I can pay. For the freedom of my father, I would pay that willingly."

Freize leaned toward his ear. "It's not really yours," he reminded his friend. "How will it be when Milord wants you to account for it?"

"I have to use it!" Luca said fiercely. "For my father's freedom, I would steal it outright! But this is just borrowing. I will explain to Milord. I will make it up to him with the profit I will make trading in the English nobles."

The priest nodded. "I will write tonight, then, and send Bayeed an offer to pay. I expect that they will want it in English gold nobles. That is the currency they prefer, both for ransom and tribute this year. It will be five English nobles. They may settle for four and a half; the value of the English noble is rising. It would be better for us to fix the price at once. Everyone seems to think that the value of the noble is going to reach the sky."

"I can get the coins," Luca assured him. "I can pay them in English nobles."

"And I have some other news for you as well."

Luca waited.

"The man who had served with your father said that

your father had learned where his wife had been taken. He knew that your mother was enslaved as a house servant, to a family that served the emperor. Your father had seen them buy her at the auction before Bayeed bought him. It may be that she lives, that she is working for them still. If they have moved with the court then they will be in Istanbul now, God forgive them for stealing our city."

Luca almost staggered under the news. Freize took his arm. "Steady," he said. "Steady now." Carefully, he put Luca on his feet, patted his back. "You all right, Sparrow?"

Luca brushed his hand away. "My mother?"

"This is old news," the friar cautioned. "Your father said that he saw her sold to a man who looked like he might be a good master, years ago; but of course she might not still be with them now."

"But you said that she was sold to a family who were connected to the emperor's court?"

"Yes. And that is a good service, easy work. I could write to one of the court officials and inquire for her," the priest said quietly. He lifted his pen. "What is her name?"

"Clara," Luca said. "Clara Vero. I can hardly believe this. I cannot believe this. I was told they were dead when I was no more than a boy of fourteen. They were taken from our farm, just a little place. Nobody even witnessed the raid. For four years I have given up all hope of ever seeing them again.

I have grieved for them ever since. I have feared that I was an orphan without parents."

"God is merciful," the old priest said gently. "Praise Him."

"It's quite a miracle," Freize confirmed. "Amen. Bear up, Sparrow."

Luca bowed his head and whispered a prayer. "When shall I come to you again, Father?" he asked.

"I will send for you as soon as I have news, any news at all," the priest said gently. "It will be a few days before we know of your father, months before we can trace your mother. You will have to learn patience. Your servant tells me you are living in the palazzo of the de Longhi family?"

"Yes." Luca nodded. "Yes. Send for me there."

"You have come a long way from a little village, from your farm," the priest remarked. "Clearly, you have enjoyed much worldly success."

Luca, shaken by the news of his parents, was quite at a loss. He could not find a ready lie.

"My master has been lucky in trade," Freize interrupted swiftly. "We have come to Venice to trade in gold, for it is his speciality. And we have a share in a cargo that is coming in from Russia. But he was determined to see you and ask you if you could find his father. He's a most devoted son."

The priest smiled. "Perhaps you will give some of your

wealth to the Church," he said to Luca. "There are many Christians who could be ransomed back to their family, just like your father and mother, if we only had the money for their ransom."

"I will," Luca promised, shaken with emotion. Freize saw that he hardly knew what he was saying. "I will. I would want to be generous. I would want others to come home too. God knows, if I had my way, there would be no men and women in slavery and no fatherless children waiting for them."

"God be with you, then, my son"—the priest drew the sign of the cross in the air—"and may He guide your way as you trade in gold and sell your cargo. For that is a very worldly business and you will need to guard yourself against criminals."

"And no need to tell all of Venice our business," Freize said quietly. "The little farm then—the great fortune now: my master doesn't like it talked about."

"I don't gossip," the priest said gently. "My trade is in information about poor lambs lost from the flock. My work depends upon my discretion."

"Fair enough." Freize nodded and turned to follow Luca. "Much gold around here, is there?" Freize asked nonchalantly.

"I have never seen so many English gold nobles in my life before," the priest said. "Truly God is good. For the Ottomans are demanding to be paid in gold nobles and many people have given me gold nobles for my work, and their price rises every day so I can buy more souls with the lucky coins. I have traded all my savings into the gold nobles so that I can do my work, praise Him."

Back at the house Ishraq dashed in the side door to the street just as the gondola carrying Freize and Luca nosed into the water gate that opened into the front of the house. She ran up the stairs, taking them two at a time, to the girls' floor as the men were walking together, up from the water level to the main floor. She bundled capes and breeches and sturdy shoes under her bed and showed Isolde the purse of gold coins.

"How much did you get for the rubies?" Isolde asked quickly in a whisper.

"Ten and a half gold nobles," Ishraq replied. "It was the best I could do."

Isolde gulped at the thought of speculating with her mother's jewels. "I hope they gain value," she said nervously. "They were my mother's greatest treasure."

"Me too," said Ishraq. "But everyone says that the nobles will be worth more, even tomorrow. People are gambling on good prices tomorrow even now, as the market is closing. We could sell them at a profit tomorrow and get the rubies back."

Isolde crossed her fingers and tapped them against

Ishraq's forehead in an old silly game from their childhood.

"Lucky luck," Ishraq replied. "You go on down to him, I'll put this purse under the mattress."

As Isolde entered the room Luca's face lit up, and he took her hands as he told her that he thought he might be able to ransom his parents. "This is wonderful news," she said. "This is the greatest thing that could happen for you."

For a moment they stood handclasped, and he realized that he had been hurrying home just so that he could tell her this news, that as soon as he had heard it, he had wanted her to know too.

"You understand," he said wonderingly. "You understand what this means to me."

"Because I lost my father too," she said gently. "Only mine has gone from me forever, into death. So I do understand how you can long for him, how his absence has been a grief for all of your life. But if your father can return to you, if your mother can come home, what a miracle that would be!"

"I would leave the Church," Luca said, almost to himself. "If they were to come home, I would leave the Church to live with them at our farm once again. I would be so proud to be their son and work in their fields. I would want nothing more."

"But your work—the Order of Darkness? They say that you have a great talent for understanding, that you must go throughout the world and read the signs for the end of days. Brother Peter says it is your gift and your calling. He says you are the greatest Inquirer he has ever seen at work, and he has traveled and advised many Inquirers."

He smiled at the praise. "Really? Did he say that?"

"Yes!" She smiled ruefully. "When he was scolding me. He even told me that I must not distract you from doing God's work. That you have a calling, a vocation. He says you are exceptional."

"Even so, I would go back to my father and mother if they were to be free and come home. Of course, I would complete my mission here, I would not leave anything undone. But if my parents were to come home, I would never want to be parted from them again. I wouldn't want to be exceptional, I would want to be an ordinary son."

She nodded. Of all of them, Isolde understood homesickness. On the death of her father, her brother had cheated her out of her lands and the castle that was to have been hers. "But you know, we can never really go back," she said gently to him. "Even if I raise an army from my godfather's son and defeat my brother and get my lands returned to me, even if I ride into my own castle gate and call it mine once more, it will never be the same. Nothing can ever be as it was. My father would still be dead. My brother would still have betrayed me. I would still be alone in the world but for Ishraq. I would still have known grief in the loss of my father and anger in the betrayal of my brother. My heart would still be a little hardened. I would not be the same, even if the castle still stood."

"I know," he said. "You're right. But if my parents could return home, or if you could live where you belong, then, in our own ways, in our own places, we could make new lives for ourselves. New lives in the old places. New lives where we truly belong. We could start again, from where we began."

She understood at once that their lives would take them in very different directions. "Oh Luca, if I were to win Lucretili back, I would live very far from your farm."

"And I would be such a small farmer, I could never even speak to such a grand person as the Lady of Lucretili. You would ride past my farmhouse and not even look at me. I would be a dirty farmer's boy behind an ox and a plow, and you would be on a great horse, riding by."

Without exchanging another word they both thought— yes, whatever new life is ahead of us, we can never make a life together—and quietly, they released their clasped hands.

"We can't neglect our mission." Brother Peter came into the room and saw them turning away from each other. "That's the main thing. That's the only thing. I am glad that you have traced your father, Luca. But we must remember that we have work to do. We have a calling. Nothing matters more than tracing the signs of the end of the world."

"No, I won't forget what I have come here to do," Luca promised. "But since Milord commanded us to trade and even gamble, this is a chance for me. I need to earn some gold on my own account. I will need a small fortune to ransom both my parents."

"You might get it by trading," Ishraq remarked, coming into the room. Isolde shot one guilty look at her. "If you were to buy English nobles now, everyone says they will be worth twice what you pay for them, by only next month. This is a way to make money that is like magic. You buy now, and you sell in a month's time and someone gives you twice what you paid."

"But how?" Isolde asked nervously, directing the question to Luca. "I see that it happens, I see that half of Venice is counting on it happening—every day a little profit is added. But how does it happen?"

"Because everyone wants the English nobles, and they think that there are more buyers than coins to be bought," Luca said. "It is like a dream. Everyone buys, expecting to make a profit, and so the value goes up and up. It could be anything that they are running after. It could be nobles or shells or diamonds or even houses. Anything that can be exchanged for money—so that its value can be seen to increase. If more people want it, they outbid each other, and the price rises."

"But one day it will burst like an overfull bladder," Ishraq predicted. "The trick is to make sure that you have sold before that day arrives."

"And how do you know when that day comes?" Luca asked her, and was surprised to see the anxious look that passed between the two young women.

"Why, I was hoping you would know," Isolde confessed. "We have bought some nobles."

"You have?" Luca laughed. "You are speculators?"

The girls nodded, wide-eyed as if they had frightened themselves.

"How much?" Luca asked, sobering as he saw how serious they were.

"Ten and a half nobles," Isolde confessed.

He made a soundless whistle. "How did you get them?"

"I sold my mother's rubies," Isolde confessed. "Now of course I am afraid that I will never be able to buy them back."

"Will you tell us when you think we should sell?" Ishraq asked him.

He nodded. "Of course, I'll do my best. And we'll be in the market every day, watching the prices."

"And they are gold, solid gold—we tested them," Ishraq reminded him. "Whatever happens they can't fall below the value of gold."

"Perhaps Luca will win his fortune?" Brother Peter said, turning to them with a letter in his hand, deaf to their conversation. "Luca, you have been invited—actually, we have all been invited—to an evening's gambling, in a neighboring palace, the day after tomorrow. A letter of invitation came while you were out. Our name seems to have gotten about already, and the lies we have told to pass as a wealthy family. There was an invitation to a banquet also."

The two girls looked up.

"Shall we go?" Luca asked.

"I think we have to," Brother Peter said heavily. "We have to mix with people who have these gold nobles to discover where they come from and how much English gold is circulating. Milord himself said that we would have to gamble to maintain the appearance of being a wealthy, worldly family. I shall pray before we go out and when we come back. I shall pray that the Lord will keep me from temptation."

"For any woman is certain to fling herself at him," whispered Ishraq to Isolde, prompting a smile.

"And shall we come?" Isolde asked. "Since I am to play the part of your sister?"

"You are invited to visit with the ladies of the house." Brother Peter handed over a letter addressed to Signorina Vero.

"They think I have your name!" Isolde exclaimed to Luca and then suddenly flushed.

"Of course they do," Brother Peter said wearily. "We are all using Luca's name. They think I am called Peter Vero, his older brother."

"It just sounds so odd! As if we were married," Isolde said, red to her ears.

"It sounds as if you are his sister," Brother Peter said coldly. "As we agreed that you should pretend to be. Will you visit the ladies while we go gambling? Ishraq should accompany you as your servant and companion."

"Yes," Isolde said. "Though gambling and a banquet sound like much more fun than visiting with ladies."

"We are not going to have fun," Brother Peter said severely. "We are going to trace false gold, and to do this we will have to enter into the very heart of sin."

"Yes indeed," Isolde agreed but did not dare look at Ishraq, whose shoulders were shaking with suppressed laughter. "And we will do our part. We can listen for any news of gold while we are talking to the ladies, we can ask them what their husbands are paying for the gold nobles on the Rialto and where they are getting them."

The next morning, Freize, Luca and Brother Peter went again to the Rialto Bridge to see the money changers. "How will we know how much gold they keep by them?" Brother Peter asked anxiously as the gondola wove its way through the many ships. "We need to demand enough to make them go to their suppliers, so that we can see where they go. But how shall we know how much to ask for?"

"I saw only one chest behind the Jewish money changer, when we went before. I don't think he carries many coins into the square. But I don't know what he might keep at home," Freize said.

"Brother Peter has shown me the manifest for the cargo that Milord has given us," Luca volunteered. "It's due to come in from Russia next week. We'll get a quarter of the cargo of a full-size ship. We are talking about a fortune."

Freize whistled. "Milord has this to give away? What's the ship carrying?"

"Amber, furs, ivory."

"How is Milord so wealthy?" Freize asked. "Is he not sworn to poverty like the brothers in our abbey?"

Brother Peter frowned. "His business is his own concern, Freize; nothing to do with you. But, of course, he has the wealth of the Holy Church behind him."

"As you say." Luca adjusted his view of his mysterious master yet again. "I knew he had great power. I didn't know he could command great wealth too."

"They are one and the same," Brother Peter said dolefully. "Both the doorway to sin."

"Indeed," Freize said cheerfully. "And clearly none of my business, dealing as I do with petty power and small change."

"We'll say that we want to trade the cargo for gold, as soon as the ship comes in," Luca decided. "We'll ask them if they keep enough gold in store. I'll show them the manifest if I need to. We'll have to match our words to what seems most likely and make it up as we go along."

Brother Peter shook his head. "I am lying every time I draw breath in this city," he said unhappily.

"Me too," Freize said without any sign of discomfort. "Terrible."

The gondolier drew the craft up to the steps and held the boat alongside the quay. "Shall I wait?"

"Yes," Luca said as he stepped ashore.

"The ladies will not need the gondola?"

"The ladies will not go out," Brother Peter ruled. "They could only go to church in our absence, and they can walk to San Marco."

The gondolier bowed in obedience as the men went up the quay's steps to the busy square. Freize looked around at once for the pretty girl who gambled with the cups and ball. She was kneeling before the game, a square of pavement sprinkled with white sand, the three cups tipped upside down before her. Her taciturn father was standing nearby, as always.

"I'll just be a moment," Freize excused himself to Luca and Brother Peter, and went over to her. "Good morning, Jacinta," he said and was rewarded by a bright smile. "Good morning, Drago Nacari," he said to her father. "Are you busy today?"

"Busy as always," she said, smoothing the sand and resetting out the cups. Freize watched as she put the cloudy marble under one cup and then swapped them round and round, swirling them quickly until they came to rest. He watched a few times, and then he could resist temptation no longer.

"That one," Freize said with certainty. "That one, I would put my life on it."

"Just put your pennies on it," she said with a quick upward flash of her brown eyes. "I don't want your life."

"It's the right-hand one," Luca said quietly beside him. "I was watching. I am certain."

"Whatever you think," the girl said. "Why don't you both bet?"

Luca put down a handful of small coins on the right-hand cup but Freize put down all the contents of his purse on the center cup.

She laughed as if a customer's winning gave her real pleasure, and she said to Freize: "Your friend has quicker eyes than you! He is right." She scooped up all the money before the central cup that Freize, and most of the crowd, had chosen, and to Luca she counted up his *piccoli* and handed him a quarter English noble. "Your winnings," she said. "You get your stake back three times over."

"It's a good game to win," he said, taken aback to have one of the English coins passed into his hand as if it were ordinary currency.

She misunderstood his hesitation. "That's a quarter English noble. It's as good as a half ducat," she said. "It's a good coin."

"I hope you're not questioning the gold coins?" someone asked from the crowd.

"Not at all. I'm just surprised by my good fortune," Luca said.

"It's a rare game to win," Freize grumbled. "But a clever game, and a pleasure to watch you, Jacinta."

"Have you come to see Father Pietro again?" she asked. "For he doesn't come till the afternoon."

"No, my master here is a trader. He is arranging to sell a great cargo that will come in any day now," Freize said glibly. "Silks. Wouldn't you love a silk dress, Jacinta? Or ribbons for your shiny brown hair?"

She smiled. "Oh very much! Shall you gamble them on my cups and ball? A dress for me if you lose three times over?"

Freize grinned at her. "No, I shall not! You would get a wardrobe full of dresses, I am sure, a shipful!"

She laughed. "It's just luck."

"It's a very great skill," Luca told her. He lowered his voice: "But I will tell you a secret."

She leaned forward to listen.

"I did not see that the marble was under the right-hand cup—your hands move too swiftly for me to see. I should think you are too quick for almost anyone. But I guessed that it would be the right-hand cup."

Her eyes narrowed as she looked at him. "A lucky guess?"

"No. A guess based on what I could see."

"And what did you see?"

"You're right-handed," he told her. "And the strongest move is to push away, not pull toward. When you move the cups around, you favor the cup with the hidden marble, and you favor the movement to your right. Three times out of the seven that I watched, you sent the cup with the marble to your right. And at the end of the day, when you're a little tired, I should imagine that you favor your right even more often."

She sat back on her heels. "You counted where the cup ended up? And remembered?"

Luca frowned. "I didn't set out to count," he explained. "But I couldn't help but notice. I notice things like patterns and numbers."

She smiled. "Do you play cards?"

Luca laughed. "You think I could count cards?"

"I'm sure you could," she said. "If you can count cards and remember them, you would win at Karnöffel. You could play here, on the square. There is a fortune to be won— everyone here has money in their pockets, everyone believes that they might be lucky."

Luca glanced back to Brother Peter, who was waiting for them with an air of wearied patience. "I don't gamble, my brother would not like it. But it is true that I would be able to remember the hands."

"If you learned a set of numbers, how many would you be able to remember?" she asked.

He closed his eyes and imagined that he was a boy running down a portico with colonnades of numbers flicking past him. "I don't know, I've never tried. Thousands, I think."

"Sir, do you see numbers in colors?"

It was such an extraordinary question that he hesitated and laughed. "Yes, I do," he confessed. "But I think it is a rare illusion. An odd trick of the eye, or perhaps of the mind. Who knows? Of no use, as far as I know. Do you see numbers as colors?"

She shook her head. "Not I. But I know that some people who can understand numbers see them in colors or as pictures. Can you understand languages at first hearing?"

He hesitated, shy of boasting, remembering the bullying he suffered when he was a child for being a boy of exceptional abilities. "Yes," he said shortly. "But I don't regard it."

She turned and summoned her father to come closer with a toss of her head. Drago Nacari came over and shook Luca's hand in greeting. "This is my father," Jacinta introduced him. To her father she spoke in rapid French: "This young man has a gift for numbers and for languages. And he is a stranger new-come to Venice, and he came to us today."

Drago's grip on Luca's hand suddenly tightened. "What chance! I have been hoping and praying that such a man like you might come along," he said.

"Last night I had a dream," the girl said quietly to Luca. "I dreamed that a deer with eyes as brown and bright as yours came into the San Giacomo Square, stepping so that its hard little hooves echoed on the Rialto Bridge, and the square was a meadow and it was all green."

"He's a wealthy trader," Freize interrupted. "Just playing the game for fun. Not a gambler. Not likely to be any help to you in your line of work. Not like a deer, not like a deer at all."

"Do you understand me?" Drago asked Luca in Latin.

"I speak and read Latin," Luca confirmed. "I learned it when I was in my monastery."

"Do you understand me?" Drago asked him in Arabic.

Luca frowned. "I think that is the same question," he said tentatively. "But I don't speak Arabic. I'm just guessing."

"Well, you won't understand this," Drago said in Romany, the language of the traveling Egyptians. "Not one word of what I say!"

Luca laughed. "Now this is just lucky, but some Gypsies came to my village when I was a child," he said. "I heard them speak and understood at once."

"Do you know the language of birds?" Drago asked him very quietly in Italian.

Luca shook his head. "No. I've never heard of it. What is that?"

"I am studying some manuscripts that puzzle me," Drago Nacari remarked without answering the question. "There are numbers and strange words and something that looks like code. I said—only last night—that I must pray that God sends me someone who can understand numbers and languages, for without some help I will never make head nor tail of them. And then my daughter dreamed of a deer, walking over the Rialto Bridge. And today you come to us."

"Why would the dream mean me?" Luca asked.

Jacinta smiled at him. "Because you are as handsome as a young buck," she said boldly. "And the deer walked like you do, proudly and gracefully, with his head up, looking round."

Freize leaned forward. "I too am a young buck," he said quietly to her. "Perhaps it was me that you dreamed of? A buck, or at least a horse? Or a handsome ox. Steady, and well-made. When he was a boy I nicknamed him Sparrow because he was so slight, long-legged and half starved."

"You do indeed resemble a handsome horse," she said with a sweet smile. "And I liked you the moment we met."

"What sort of manuscripts?" Luca could not hide his interest.

"This is like a book with pictures and writing. But the pictures are of no plant or person that I have ever seen, and I cannot understand the language of the writing around them."

"Have you taken them to the university here, or in Padua?"

The man spread his hands. "I am afraid to do so," he admitted. "If these manuscripts contain secrets and are profitable, then I should like to be the one who profits from them. If they are heretical then I don't want to be the one to bring them to the Church and be punished for it. They will ask me where I got them, they will ask me what they mean. They may accuse me of forbidden knowledge, when I know nothing. You see my dilemma?"

"Are these on the list of banned books?" Freize asked cautiously. "My master can't read anything that might be heresy."

The man shrugged. "As I can't even translate their titles. I don't know what they are."

"Why would you trust me?" Luca asked.

Drago smiled. "If you translate them, you will be translating a few pages of a very long book. They would make little sense to you. You'd have to be a philosopher to begin to understand them. You say you're a trader. It's a quicker way to a fortune than studying the wisdom of the ancients. But I would promise you a share in anything I discovered through your scholarship."

"I would certainly be most interested to see them," Luca said eagerly. "And we are traveling with a lady . . ."

"His sister's companion," Freize added, trying to maintain the fiction of their identity. He leaned his shoulder heavily against Luca. "And see, your brother is waiting for us and getting impatient."

Luca glanced over his shoulder to Brother Peter, who was looking frankly alarmed at the time they were spending with street gamblers. "Yes, just a moment. The lady that I mean is my sister's companion. She is half Arab, and could help us with the Arabic. She studied in Spain at the Moorish universities and is very well-read. She was educated as a true scholar."

"An educated woman?" Jacinta asked eagerly, as if it were not a contradiction in terms.

"Shall I bring the manuscript to your house?" Drago Nacari asked him.

"Come," Luca invited him. "Come this afternoon. I should be most interested to see it."

"We will come as soon as we have finished here," Drago promised. "After Sext."

"Agreed," Luca said.

The man bowed and Jacinta knelt once more and brushed the sand over the square of the paving stone. Freize dropped down to his knee to say a quiet good-bye to her. "So shall I see you this afternoon? Will you come with your father?"

"If he asks me to come," she replied.

"Then I shall see you again, at our house, the Ca' de Longhi."

She smiled. "Either there, or I am always here in the morning. Perhaps tomorrow you will come and place a bet and you will be lucky."

"I am very lucky," Freize assured her. "I was snatched by a terrible flood and I came home safe. I was in a nunnery where everyone was half mad and I came out unscathed, and before all of that I was apprenticed as a kitchen lad in a country monastery and the only boy that I liked in the whole world was summoned to Rome and turned into a lord and he took me with him. That's when I got my lucky penny."

"Show it to me again," she demanded, smiling.

He produced it from a pocket in his shirt. "I keep it apart from my other money now, so I don't spend it by accident. See? It is a penny minted by the Pope himself in the year of my birth. It survived a flood with me and I didn't spend it as I found my way home. Lucky through and through."

"Will you not bet with it?" she asked. "If it's so lucky?"

"No, for if it were to fail just once and I were to lose it, it would break my heart," Freize said. "And all my luck would be gone. But I would give it to you . . . for something in exchange."

"Lend it to me," she said, smiling. "Lend it to me and I promise I will give it back to you. As good as before but a little better."

"A keepsake?" he asked. "A sweetheart's keepsake?"

"I won't keep it for very long," she said. "You'll have it back, I promise."

At once he handed it over. "I shall want it returned with a kiss," he stipulated.

Shyly, she kissed her fingertips and put them against his cheek.

"See how lucky I am already!" Freize beamed, and was rewarded by a flash of her eyes from under her dark eyelashes as he jumped up and followed Luca.

Luca led Brother Peter and Freize across the busy square to the line of money changers whose long trestle table was set back under the portico, each trader seated, with a young man with a stout cudgel or a menacing knife under his belt standing behind him.

"That's the one, on the left," Freize prompted him. Luca went toward the man whose tall hat and yellow round badge showed him to be a Jewish money changer. He sat alone, at the end of the row, separated from the Christian money men by a little space, as if to indicate his inferior status.

"I would talk business with you," Luca said pleasantly.

The man gestured that Luca might sit as his boy brought a second stool. Luca sat, and Brother Peter and Freize stood behind him.

"I am an honest man of business," the money changer said a little nervously. "Your servant will confirm that I gave him a fair exchange for his coins when he came the day before yesterday. And actually, the value has risen already. I would buy the English nobles back from him and give him a profit."

Freize nodded, and smiled his open-faced beam. "I have no complaint," he said cheerfully. "I'm hanging on to them and hoping they will rise in value again."

"I have a share in a ship coming in from the East, carrying Russian goods," Luca said, leaning toward the money changer so that no one else could hear. "I want to prepare for the sale of the cargo, as soon as it comes into port."

"You have borrowed against it?" the money changer asked acutely.

"No!" Brother Peter exclaimed.

"Yes," Luca said, speaking simultaneously.

They exchanged an embarrassed look. "My brother denies it, for he hates debt," Luca explained quickly. "But yes, I have borrowed against it, and that is why I want to sell it quickly, as soon as it enters port, and for gold nobles."

"Of course," the man said. "I would be interested in buying a share, but I don't carry that many nobles to hand. I keep my fortune in different values. You would accept a payment in silver? In rubies?"

"No, I only want gold," Luca said. "My preference would be gold coins. These English nobles, for instance?"

"Oh, everyone wants English nobles, they are driving up the price! It's ridiculous."

"Perhaps. But that makes them better for me. I want to get them while they are rising in price. The value of my cargo would be perhaps a thousand English nobles?"

The merchant lowered his eyes to the table before him. "A very great sum, Milord!"

"It is easily worth that." Luca lowered his voice. "Almost all furs."

"Indeed."

"Squirrel, fox, and beaver. I told my agent to only buy the very best. And some silks and amber and ivory." Luca spread the cargo manifest on the trader's table, letting him see the goods that had been ordered.

The trader nodded. "So. If your cargo is as good as you describe . . ."

"But I will only sell for the English nobles."

"It would take me a few days to get that sum together," the money changer said.

"You could get the full amount?"

"I could. When would your ship come in?"

"It's due next week," Luca said. "But, of course, it could be delayed."

"If it is very late, you will find the gold nobles have risen in value and I will only be able to pay for the cargo at the current value of the nobles. But I will offer you a fair price for the furs, and I am very interested in the amber. I will pay you a deposit now, if you would let me have first look at the goods, and first offer?"

"You perhaps want a pound of flesh as well?" Brother Peter demanded irritably.

The merchant bent his head, ignoring the insult. "I will offer in English nobles."

"But where will you get so many coins?" Brother Peter asked. "From these other money changers?"

The trader looked along the row of little tables. "They don't like to work with me except for an extreme profit," he said. "And it is not always good for a man of my religion to do business with Christians."

"Why not?" Brother Peter asked, bristling.

The Jewish money changer gave him a rueful smile. "Because, alas, if they decide to deny a debt, I cannot get justice."

"Even in Venice?" Luca asked, shocked. He knew that

all of Christendom was against the Jews, who only survived the regular riots against them because they lived in their own areas under the protection of the local lord; but he had thought that in Venice the only god was profit, and the laws protecting trade were rigidly enforced by the ruler of Venice, the doge.

"It is better for people of my faith in Venice than elsewhere," the merchant conceded. "We are protected by the laws and by the doge himself. But here, like everywhere, we prefer to work only with men we can trust. And anyway, I can get all the gold nobles I need without going to the Christian money changers."

"You will go to the Arab bankers?" Brother Peter was suspicious. "You will go to gold merchants? We don't want the whole of Venice knowing our business."

"I will say nothing. And it does not matter to you where I get the nobles as long as they are good. I go to my own merchant. Only one. And he is discreet."

"And the English nobles are the best currency, aren't they?" Luca confirmed. "Though it is surprising that there are so many of them on the market at once."

The man shrugged. "The English are losing the war against France," he said. "They have been pouring gold into France to pay for their army in Bordeaux. When they lost Bordeaux last summer, the city was sacked and the campaign funds disappeared. As it happens, the money chests all came here. These things happen in wartime. That's their sorrow and our gain, for the coins are good. I have tested them myself, and I can get them at a good price."

"And who is your supplier?" Brother Peter asked bluntly.

The merchant smiled. "He would prefer Venice not to know *his* business," he said. "You will find me discreet, just as you asked me to be."

"When will you get them?" Luca asked.

No one but Luca would have noticed the swift, almost invisible glance that went from the money changer toward the street-gambling girl's father, who was helping her pack up her game, quite unaware of the money changers. But Luca was watching the Jew as closely as he had watched Jacinta playing the cups-and-ball game.

"By tomorrow," the man said. "Or the next day."

"Very good," Luca said pleasantly. "I'll come again tomorrow. Perhaps I'll have news of my ship then."

"I hope so." The merchant rose from his stool and bowed to the three men. "And please, do not speak of your ship with others till we have concluded our business."

They crossed the square together and got into the gondola, Freize throwing a casual smile and salute to Jacinta as they went by. The gondolier steered out into the middle of the canal as Freize said quietly: "Put me down on the far side. I'll stick to the merchant like glue and come home to report later."

"Take care you're not seen," Luca cautioned him.

"Carnival!" Freize said. "I'll buy a mask and a cape."

"Just follow him," Luca said. "Don't try to be a hero. Just follow and watch and then come home. I don't expect us to solve the mystery in one step. Things might not be as they appear."

"This is Venice," Brother Peter said miserably. "Nothing is as it appears."

As the two men set off for home in the gondola, Freize strolled back to the Rialto Bridge, pausing only to buy a handsome dark red cloak, a matching elaborate mask and a glorious big red hat in one of the many stalls that lined the bridge. He put them on at once and went down the steep steps of the bridge and into the Campo San Giacomo. Jacinta and her father had already finished for the day, and gone away. As Freize looked around he saw the money changer picking up his papers, locking them in his box and gesturing to his young guard to carry box and table away. He himself carried the two little stools.

With the enormous red hat bobbing gently on his head, and the mask completely obscuring his face, Freize was confident that he would not be recognized, but realized that he was rather noticeable, even among the flamboyant carnival costumes, as he watched the money changer weave quietly through the crowds around the Rialto Bridge and make his way inland.

"Now then," Freize admonished himself, pulling the hat off his head and crushing the bobbing peak down into the brim and snapping off three overarching plumes, to make an altogether smaller and more modest confection. "I think I made the mistaking of buying a hat out of vanity and not from discretion. But if I fold it like so . . ." He paused to admire the reduced shape. "That's better, that's surely better now."

Freize followed the money changer and his lad at a safe distance, ready to step into a doorway if the man looked round, but the old man went steadily onward, and his page boy led the way, never looking back. They went down one dark street after another, twisting and turning around little alleyways to find the way to little wooden bridges, some of which had to be lowered by the young man for the merchant to cross and then raised up again so that the water traffic was not delayed. At the larger canals the pair had to wait at the steps leading down to the water for a flat-bottomed boat to ferry them across for the price of a *piccoli*. Freize stood behind them, shrinking into the shadows, waiting for them to cross and go on their way, before he whistled the boat back to ferry him over. He had to fall back and was afraid then that he had lost them, but he heard their footsteps echoing on the stone quayside as they went under a bridge, following the canal, and he could hurry after them, guided by the sound. It was a long and rather eerie walk, through the quiet dark back streets of the city with every path running alongside a dark silent canal, and the constant sound of the splash of water against weedy stone steps.

Freize was glad to arrive at a corner, just in time to see them knocking on the side door to a house on the very edge of the Venice ghetto, where the air was smoky and dark and the canals were cloudy with the soil of the tanneries and stained with dye from cloth. All the dirty work of the city was done in this area, and the Jews of the city were confined here at night behind the ghetto walls and a bolted gate. Freize peered around a corner and saw the door of the house open, and in the candlelight that spilled out he saw the pretty young woman, Jacinta, admit the two men into the house.

"The gambling girl," Freize remarked to himself. "Now that's a little odd. There's no great fortune to be made taking small coins from playing cups and ball, and yet—that's a pretty big house. And the money changer has come here as his first call when he wants a lot of gold nobles."

He pulled his big hat down over his mask and waited, leaning back in a darkened doorway. After nearly an hour the

Jewish money changer came out, followed by his lad, and the two of them went through the narrow gate into the ghetto. Freize did not dare follow, knowing that he would be conspicuous among all the dark-suited men who wore the round yellow badge. But he waited outside the gate and watched as the money changer and his boy turned sharply right, into a tall thin house that overlooked the dark canal. Over the doorway swung the three balls, the ancient insignia of the money changer and lender.

"Hi, lad, tell me, who lives in there?" Freize asked a passing errand boy, who was clattering along the street with some newly forged metal rings for barrels, slung like hoops over his shoulder.

Freize pointed at the house behind the ghetto gate, and the boy glanced back over his shoulder. "Israel the moneylender," he said shortly. "He has a stall in the Campo San Giacomo, every day, or you can tap on the door and borrow money any time, night or day. They say he never sleeps. And if he ever did, his wealth is guarded by a golem."

"A golem? What's that?"

"A monster made from dust, obedient to his every word. That's why nobody ever burgles his house. The golem is waiting for them. It has the strength of ten men, and he controls it by the word on its forehead. If he changes a letter of the word, the golem crumbles to dust. But if the golem attacks you, it goes on and on forever, until you are dead."

"Inconvenient," Freize commented, believing none of this. He fell into step beside the young man as they crossed the wider square outside the ghetto. "And do you know who lives in that house?" He pointed to Jacinta's house, where the moneylender had visited for an hour.

The boy broke into a trot. "I can't stop, I have to get these to the cooper by this afternoon."

"But who lives there?"

"The alchemist!" the boy called back. "Nacari, the alchemist, and the pretty girl he says is his daughter."

"Are they guarded by a golem?" Freize shouted after him in jest.

"Who knows?" the boy called back. "Who knows what goes on in there? Only God, and He is far, far away from here!"

"And you are certain that they didn't see you?" Luca demanded. Freize was proudly reporting on his work as the group ate dinner together, the doors closed against eavesdroppers. Freize's plate was piled high: his reward to himself for good work well done.

"They did not, for I didn't go near the Nacari house. And I am certain that the money changer did not see me, nor his page boy."

Luca looked at Brother Peter. "And the boy on the street called Nacari an alchemist?"

Brother Peter shrugged. "Why not? He's a street gambler, we know that for sure. He could equally be a magician or a trickster. A bloodletter, an unqualified physician, perhaps a dentist? A trader in old manuscripts and in love potions? Who knows what he does? Certainly nothing known and certified with a proper license from the Church."

There was a silence. It was Isolde who said what everyone was thinking. "And perhaps Drago Nacari is a coiner as well as everything else. Perhaps he's a forger."

"We tested the coins ourselves," Luca reminded her.

"That only proves that some of them are good."

"But why would they make English gold nobles?" Ishraq asked. "Wouldn't he do better to make gold bars?"

"Not necessarily," Brother Peter said. "If you forged gold bars then most of your customers would buy them to have them worked at once, into gold goods or jewelry. That's when you'd be in danger of them discovering the base metal inside the bar. But if you forge perfect-looking coins—especially some with a persuasive story behind them—English nobles made in the Calais mint to pay the English soldiers—it all makes sense, and you can release the coins into the market. We know that they are traded against Venetian ducats at two to one. And the money changer said they were rising in price."

"But we tested them," Luca reminded him. "Others must test them and find them good."

"Perhaps they are very good forgeries," Brother Peter said suspiciously. "At any rate, no one says anything against them."

"They're still rising in price," Ishraq confirmed. "I looked today. They're up again."

Isolde shot her a quick smile. "You are a trader," she whispered.

"But what would such a man buy instead?" Luca wondered aloud. "If you sell your forged gold coins? What do you buy with the profit? How do you take the profit?"

"Jewels," Isolde guessed. "Small things that you can easily take away if you get caught."

"Books," Ishraq volunteered. "Alchemy books so that you can practice your art. Old manuscripts, as we know he has. Precious ingredients for your craft."

"Horses," Freize said. "So you can get away."

Luca exchanged an affectionate glance with his friend. "And because you'd always buy horses."

Freize nodded. "What would you buy?" he asked Brother Peter curiously.

"I'd buy masses for my soul," Brother Peter answered. "What matters more?"

There was a brief respectful silence. "Well, they don't look like wealthy people," Freize said. "There's the daughter working every morning in the street for handfuls of silver, and she's not wearing gold bracelets. She said she would gamble with me for a silk dress. She answered the door as if they didn't have a maid. But they have that big house. It doesn't add up."

"How can we find out more?" Luca puzzled aloud. "How can we find out what they're doing?"

"We could break in," Ishraq volunteered. "We know that they are out every morning, gambling at the Rialto. The father is always there with her, isn't he? And Freize thinks they have no maid."

"They've been there every morning, that we've seen so far," Freize said cautiously. "And he is coming here this afternoon. They have a manuscript to show Luca."

"They asked me if I would look at it. I said you might be able to read it, if it is in Arabic," Luca said to Ishraq.

"Is it about alchemy?"

"He said it was a mystery to him. But obviously it is something strange. He does not want to take it to the university nor to the Church."

"Well, I can try to read it with you this afternoon. And tomorrow morning why don't you go to the square and gamble with them, keep them there, while I go to the house and break in?"

"You can't go alone," Isolde said. "I'll come with you."

"No, that would be to walk straight into danger." Luca was instantly against the idea.

"And immodest to go wandering round the streets of Venice in carnival time," Brother Peter said crossly. "We have already agreed that it shouldn't be done. The young women must stay indoors like Venetian ladies."

"Carnival time is the very thing that makes it possible,"

Ishraq replied. "We can go disguised. I can dress as a young man, and Freize can come with me as my servant. You and Brother Peter go and gamble, and since they have never seen Isolde; she can go separately from both of us and act as lookout. If they pack up early or start to come home, she gets ahead of them, runs ahead of them, and brings us warning at their house so we can get out and away."

"You'll just go in, have a look round, and come away again," Luca ruled.

She nodded. "I'll get in through a window and open the door for Freize."

Luca hesitated. "Can you do that? Can you climb up a house wall and get in through a window?"

Isolde smiled. "She climbs like a cat," she said. "She was always getting in and out of the castle without the sentries knowing."

Luca glanced uncertainly at Brother Peter, whose face was dark with disapproval.

"We are to go gambling in the square while a woman in our care is breaking into a house?" Brother Peter demanded. "And no doubt thieving? While a young lady, a noblewoman, the Lady Isolde of Lucretili, acts as a lookout? Like some kind of gang of thieves?"

"So that we can write Milord's report," Luca reminded him. "He told us we were to find out where the English gold nobles were coming from. We're on the way to discovering the source."

Brother Peter shook his head sadly. "It's hard for me to countenance sin," he said. "Even for a great cause. Milord is our commander and the Order of Darkness is pledged to understand the rise of heresy, the signs of darkness, and the coming of the end of the world. Often in this work I have had to study terrible sin. But never before have I had to be a party to it."

"It's hardly terrible sin; you're only gambling for *piccoli*," Freize said cheerfully. "We might have to do far worse. And anyway—look on the bright side—you might win."

The five of them waited in their grand palace for the arrival of the alchemist and his daughter. Isolde was confined upstairs and so she peered down the great marble staircase, hoping to glimpse the stranger when he came up the steps from the water gate. Ishraq was waiting on the first floor in the dining room, which they had equipped as a study, with paper and pens laid out on the dining table. Freize, dressed in a dark suit and looking like a servant, was ready to greet the alchemist as his boat came into the private quay and to usher him upstairs. Brother Peter had shut himself in his room to write the report to Milord, and Luca was holding his chip of glass up to the light and idly measuring and drawing half arcs of rainbows while gazing out over the Grand Canal.

"I think that's him," he said to Ishraq as a small gondola detached itself from the seething traffic of the Grand Canal and turned toward the water gate of the palazzo. Luca crossed to the door with three swift steps. "Freize!"

"Ready!" came the shout from the lowest level of the house. Luca turned and looked upward to the second floor and caught a glimpse of Isolde's smile before she stepped back, out of sight. It was as if she had sent him a message of encouragement, or blown him a kiss; the smile was for him alone as if she was saying that she had faith in him.

He heard Freize greet the man and, looking down, saw him leading the dark-robed man up the stairs to the first floor. Luca went forward to greet him with his hand held out.

"Drago Nacari," he said. "Thank you for coming."

"Luca Vero," the man replied formally. "Thank you for inviting me to your home."

They entered the room, and Ishraq rose up from her seat behind the table. She was wearing her Moorish dress: tunic and pantaloons, her scarf covering her hair and half veiling her face. She bowed to Drago Nacari, and he took off his hat and swept a bow to her.

"This is my sister's companion, Mistress Ishraq," Luca introduced her. "I thought she might be able to help us with your manuscript. She speaks Arabic and Spanish, and she is a scholar."

"Of course," the man said. "I am honored to meet you."

"Did you not bring your daughter with you?" Ishraq asked.

"No," he said. "She is studying at home."

The three of them sat at the great table, Drago at the head, and Luca and Ishraq on either side of him. He was carrying a satchel and he put it on the table, unfastened the ties and slid out a sheet of parchment painted with beautiful symbols and plants, and closely written with a clerk's well-wrought handwriting.

"Where did you study?" he asked Ishraq politely. "Do you recognize any of this?"

"I was in the service of the Lord of Lucretili," she said. "He was a great crusader lord, and he took an interest in the people and the learning of the Moors. He took me to Spain to study with the philosophers at the universities. I was allowed to study geography and astronomy, some medicine and languages. It was a great privilege."

He bowed his head. "I have studied in Egypt," he said. "I read Arabic, but I cannot understand this. It is definitely an alchemy text. I know that much for certain. So we may expect certain things."

"What things?" Luca said.

"A mixture of symbols and numbers and words," the man answered. "Alchemists have symbols, special signs for many elements, and for many processes." He pointed to one symbol. "That means to heat gently, for instance; any alchemist would recognize it."

"Do you think this is a recipe?" Luca asked. "An alchemy recipe?"

Drago spread his hands. A small gold ring on his finger caught the light. "That, I don't know," he said. "I hope so, of course. I hope it is a recipe for the one thing, the greatest thing, the thing we all seek."

"And what is that?" Luca asked. He was scanning the first page of the manuscript, trying to see what words stood out. Nothing was recognizable; he could not even see a pattern.

"Of course, we all seek the stone," the man said quietly. "The philosopher's stone."

"What is that?" Luca asked.

Drago glanced at Ishraq to see how much she knew of the stone.

"It is the stone that changes base material to gold," she said quietly. "And water thrown on the stone when it is hot becomes the elixir of life, it can prolong life perhaps forever, it can make the old young, it can make the sick well. It is the one thing that all alchemists hope to make. It would solve all the troubles of the world."

"And you trust me to translate this with you?" Luca asked Drago Nacari. "If we could understand it, this document might mean the end to death and the beginning of limitless wealth for any one of us, for all of us." For a moment he thought what he would do if he had the stone and could command a fortune, an unstoppable fortune. He thought he would buy the freedom of his parents, of all slaves. Then he would buy the castle of Lucretili and give it to Isolde. Then he would ask her to marry him, he would be a man so rich that he could propose marriage to her. He broke off from his dream with a short laugh. "Already I am dreaming what I would do if I had the stone and could make gold," he said. "Why would you trust us strangers with this?"

"This is only one page of many," Drago said. "And it's not a recipe for stewing oysters, it's not easy. Even if you were to read every word, you still would be far from making the stone. To make the stone you would need to study for years. You need to purify yourself and everything you touch. I have been working for decades and only now am I starting to be ready. You may be very clever—Jacinta says that you have quick eyes and a good ear, and, of course, she dreamed of you—but you have not studied for years, as I have done."

Ishraq smiled. "And also there is the question of desire," she said.

"Desire?" Luca repeated the single inviting word.

Drago Nacari nodded. "You *are* learned, then," he confirmed to Ishraq.

"If you desire wealth, if you are bound to the world by greed, then you cannot find the stone for you are not pure in heart," Ishraq explained. "The only man or woman who can find such a thing would be he or she who wanted it for others. Someone who did not want it for themselves. It is the purest thing in the world, it cannot be discovered by someone with dirty hands, it cannot be snatched in a greedy grasp."

Luca nodded. "I think I understand. So let's have a look at it."

"It's not Arabic," Ishraq said. "Though some of the symbols are like Arabic symbols." She pointed to one sign. "This one, and perhaps these."

"It's no language that I recognize," Luca said. "Have you shown it to a Russian? Or to someone from the East?"

Drago shook his head. "Not yet. I hoped to be able to understand it on my own, but I have studied it for months now, and I see that I need help."

"I don't recognize these plants," Ishraq said. "I've never even seen them, not in the garden, not in an herbal. Do you know them?"

Luca did not answer her. He was looking at the writing and scribbling something down. Ishraq immediately fell silent and looked from Luca's notes to the manuscript.

"It might be a cipher," he said. "A code."

"Based on what?" Drago Nacari whispered as if he feared being overheard.

"Based on old numbers," Luca said. "Latin numbers. I, II, III and so on. Look here." He pointed to a string of words. "These words recur: 'or, or, or, oro.' These could be code for numbers. How old is this manuscript?"

Drago shook his head. "Not more than fifty years old, I believe."

"And who was the author?"

"I don't know. I only have a few pages of it. I believe it was written in Italy, but I had it from a scholar who had a library in Paris."

"A Frenchman?"

Drago hesitated. "No. I had it from an English lord. He was a great philosopher, but he was not the author. He was . . . He was with the English court in Paris." He broke off and saw that Ishraq was scrutinizing him with a narrowed dark gaze.

"What was his name?" she asked bluntly.

"I cannot tell you."

"Was he a wise man?" she asked. "Did he know the language of birds?"

He smiled at her. "Yes, yes he did."

"What is the language of birds?" Luca asked curiously.

Drago answered him. "It is the coded speech of alchemists."

"So this book was owned by an alchemist, and it is not likely to be written in either English or French. More likely to be based on Italian or perhaps Latin?"

"And it is not a chimera?" Ishraq asked the alchemist directly. "You spend your mornings helping your daughter deceive people. This is not another deceit? Not simply a pretense? We cannot waste our time on a sleight of hand."

"My daughter earns her keep," he said defensively. "And no one is cheated. It's a fair game."

"I don't criticize her," Ishraq said. "But it's an odd occupation for a young woman whose father is hoping to find the secret to make gold from dust, who has studied—as you say you have done—for decades. In the afternoon you pursue the wisdom of ages and in the morning you play with fools."

"We did not always live as we do now, we did not always have a patron," Drago explained. "We did not always live here. We did not always have this manuscript, and the other pages—the recipe for deep transformation."

"You gambled for your living before you found your patron?"

"Yes."

"And you gamble still?"

"By way of explaining our presence here."

"Did the patron give you the house and the manuscript together?" Ishraq asked casually. "And tell you to pass as street gamblers?"

"He did. Two years ago," Drago said.

"And what does he expect for his generosity?"

"A share, of course," Drago said. "When we have the answer that he seeks. Most alchemists have a patron—how else could we afford the ingredients? How else could we undertake years of study?"

"He must be a generous man, for sure a patient man," Ishraq said, and was surprised to see no answering smile from the alchemist.

He was grave. "I don't know him at all," he said quietly. "He is my patron. He is my lord. He gives me sealed orders often through a third person. I have only met him twice. He is not a friend."

"You don't like him?" she asked acutely.

His face was closed. "I don't know him," he said.

"What's this?" Luca asked suddenly.

He was pointing to a small pen-and-ink drawing at the foot of one page. Ishraq bent close and saw that it was a dragon, tail in its own mouth, the symbol of Luca's own Order. His lord had tattooed the first part of the symbol on Luca's upper arm, as he completed the first part of his apprenticeship. The lord had promised that he would add the rest of the dragon and the detail of its scales until Luca, like Brother Peter, like Milord himself, carried the entire symbol on his own flesh: a different version from this little sketch, but clearly the same symbol.

"That is the sign of ouroboros," Drago said. "That is an alchemical sign. It means eternal life, a life that is forever renewed. The dragon feeds on itself, it eats its own tail, it drinks its own blood, it goes on forever. All is in one. One is in all."

Luca was a little pale. "I know this sign," he said. "It is an emblem for an order."

"The Order of the Dragon?" the man confirmed. "The order of my patron."

"The order that I am thinking of is known as the Order of Darkness," Luca corrected him.

"Darkness," the man repeated softly. "The darkness of the first matter, of Al-Khem, which gives its name to alchemy, the primary material that changes into one thing, and then another, into two and then three, and finally into the stone, into gold. Everything comes from darkness. This order is well named if it makes the journey from darkness to gold."

"They hope to go from ignorance to understanding," Ishraq murmured.

Luca shook his head as if to clear his thoughts. "What does this mean?" he asked. "You speak as if everything is connected with everything else."

Drago Nacari smiled. "Without a doubt it is," he said.

"Luca here knows of an order that is called the Order of Darkness," Ishraq said slowly. "The Order is commanded by his lord. We don't see his face. It exists to discover the end of days, the end of the world, the end of all things, of life on earth. Now you show us its symbol: the dragon eating its own tail, a sign of eternity, of life itself. You speak of the Order of the Dragon, and you too are commanded by a lord who you don't know."

"Many great men work in secret," Nacari volunteered. "In my business, everyone works in secret." He rose to his feet. "Shall I leave this page with you for you to study?"

"If you will," Luca said.

"But show it to no one else," he said. "We don't want it to fall into the hands of those who might use it against the world. Since we don't know what it says, it could be something that does not transmute to purity and good, but something that goes the other way."

"The other way?" Ishraq repeated. "What other way?"

"Into the shadow of darkness, into death, into decay," he said. "Into our destruction and the end of man. Into what you call the end of days. The dark is as real as light. The other world is just a fingertip away. Sometimes I can almost see it."

"Do you see any signs of the end of days?" Luca asked him. "I have a mission to know. Do you think the world is going to end? The infidel is in Constantinople, his armies have entered Christendom—is Christ going to come again and judge us all? Will the world end, and will He harrow hell? Have you seen signs of it in your work? In the world that you say is just a fingertip away?"

The man nodded as he turned toward the door. "I think the time is now," he said. "I see it in everything that I do. And every day I have to conquer . . ."

"Conquer what?" Ishraq asked him when he broke off.

"My own fears," he said simply. He looked at her directly, and she was sure that he was speaking the truth. "These are dark times," he said frankly. "And I fear that I serve a dark master."

Next morning the little group divided. Ishraq, dressed in the costume of a young man about town, with a dark black cape around her shoulders, her long hair pinned up under a broad black velvet hat, and a black and silver mask on her face, set out with Freize in attendance as her squire, taking a passing gondola to the quay near to the Nacari house at the edge of the ghetto. Luca and Brother Peter took the house gondola to the Rialto Bridge, and Isolde, dressed as modestly as a nun, with her face hidden beneath a great winged hood, walked down the alleyways and over the little bridges to the San Giacomo Church on the square beside the Rialto Bridge. She took up a position under the portico of the church and watched as Brother Peter and Luca strolled into the square, and went to watch the cups-and-ball game.

"Have you come to try your luck, my masters?" Jacinta asked, as pleasantly as always. She smiled at Luca. "My hands are quick today. I think I shall outwit you."

Luca chinked silver *piccoli* in his hand. "I think I am certain to win," he said.

She laughed. "Watch carefully, then," she invited him, and as a small crowd gathered round she put the gleaming marble ball under an upturned cup and moved the cups slowly, and then at dazzling speed, until they came to rest, and she sat back, smiled and said: "Which cup?"

Isolde glanced out of the square, down the maze of streets and waterways so that she should be certain which way she would have to go if she had to run before the Nacaris to warn Ishraq and Freize, and then bowed her head as if saying her prayers. She found she was truly praying for them all. She prayed for her own safety: that her brother's men had gone back to Lucretili and her brother would give up his pursuit. She prayed for Luca's quest to find his parents, and for her own mission to get back to her home. "Please," she whispered, "please let us all be safe and not exposed to danger nor be a danger to others." She tried to concentrate, but she found her mind strayed. She fixed her gaze on the image of the crucified Christ, but all she could think of was Luca—his face, his smile, the way that she could not help but be near him, lean toward him, hope for his touch.

Guiltily, she shook her head and pinched her clasped hands. She closed her eyes and bowed her head again to pray for the safety of Ishraq and Freize as they went, disguised, to the Nacari house.

Ishraq and Freize were far from needing prayers, gleefully excited by their mission as they approached the tall crowded houses just outside the Jewish ghetto. Ishraq loitered behind as Freize went boldly up to the side door, which stood on the quayside, and hammered on the knocker. There was silence from inside.

"Anybody in?" Freize shouted.

A woman from the far side of the narrow canal threw open her shutters and called down. "They're at the Rialto, they're there every morning."

"Can their maid not let me in? Don't they have a page boy?"

"They have no maid. They have no servants. You'll have to go to the Rialto if you want them."

"I'll go there then and find them," Freize called back cheerily. "I'll go now. Thank you for your help."

"Pipe down," the woman advised rudely and slammed her shutters.

Freize exchanged one wordless glance with Ishraq and set off, apparently in the direction of the Rialto Bridge. As quiet as a cat, Ishraq tried the handle of the door in the garden wall. She felt it yield, but the door would not open. Clearly, the Nacaris had locked it behind them when they left the house. Ishraq dropped back, took a short run at the garden wall and leaped up, her feet scrabbling to find a purchase on the smooth wall, until she got her knee on a branch of ivy and heaved up to the top of the wall and dropped down on the far side.

She was on her feet in a moment, looking alertly all around the garden in case anyone had heard her. Already she had identified the tree that she would climb if a guard dog came rushing toward her, or a watchman, but there was silence in the sunlit garden, and a bird started to sing. On tiptoe, Ishraq went toward the house and tried the door that led from the garden to the storeroom. It was locked and the shutters were closed on the inside. She turned to her right and tried the shutters on the windows. They too were firmly bolted from the inside. She looked up. Overlooking the garden was a pretty balcony with a spiral stone staircase that led down to the lawn and a peach tree.

Quiet as a ghost, Ishraq slipped up the stairs and found the window to a bedroom had been left latched open. She put her slim hand into the gap beneath the window and flicked the catch. As the window swung open, Ishraq went headfirst through the opening and landed as quietly as she could in a heap on the floor.

At once she was on her feet, listening, sensing that the house was empty. She tiptoed from the room to the landing, head cocked, looking down the well of the stair. Nothing moved, there was no sound. Lightly, she ran down the stairs and unbolted the door just as Freize was walking briskly—a man with business to attend to—past the house. One swift sideways step and he was inside the house and the door was closed behind him.

They beamed at each other. Ishraq slid the bolts across the door, locking it against the street. "In case they come back unexpectedly," she said. "Come on."

They went first into the big room at the front of the house, which overlooked the canal, and found a table piled with rolls of manuscripts and some hand-copied bound books. Ishraq looked at them without touching. "Philosophy," she said. "Astronomy, and here—alchemy. These are a lot of books. It seems that he was telling the truth when he said he had been studying for decades."

"They both have," Freize corrected her. He pointed to a writing table beside the bigger table. There was a brown scarf over the back of the chair, and on the table, a page of paper with a carefully copied drawing, and a page of notes. He looked from the book to the paper. "She's translating something," he said. "She's studying too."

Ishraq came and looked over his shoulder. "Alchemists often work in pairs, a man and a woman working together for the energy that they bring," she said. "Alchemy is about the transmutation from one form into another, liquids to solids, base to pure. It needs a man and a woman to make it work, it needs the spirit of a woman as well as that of a man."

"How d'you know all this?" Freize asked curiously.

Ishraq shrugged. "When I was studying in Spain, the Arab philosophers often studied alchemy texts," she said. "One of the universities even changed from studying the philosophy of Plato to that of Hermes. They said that there was more to learn from alchemy than from the Greeks—that gives you an idea of how important the work is, how much there is to understand. But this material is far beyond me."

Freize picked up a curiously shaped paperweight, a long pyramid of sparklingly clear glass, and then found a brass stamp beneath the paper. "What's this?" Freize asked. "Their seal?"

Ishraq picked up the little gold stamp and looked at the base. It was an engraved gold picture, for stamping the hot wax of a letter or a parcel to mark the insignia.

"This looks like a royal crest, or a ducal crest. Why would the Nacaris have it to seal their letters?"

"Get a copy of it, we should show it to Luca," Freize advised. "I'll look round upstairs," he said.

She heard him going quietly upstairs and the slight creak of the door as he put his head into the two bedrooms, then the slight noise as he went upward to the empty attic bedrooms for the servants. She was so intent on her work of heating the sealing wax at the embers of the fire, and dripping the melted wax onto a spare sheet of paper, that she hardly noticed as he came down the stairs again and went to the backroom, the storeroom. She pressed the seal into the wax and saw the clear image. But then she heard him say urgently: "Ishraq! Come and see."

Replacing the stick of wax just as it had been, putting the seal back into its velvet-lined case and waving the page to dry the cooling wax, she went to the storeroom at the back of the house and froze as Freize heaved open the heavy door.

The room was no longer the homely store of a small Venice house, it was an alchemist's workplace. The place stank of decay and rotting food, and a subterranean smell of mold and vomit. Ishraq put a hand over her nose and mouth, trying to block the stench. Next to the doorway, a great round tank with a wooden lid bubbled and gave off a rich stink of death.

"My God," Ishraq said, gagging. "It's unbearable."

Freize shot one horrified look at her. "It smells like a midden," he says. "Worse than a midden, a plague ground. Why are they cooking it?"

Under the window, before the locked shutters, was a stone bench. On its flat surface had been carved four small circular depressions, each one filled with charcoal, ready for burning, each one ready with a tripod and a pan, or a small cauldron. On the shelves were strange-shaped metal baths, and some expensive glass containers, with spouts and tubes for pouring and distilling liquids. Standing on the floor in massive coils, and towering as tall as Ishraq, was a great glass distillation tube with its dripping foot oozing a yellow slime into a porcelain bowl. On a big table in the center of the room there were trays of candle wax, some with flowers or herbs facedown into the wax as their essences drained away.

Freize looked around, his face pale, his eyes darkening with superstitious fear. "What is this? What in God's name are they doing here?"

Under an airtight bell jar that stood in a shallow bath of water, there was a small brown mouse on a platform, sitting up and cleaning its whiskers, beside a burning candle.

"Are they roasting it?" Freize whispered. "Killing it, the poor little creature?"

Ishraq shook her head, as shaken as her friend. "I don't know. I've never seen anything like this before."

The stone hearth beneath the chimney had been raised to waist-height—as high as a fire in a forge—and great bellows beside the chimney and cracks in the stone fire-back showed that it had been heated beyond bearing. Now it had burned down to red embers, but they could see that in the gray ashes there were hundreds, perhaps thousands, of the *piccoli* silver coins, glowing like a thousand little eyes, pooling as they cooled into strange ominous shapes.

"What are they doing to the money?" Freize demanded.

Ishraq shook her head in bewilderment.

A range of shelves held the dried bodies of small animals: trapped mice, rats bought from the rat catcher and missing their tails, birds with their heads flopped to one side, a desiccated nest with four dried-out nestlings, and jar after jar of dead insects of all sorts. Freize made a face of disgust. "What do they do with these? Is this for alchemy? Is it magic? Are they killing things here for sport, for devilment?"

Once more Ishraq shook her head. "I don't know." She turned her eyes from the little limps bodies and could not suppress a shiver.

Against one wall was an empty chair, as tall as a throne, draped in purple velvet, with a purple velvet cape and robe beside it. Turned to the wall was a hammered silver mirror.

"What's that for?" whispered Freize. "Who is that for?"

"It might be for scrying," Ishraq replied. "Foreseeing the future. If one of them has the gift of Sight."

"What would they do then?" Freize asked in fascinated horror.

"Look in the mirror, see visions," Ishraq answered briefly.

Draped around the mirror was a tentlike structure with curtains that could be let down for privacy, and before it was a small table like an altar. Above it was pinned an illuminated manuscript in green ink:

"'The Emerald Tablet.'" Ishraq read the Arabic symbols. She turned to Freize. "These are the rules of alchemy," she whispered. "It says: these are the commandments that guide all seekers of this truth."

"What does it say?" Freize asked. "Does it tell you what to do? Does it say how to make gold?"

Ishraq shook her head, her eyes dark with fear. "I can translate it for you, but I can't explain it," she warned him.

"So tell me!" he said.

"'Rule one,'" she read. "''Tis true without lying, certain and most true: that which is below is like that which is above, and that which is above is like that which is below, to do the miracles of one only thing. And as all things have been, and arose from one by the mediation of one: so all things have their birth from this one thing by adaptation.'"

Freize looked back over his shoulder at the dead animals on the shelves. "What does it mean?" he asked unhappily. "For I can understand nothing but cruelty here."

"These are mysteries," Ishraq told him. "I did say that I can't explain it."

"You did," Freize confirmed. "And you spoke fairly then. Can we go now, d'you think?"

Ishraq looked round. "We should search for the gold nobles," she reminded him.

"God knows what we will find if we open these boxes," Freize said anxiously. "Dead grandmothers, if not worse. The lad said there was a golem to guard the Jewish banker. I thought he was joking."

"A what?" Ishraq asked, suddenly intent.

"A golem. A sort of guardsman, a monster with a word of command on his forehead."

Despite herself Ishraq shivered.

"Let's go," Freize urged her.

"Wait," she said. "We've got to see . . ."

On the table were two tablets of wax with strange insignia drawn on their surfaces, and under the table, covered in a velvet cloth, was a chest. Ishraq bent down and tried to slide the bolts. They did not move. It was somehow locked.

"Don't," Freize said bluntly. "Don't force it open. What if there is . . ." He broke off. He realized he could not imagine what the alchemists might have in a small locked chest.

On the farthest wall a great glass vessel suddenly released a gush of foul-smelling liquid into a tray. They both jumped nervously at the splashing sound. Then they saw that below the big table was another closed box, broader than the one beneath the altar. This one was unlocked. Ishraq tried it, and Freize stepped forward to help her lift the heavy lid. She glanced at him and saw his face screwed up in a grimace of fear at what they might find. Even with the lid opened, Freize still had his eyes closed.

"Look," she whispered, quite entranced.

Freize opened his eyes. "Now, will you look at this?" he whispered, as if it were his own discovery and he was showing it to her. "Will you look at this?"

Inside the box was a metal tray with a dozen indentations, almost like a sweetmeat maker would use to make little bonbons. But each indentation was beautifully wrought. They were molds. Freize squinted to be sure what he was seeing. "Molds for coins," he said. "Molds for English nobles. See the shape of them? See the picture on the molds? The king in the boat and the rose?"

"So they really are coiners," Ishraq whispered. "Alchemists, as we have seen; but they are coiners as well. Practicing magic and crime side by side. They really are." She looked around. "I wouldn't have thought it. But they really are coining gold nobles. So they make them here, at this forge. But where do they keep the coins? Where's the gold?"

"Hadn't we better get out of here?" Freize suggested. "If they come back and catch us, God knows what they might do. These are not simple magic makers, these are a couple turning over a fortune."

"Let's be quick," Ishraq agreed. Freize closed the lid on the box of molds, looked around the room and saw for the first time, set low on the floor, the arched entrance to the cellar.

"See that?" he pointed it out to her.

"Can we open it?" Ishraq was there in a moment. The half-door was locked. Ishraq looked around for the key as Freize bent down, put the sharp blade of his knife in the keyhole, and turned carefully. There was a series of clicks and the door swung open. Ishraq raised her eyebrows at Freize's convenient range of criminal skills.

"You didn't learn that in the monastery."

"I did, actually," he said. "Kitchen stores. I was always hungry. And Sparrow would have faded away if I hadn't fed him up."

Ishraq bent down to swing the door outward and peer through. The door was so low that she had to go down on her hands and knees and then lie on her belly and squirm forward.

"What can you see?" Freize whispered behind her.

"Nothing, it's too dark," she replied, coming back out again.

He turned to the chimney and lifted down a rushlight, lit it at the fire and handed it to her. Ishraq thrust it into the dark opening, wriggled her shoulders through and looked down. Freize held her feet.

"Don't fall," he warned her. "And don't for pity's sake leave me here."

Fitfully, the flame flickered, illuminating the dark moving water at the end of the stone quay, immediately below her, and on the stones a glint here, a blaze of reflected light there, and then finally a cold draft of air blew the light out altogether and left her in damp blackness with nothing but the eerie slap of the dark waters to warn her of the edge of the quay.

"What can you see?" Freize's voice whispered from the room behind her. "Come back! What can you see?"

"Gold," Ishraq said, her voice quiet with awe. "An absolute fortune in sacks and sacks of gold nobles."

Brother Peter and Luca watched the gamblers at their place and then went into the San Giacomo Church. As they had expected, Father Pietro was kneeling at a side chapel before the flickering flame of a candle placed at the feet of an exquisite statue of the Madonna and Child. Both men bent a knee and crossed themselves. Luca went to kneel in silence beside the priest.

"You do not disturb me, because I was praying for you," Father Pietro said quietly, hardly opening his eyes.

"I suppose that it's too soon for any news?"

"Perhaps tomorrow, or the next day. You can come to me on the Rialto or I can send you a message."

"I'll come to you," Luca promised. "I hardly dare to pray for the safety of my father, I hardly dare to think that he might come home to me."

The priest turned and made the sign of a cross over Luca's bowed head. "God is merciful," he said quietly. "He is always merciful. Perhaps He will be merciful to you and your father and your mother."

"Amen," Luca whispered.

Father Pietro looked up at the serene face of the Madonna. He smiled at her, as a man who knows that his work is blessed. Luca thought that a more superstitious man would have thought that the beautiful statue smiled back.

"Thank you, Father Pietro," he said. "I thank you from the bottom of my heart."

"Thank me when your father holds you in his arms, my son," the priest replied.

Luca and Brother Peter completed their prayers and went to the back of the church and quietly opened the great wooden door and slipped out together.

Luca squinted at the brightness of the sunlight on the square, looked in one direction, and then another, and then quietly said: "Oh no."

The place where Jacinta had laid out her game earlier was empty. Drago and his daughter were missing.

And Isolde, their lookout, had vanished into thin air.

Isolde, her long skirt bunched into her hand, was running as fast as she could, through the narrow alleyway, her feet pounding on the damp cobblestones of the poorer streets, speeding up as she crossed a square paved with flagstones. She had watched Jacinta play for a crowd of people and

Nacari stand over her, and then suddenly, without a word of warning, far ahead of their usual time, they had packed up the game, stepped to the quayside and hailed a passing gondola.

Isolde, her breath coming short, hammered over the little wooden bridges, hailed the ferryboats in a panting shout, and then raced down the road from the bridge to where the Nacaris' tall house stood by the ghetto, trying to beat them by running the shortcut that Freize had described to her, while the gondola went round by water.

She recognized the house at once from Ishraq's drawing and hammered on the door. "Freize! Ishraq!" she shouted. "Come away!"

In the quiet house, the hammering on the door was shockingly loud. In the storeroom, Ishraq and Freize, locking up the hatch, both jumped in fear at the explosion of noise. Freize's first terrified thought was that the mysterious golem had come for them, as Ishraq started for the hall. "It's Isolde," she said.

"Open the door, quick," Freize said. "She'll turn out the watch in a moment."

Ishraq raced along the narrow hall and slid the bolts to throw open the door.

"They've left the square, they could be coming here!" Isolde gasped. "I don't know where they're going, they took a gondola. I ran as fast as I could." Her nun's hood had fallen from her head, and her blonde hair was tumbling down around her shoulders. She was panting from her run.

Ishraq at once put her arm around her friend's shoulders as if to leave at once. "Come on," she said to Freize. "Let's go."

"Not out of the front door, they left it bolted from the inside," Freize reminded her.

As she hesitated, Isolde glanced down the narrow canal and saw the frightening silhouette of the shadow of the prow of a gondola on the canal wall, just as it was about to turn the corner and see them, on the doorstep of the house. They heard the gondolier cry a warning: "Gondola! Gondola! Gondola!"

"Too late!" Isolde whispered. "We'll have to go inside."

They slipped back into the hall, closing the front door behind them.

"Out through the garden," Ishraq hissed. "Quickly, or they'll see us as they come in."

She drew Isolde through the house as Freize bolted the door to the street.

"My God, what is that smell?" Isolde hesitated and put her hand over her mouth as they went past the open door to the storeroom. "It's like death."

"Quick," Ishraq said, closing the door and leading the

two of them through the living quarters and out through the door into the little courtyard garden.

"You go," she said. "I'll lock up behind you and come out through the bedroom window."

"I'll go!" Freize volunteered. "You get out."

He was too late. Ishraq was already racing up the stairs to the upper room. Freize turned to Isolde. "We'll have to get over the wall," he whispered. "The garden door is locked and they have the key." He cupped his hand for Isolde's shoe. "Come on," he said. "Like getting up on a horse!" Isolde stepped up, and he threw her upward so that she caught the branch of the tree and heaved herself up to the top of the wall. Arduously, Freize hauled himself up beside her and then paused. They both clung to the top of the wall and watched, horrified, as below them, the Nacaris, father and daughter, walked to the garden door, produced a key and let themselves in. They opened the door to the house, and went inside.

"What can we do?" Isolde whispered. "We have to get her out!"

"Wait," Freize advised.

Ishraq, in the house, went swift-footed silently up the stairs. She heard the garden door open and the Nacaris come in. She heard Jacinta remark on the coldness of the day and then she heard, frighteningly clear, Drago say: "What's that noise?"

Silently, Ishraq slid across the treacherous floorboards to the bedroom window and eased herself out. She flung herself down the spiral stone staircase to the garden and saw her two friends, poised on the top of the wall.

"Get down!" she hissed. "They're in the house. They'll see us if they look out of the window!"

Freize jumped down into the street and reached up for Isolde, who dropped down into his arms as Ishraq stretched for a low-bending bough, and swarmed her way upward. As soon as she was at the top of the wall, she too lowered herself down and then jumped clear.

They were facing a small tributary canal, and farther down the water was a little wooden swing bridge.

"This way," Isolde said, pulling up the hood of her robe over her blonde hair and leading the way at a brisk walk. She wiped her face with her sleeve. "I haven't run so fast since we left Lucretili," she remarked to Ishraq.

"You always were fast," her friend said. "Faster than me. Now I should teach you to fight."

Isolde shook her head in a smiling denial.

"She doesn't like the thought of hurting people," Ishraq explained to Freize.

The three of them crossed the bridge and started along the quay on the far side.

"I don't think I will ever have the stomach for fighting,"

Isolde remarked. "I can't bear it. Even that scramble has left me trembling. And now, I'd better walk home on my own."

"Will you be all right?" Freize asked, torn between his desire to escort her to safety and maintaining the deception of being Ishraq's servant.

"Oh yes," she said. "I tremble very easily, but I'm not a coward."

"I should go with you," he hesitated.

Ishraq laughed. "If there's any trouble, she can run," she said. "She can certainly run faster than you."

Isolde smiled. "I'll go on ahead and see you at home."

Freize and Ishraq strolled home together, along the Grand Canal, Ishraq careful to swagger ahead of Freize like a young prince, right until the moment when they came to the quay, which ran to the side door of their house. Then she glanced left and right, checked that there was no one at the windows and no one on the canal and slipped down the street and scurried into the side door.

Isolde leaped up from where she had been sitting at the door and hugged her friend. "Good! I was waiting for you. The others are home too." She called across the stone hall, "They're back!" as Freize came through the side door and Luca and Brother Peter opened the doors to their rooms.

"Come in," Luca said. "How did you get on?"

Brother Peter recoiled in horror from Ishraq's young prince costume. "She should change her clothes," he said, covering his eyes. "It's heresy for a woman to dress as a man."

"I'll be one moment," Ishraq promised.

She raced up the stairs, taking them two at a time, just like a boy, and they could hear her hurling her clothes into a chest and scrabbling into a gown. She came running downstairs with her dark hair tumbling down, and only at Brother Peter's scandalized glare did she twist it into a casual knot and pin it at the nape of her neck. Luca smiled at her. Anyone but the old clerk would have been struck by her agile grace in boys' clothes and her careless beauty when she was dressed once again as a girl in a conventional gown. "I like you in costume," he said.

"It's against God's will and the teaching of the Church," Brother Peter said. "And certainly a doorway to sin."

"Well, it was useful," Ishraq defended herself. "So tell me about the square, was everything all right?"

"Everything," Luca said shortly. "We gambled, she won, as usual, took a small purse of silver coins for the morning's work and gave them to her father. We spoke to the money changer, and he said he would have enough nobles for us when the ship comes in. He says he has made an arrangement and has about a thousand gold nobles to hand. We saw

Father Pietro in church. He's had no reply yet. Then it was dreadful when we came out of church and saw that they had left early. And then Isolde was gone too! But I see you're safe. How did you get on? Did you have to break into the house?"

"I got in through an open window," Ishraq said. "And then I let Freize in. They may have suspicions. They might have thought that they heard something; but they can't be sure that anyone was ever inside.

"They don't have a servant—well, they can't have one. They daren't have one. The storeroom is completely devoted to alchemy. It reeks of magic and decay. Any servant would report them at once. In the main room, where they study, there were more pages like the one they brought to us. There were about ten pages that I could see. I couldn't read any of them. Plants that are unknown, language that you can't even spell out. And I copied this." She put the piece of paper in front of Luca. "I thought it was odd that they should have such a seal."

He scrutinized it. "I wouldn't know whose seal it is," he said.

They both turned to Isolde, whose family had their own crest. She recognized it at once. "Oh! That's the seal of one of my godparents," she exclaimed.

"Count Wladislaw? Of Wallachia?" Brother Peter asked respectfully.

"No," she said. "Another one. My godmother."

"How many do you have?" asked Freize. "How many does a girl need?"

She shrugged with a smile. "My father was very, very well connected. This godmother was very grand indeed. She was the wife of John, Duke of Bedford, Regent of France. She was Jacquetta, the Dowager Duchess."

"Who?" Freize asked.

"Her husband was brother to the great king of England, Henry V, who conquered France for England. John the Duke was regent in France when the little prince of England came to the throne," she said. "When the French rose up under their king Charles VII, he fought them, and he captured their leader, Joan of Arc."

"Yes," Luca said, recognizing a part of the story that he knew. "I know who you mean, I've heard of him. He burned Joan of Arc as a witch."

"The Church judged that she was guilty of witchcraft and heresy," Isolde remarked. "But I never met the duke—he died when I was still a baby. They say that he ruled France like an emperor. He maintained a huge army, he had magnificent palaces in Paris and Rouen, he made the laws, he issued coins. After he died, his widow, my godmother, remarried. She lives in England now, at the court of Henry VI."

"But why would these street gamblers have the duke's

seal?" Brother Peter asked. "They have forged it, presumably, but why would they want it?"

"Would it be to seal the chests of gold?" Isolde asked. "That they say is English gold? Chests from the English mint would have the regent's seal on them, wouldn't they?"

Everyone was silent, and then Luca reached across to her and grasped both her hands. Ishraq rescued the paper with the copied seal as it slipped from Isolde's grip.

"Brilliant," he said. "That's so brilliant. They seal it with his crest so that it gives credence to the forged gold being genuine English nobles. Because the duke would have been in charge of the mint at Calais. He would have commanded them to make gold, he would have shipped the gold out to the soldiers. If a chest or even a hundred chests went astray, they would all have had his seal on them. Then, years later, if someone forges gold and wants to pretend that it came from the mint, they mark each coin with the mark of the mint at Calais, and they sell it in boxes sealed with the regent's seal."

Isolde glowed as he held her hands, the two of them standing, quite still, as if they had forgotten the others in the room.

"But are they really making gold?" Brother Peter asked dryly. "Before we get so excited about these imaginary chests? Sealed so cleverly with this imaginary seal? And this brilliant guess as to why they have the seal. Is there any gold there?"

"Oh yes," Freize said smugly. "Don't you worry about that. There's sackfuls of the stuff. Sackfuls of it. And Ishraq found it."

"You did?" Luca turned to her.

"We went to the storeroom. The whole place is used for alchemy," Ishraq said. "The fireplace is like a forge. We saw silver still in the fire. It had been heated so hot that the chimney was cracked."

"Why would they do that?" Isolde asked. Nobody could answer.

"And we found molds for English nobles," Freize said. "It looks like they pour liquid gold into the molds."

"And then we found a cellar doorway and the sacks of gold," Ishraq said, lowering her voice. "The door is a little hatch from the storeroom, like you'd find leading to a cellar. But instead of a cellar, the half-door leads down to the quay. The sacks of gold are on a quay. Beyond is the canal, and a water door. I should think that they drop the sacks from the storeroom, through the hatch, onto the quayside and then a boatman comes and loads the gold onto a boat."

"How much gold?" Brother Peter asked. "How much did you see?"

"I saw two sacks that were open and perhaps four behind them that had been sewn up. A fortune," Ishraq said.

Luca dropped into a seat at the window. "Great work," he said to Ishraq and Freize. "Great work."

He turned to Brother Peter. "So is our mission complete?" he asked doubtfully. "We were told to find the source of the gold and answer whether it was a theft or gold mined from a new source. We can tell Milord it is a forger, and that we have found the forge."

"But we don't know how they actually make the nobles," Freize pointed out. "We saw the molds. But we didn't see any gold ore."

"D'you think that it's possible that they have found a way to refine it from silver?" Isolde asked. "From the silver they had in the forge? She wins a lot of silver every day. Every day they go home with pursefuls of little silver coins."

"The coins in the fire!" Ishraq nodded at Freize.

"We must write our report," Brother Peter decided. "And we will have to turn them in to the authorities. Milord was clear to me that we must inform the doge's officials as soon as we had identified the forger."

Awkwardly, he turned to Ishraq. "I was ungracious about your disguise," he said. "You have done great work for the Order. You were brave and enterprising." He hesitated. "And you make a very neat young man," he conceded. "You don't look heretical at all."

"Bonny," Freize said admiringly. "She looks good enough to eat." He was rewarded by Ishraq's surprised giggle. "And she climbs like a clever little monkey," he said. "If you wanted a burglar for a wife, she would be the very one."

"But it does not mean that you can dress up and go out every day," Brother Peter continued. "This was an exception. And tonight, in any case, the two of you will go out as modest and elegant young ladies. Our reputation as a wealthy young family all depends on your behavior."

"Oh, the party!" Isolde exclaimed. "With all this, I had completely forgotten about it."

"Keep your ears open for any mention of gold," Brother Peter ordered. "And remember that you are young ladies of good family, kept very strictly at home." He looked at Isolde as if he had more confidence in her playing the part of a well-behaved young lady than Ishraq. "I am looking to you, Lady Isolde, to set an example," he said.

Isolde curtsied modestly and shot a hidden laughing glance at Luca. "Of course," she said.

The five of them set out all together in the gondola. Freize would wait for them, with the other servants in the servants' room. The gondola would wait at the quay beside the house for them, bring back Ishraq and Isolde from their visit, and then go out again for Luca and Brother Peter. The men thought they would be out till late, perhaps past midnight.

The men were wearing the hoods of their capes over their heads, and dark plain masks over their eyes. Isolde could see only Luca's smiling lips as he looked at her strange beauty. She had a dark blue cape with a dark blue hood pulled over her fair hair. She wore a mask that covered her forehead, eyes and nose, so that her dark blue eyes gleamed at him through the slits of the mask. Blue feathers sprouted from the side of the mask and curled like a high question mark around her head. She looked exotic and strange and lovely. Beside her, Ishraq in black was like a beautiful sleek shadow, only her mouth showing below a black mask that was shaped like a dark moon and starred with silver.

Luca leaned toward Isolde and whispered to her, his mouth against her ear. "I have never in my life seen anyone as beautiful as you," he said.

Isolde, quite entranced, turned and smiled at him, her dark eyes gleamed through the slits in the mask. "Meet me," Luca whispered to her. "Meet me tonight. As soon as we can get away from this party."

The city was in carnival mood, every window overlooking the Grand Canal bright with candlelight, and every dark canal and quayside busy with bobbing gondolas. Sometimes they glimpsed a couple entwined in the double seat of a gondola, their hoods drawn forward to hide their kisses, their hidden hands seeking to touch. In some, a pair of lovers had gone into the cabin of the gondola and closed the door, leaving the gondolier to idle in the stern, keeping the ship steady in the water as the clandestine candlelight shone out of the slats of the cabin. Brother Peter turned his head away and crossed himself to prevent the infection of sin.

On the quayside, as their gondola approached the palace, they could see a huge crowd, beautifully dressed in the extraordinary costumes. Men dressed as monsters and angels, women in silks of every color towering high as they stood on the chopines that were the mark of a fashionable lady. Some of them were dressed so brightly, and stood so proudly, that it was clear, even to the young travelers, that the women were showing themselves off for sale. They were the famous Venetian courtesans, and it would cost a man a small fortune to spend a night with one of them, traded like everything else in this expensive city.

Everywhere people were mingling, talking, flirting behind their masks, sometimes pushing their masks on top of their heads to expose their lips for a stolen kiss, sometimes, turning away into a quiet garden or a darkened doorway. Isolde glimpsed the smiling face of a woman as a man took her hand and led her into the shadows. At the quayside, she saw a man lightly step from one rocking boat into another, laughing like a child on stepping-stones, invited by the wave of a silver glove.

It was irresistibly exciting. Every gondola burned a torch at the stern, or carried a swinging lantern at the prow, and the young women could see that men and women were making assignations on the water, and then their gondolas would slip away together to the darker side canals, where they would drift side by side so that the women could flirt behind their painted fans and the men make extravagant promises.

On the white stone quayside, the wooden patten shoes

of the women clattered like castanets as if they were inviting men to come and dance. Bursts of music came from one doorway and another, and they could hear the bright laughter of men and women. Isolde exchanged one longing glance with Luca as if she wished that the two of them could go somewhere alone together and dance and laugh and kiss.

"Isolde," Ishraq whispered a warning to her. "Your mask doesn't hide what you are thinking. You look as if you are ready to sin like a Venetian."

A ready flush rose from Isolde's neck to her cheeks. "Ishraq," she said quietly. "I have to kiss him again. I think I will die if I don't kiss him."

Ishraq gasped. "But you said . . ."

The great water gate to the palace stood open, the bright torches reflected in the glassy waters of the canal as the gondolas queued to enter the palace and leave the guests on the red carpet that stretched extravagantly, to the brink of the lapping dark water.

"It is like a strange other world," Isolde marveled. "So much wealth and so much beauty."

"So much sin!" Brother Peter mourned quietly.

At last it was their turn and their gondola slid through the archway and drew up to the palace steps. Brightly costumed servants stepped forward to steady the craft, but before they could get out, Isolde glanced back to the canal and saw a gondola with four beautiful women hesitate at the entrance behind them, the women exquisitely painted and rouged, and wearing high headdresses and exotic masks. One of them waved a lazy hand to Luca and called out the name of her house. "On the Grand Canal," she said. "Come at midnight when you leave here!"

"Sin all around us," Brother Peter said, shaking his head in horror.

"I know what I said about never kissing a man before marriage!" Isolde whispered fervently to Ishraq as she rose to her feet and pulled her hood forward. "But that was weeks ago, it was before we pretended to be married. And then he kissed me, so I know what it's like now, and besides it's carnival, and everyone, everywhere we go is courting and making love.

"Don't you see it?" she urged her friend. "Don't you feel it? It's as if the very air is caressing the skin of my neck, is touching my lips. Don't you feel it? I can hardly breathe for it."

Isolde stepped out of the gondola and stood at the water's edge. Ishraq was helped on shore and took her hand and held it tightly as they waited for the two men to disembark. "Isolde, what are you going to do?"

Isolde's dark blue eyes glittered like sapphires through the dark blue of her mask. "Will you help me?"

"Of course! Always! But not to disaster . . ."

"We'll follow you as you go in," Brother Peter said, getting out of the gondola and gesturing that the two young women should lead the way up the stairs to the inside of the palace. Isolde, as if recalled to the proper behavior for a young woman of a noble family, tightened the tie on her mask and went up the marble steps and into the brightly lit house.

They were expected, and at once a lady-in-waiting took the two young women up the sweeping stairs to the upper floor where the lady of the house was entertaining her friends. Manservants greeted Luca and Brother Peter and took their capes and hats, leaving them in their dark masks, and showed them up to the first floor. Freize, always at his happiest when he was heading toward dinner, stepped into the servants' hall at the canal side.

As she climbed the stairs, Isolde looked back and saw Luca swallowed up by the crowd of young men, and heard the rattle of dice and a cheer as someone won a small fortune at cards, and a ripple of laughter from the courtesans who would entertain the men while the ladies had to go up to the next floor.

"Greetings, how pleasant to meet you." The lady of the

house, Lady Carintha, came forward and took their hands. She was an elegant woman, dressed in dark blue, almost the match of Isolde's gown, except that hers plunged low at the front and almost slid off her broad shoulders in an open invitation. Her shining gold hair was piled up on the top of her head, in a swirl of blue silk, except for three ringlets that fell over her creamy naked shoulders. Her eyes, a calculating blue, scanned the two young women, and her rouged mouth smiled without warmth.

"You can take your masks off now we are indoors and among friends." She exclaimed at their beauty. "Oh my dears! How you are going to break hearts in this wicked city of ours! One of you so very fair and one so very dark, no man could resist the two of you. Most of them will want both of you together!"

She drew them forward and introduced them to other ladies, who were drinking wine from brightly colored glasses and eating small sweet pastries. "Some wine?" She pressed a couple of glasses on them. "But I daresay I should not praise your looks, for you will have heard it all before. You will have dozens of lovers already, you must tell me all about them."

"Not at all," Isolde said, flushing.

The lady laughed and patted her cheek. "Only a matter of time for both of you, only a matter of moments, I swear it. Indeed! Why not tonight? I can't believe how beautiful you are, and you match so well together. You must always go around together, you are each a perfect foil for the other." She turned to Ishraq. "You must have a lover, I am sure! Someone who prefers brunettes?"

Ishraq shook her head, not at all flattered by the woman's cloying warmth. "No. We have been brought up very carefully. I have no husband."

"Someone else's husband, then?" someone suggested, prompting laughter from all the ladies.

"My lady's brother is very strict," Ishraq said, hiding her irritation behind a polite smile. "We go out very little."

"The older brother, yes! You can see it clearly. No one would invite him for an affair of the heart. But the other brother, the younger one, Luca Vero, now he cannot be so very virtuous? Surely? Don't disappoint me! He is truly a man that turns heads! No one as tempting as that could be monkish."

Someone else laughed and agreed. "Turns heads! I'd turn down the sheets!"

"We were looking out of the window at him! We are so jealous of Carintha, having him for a neighbor," one of the ladies told Ishraq, squeezing her elbow. "We've all laid bets on her taking her own gondola and serenading him! She would, you know. She's quite shameless! If she sets her heart on him, she'll have him!"

They laughed, again, as Ishraq silently detached herself from the stranger's hold.

"You'd open your front door for me, wouldn't you?" Lady Carintha asked, putting her hand on Isolde's arm. "Open the door and let me run up the stairs to your brother's room?"

Isolde gave a little shiver, but did not shake off the unwelcome caress. "I am sorry. I would not be allowed," she said shortly.

"Then he'll have to give me a key himself!" Her ladyship smiled and turned to take a glass of wine. Ishraq saw Isolde grit her teeth, and tweaked her sleeve to remind her to be polite to her hostess.

"Make sure you tell him that I shall visit." Lady Carintha turned back and whispered to both girls. "I am absolutely serious. I had one look at him and I knew who would be my lover for this *Carnevale*. Good Lord, I might not be able to give him for Lent!"

Isolde made a little exclamation and tore herself away from Lady Carintha's touch. Her ladyship hardly noticed.

"I've never failed," she went on to one of her friends, ignoring Isolde's half-turned back. "I've never failed to capture a young man once I've set my heart on him. Do you think he is a virgin? That would be too delicious! I should be as innocent as him! You know I think I would tremble. D'you know I think I would gasp?"

"Surely, he can't be!"

"Not with looks like that!"

"Someone must have beaten you to it, Carintha!"

"This is unbearable!" Isolde exclaimed in an undertone to Ishraq.

"Be patient," she replied. "We only have to stay for an hour. And have you seen her earrings?"

"What about them?" Isolde said crossly.

"Half English nobles," Ishraq pointed out. "Drilled and mounted as earrings."

There was gambling in this salon too, and conversation, though there was little to talk about but fashion and love affairs. Isolde drew Ishraq away from the spiteful women and toward the gambling tables. There were musicians playing in one corner and half a dozen women dancing listlessly together.

"I am afraid that I have no money," Ishraq confessed to Carintha, who followed them, sipping greedily from her wineglass. "I did not think to bring any. Though I changed some money only a few days ago. I bought English gold nobles. I changed all that I had into English nobles, do you think that was wise?"

"Oh! Aren't they divine? They're all I use now," Carintha replied. "As clean as if someone had washed them for me. Have you seen my earrings?"

"She just remarked on them," Isolde said.

"Aren't they lovely?" Lady Carintha turned her head one way and another so that they could see. In her ears, dangling from a gold pin, were two half noble coins. "I'm having a necklace made of them too. I shall start a fashion. Everyone will want them."

"They are such pretty coins. Are they minted in Venice?" Ishraq wondered aloud, watching the play at the table and not looking at Carintha at all.

"Certainly not," she said. "They are English, through and through. My husband trades in them. They come from the English treasure house at Bordeaux. When they lost Bordeaux last year, the French captured their treasury, all the wealth of John of Bedford, the regent of France. And now they need nobles so badly in England that they are buying them back again. They have no gold at all, poor things. My husband works with all the English merchants, and they are buying up nobles by the thousand and sending them home to England." She laughed. "And every day, the poor dears have to pay more gold for their own coins because now everyone wants them!"

A woman went past her and flicked Carintha's earring, making it dance. "Delightful," she said. "Amusing."

"And where does your husband get the English nobles from?" Isolde asked lightly. "Since the English themselves don't have enough?"

"Oh, the *most* amusing Jewish banker," Lady Carintha volunteered. "You would not think, to look at him, that he had a penny to rub, one against the other. But he supplies my husband with English nobles, and so I get my pretty earrings!"

"Convenient," Ishraq remarked.

"But as for you two lovely girls," Lady Carintha went on to Ishraq, "it doesn't matter that you have no money with you. You can borrow from me and repay me next week. I shall be your banker. I should think that your credit is good enough! We all hear that the handsome young man has a ship coming in from Russia any day now! And your young lady is a great heiress, is she not?"

"Unimaginably so," Ishraq said, honest at last. "You could not imagine her fortune. Not even I can truly describe it."

The party for the ladies broke up at about ten o'clock, and they left by the outer staircase while the party for the gentlemen was still, noisily, in full swing on the first floor. Clearly—as the women rouged their lips and tied masks on their faces and slipped away in their gondolas—many of them were going on to other parties or to assignations. Lady Carintha was going to join the men, who were still gambling. She winked at her friend, and Isolde heard her whisper Luca's name.

"But we have to just go home," Ishraq remarked resentfully as Freize helped her into the gondola. "When all the world is free to walk around and do as they please."

"Let's get the gondola to drop us on the quay and walk about," Isolde suggested quietly. "Nobody will know who we are, since we have our masks and our capes, and Brother Peter is not at home to know what time we get in."

"Of course!" Ishraq exclaimed, and turned and told the gondolier to let them get out at the steps in the side canal—they would enter through the side door. The gondolier's smile and Freize's silent nod told them at once that neither young man believed for a moment that the women were going straight into the house; but it was carnival time and anything was allowed, even for wealthy young ladies. The gondolier set them down where they asked and then pushed off with Freize still aboard, to go back to wait for Brother Peter and Luca to emerge from the gambling party.

Arm in arm, the girls sauntered around the streets, reveling in their sense of freedom, in walking along the shadowy quays with the silk of their gowns swishing around their ankles, their masks hiding their faces, knowing that they looked strange and exotic and beautiful in this strange and beautiful city.

Almost every doorway stood open and there were lights and parties inside. Every so often someone called to them and invited them to come in and take some wine, come in and dance. Laughingly, Isolde refused and they walked on, loving the sense of excitement and adventure.

"What a horrible woman Lady Carintha is," Isolde remarked as they turned their steps homeward again.

"Because she said that she wanted Luca and asked you to let her into his room?" Ishraq teased. "She thinks you're his sister, she was not to know that you . . ."

"That I—what?" Isolde asked, coming to a standstill.

Ishraq was not at all intimidated. "That you would be so offended at the thought of taking her to him."

"I was offended. Anyone would be offended. She's old enough to be his mother. Ugh, with those ridiculous coins in her ears!"

"It's not because of her age or her appearance. Besides, she's not more than thirty. You were upset that she wants to take him as her lover because you want him for yourself!"

For a moment she thought that Isolde would take offense, for her friend had stopped still, and then she suddenly admitted: "It's true! I can't pretend to you or to myself any longer! I want him so much it's like a fever! I can think of nothing else but what it would be like if he were to hold me, if he were to touch me, if he were to kiss me. I know I am mad to think like this. But I can't think of anything else. He asked me to meet him, and I didn't answer, but I was longing to say 'yes.'"

"It's *Carnevale*," Ishraq said comfortingly. "It's Venice. As you said, the whole city seems to think like this. The whole city has gone mad for pleasure. And he is the most handsome young man that either of us has ever seen."

"Do you . . . desire him too?" Isolde asked, hesitating, almost as if she were frightened of the very word. "Seriously? Like I do? Are you in love with him, Ishraq?"

Ishraq laughed quietly. "Oh yes," she said. "A little. He's very attractive, I don't mind admitting it. But I don't think of him as you do. It's not as hard for me as it is for you. I can just look at him and think him absolutely desirable and utterly handsome, and then I can look away. Because he's not for me. I know that. He doesn't see me in that way, and there is no possibility of any sort of honorable love between us. And actually, very little chance of dishonorable love either! He is sworn to the Church and I am an infidel. He is in the Order to stamp out heresy and I am born to question. We could not be more different. But you . . ." She paused.

"What?" Isolde urged her on. "Me, what?"

"He's in love with you," Ishraq said quietly. "He can't take his eyes off you. I think if you said the word, he would give up the Church for you and marry you in San Marco tomorrow."

"I can't." Isolde gave a little moan. "I can't. And anyway,

he can't. He is a novice at his monastery, and Brother Peter told me that I must do nothing that would distract him from the Order of Darkness. He's one of the few men appointed to trace the signs of the end of the world and warn the Pope himself. If the world is going to end this year, it is vital that he does his work and reports to his lord in Rome. His order is our only defense against the rise of heresy and magic and the end of the world. I should not think of him in any way except as a soldier of the Church, a crusader, like my father was. I should honor him for his work. I shouldn't be thinking of him like this at all."

Ishraq shrugged. "But you are. And so is he."

"I can't stop myself thinking!" Isolde exclaimed. "And I dream! I dream of him almost every night. But I can never do anything. I would be ruined completely if I did more than kiss him. If I ever get back to my castle, I would never be able to marry any man of honor or position if it was known I had been in love with Luca. There's no point in all the danger we are risking to win back my inheritance if I have lost my honor. I could never go home to be Lady of Lucretili if I was dishonored."

"If no one ever knew . . ." Ishraq suggested.

"I would know!" Isolde exclaimed. "I would be utterly dishonored. I would never be able to offer my love to another man, I would never be able to marry. I would know always that I was dishonored, that I was not fit to be a great man's wife. I have to be able to promise my future husband an untouched heart in an untouched body."

"But can you go on like this?"

"What shall I do?" Isolde demanded with a wail. "What shall I do? When I heard her speak of coming to our house I thought I would kill her. I can't bear to let her near him. I can't bear to think of her touching . . ." Isolde clapped her hand over her mouth to prevent herself speaking. But nothing could stop her thoughts. She closed her eyes as if she could not bear to imagine what she might see: Luca and Lady Carintha together.

"If no one ever knew . . ." Ishraq repeated slowly. "If you could love him, kiss him, even lie with him, and no one ever know?"

"How could no one ever know? I would know! He would know! You would know!"

"If it only happened once? Just once. And we were all three sworn to secrecy?"

There was a long silence between the two girls. Isolde took her hand down from her mouth and whispered: "What?"

"If it only happened once. And nobody knew about it? If you and I never ever spoke of it? If you could do it, and yet let it be like an unspoken dream? Would you be satisfied if you were his lover, his first ever lover, and he yours; but he never saw your face, he never said your name, and you never admitted what you had done? Not even to me? It was a secret of the night, of *Carnevale*, and nobody remembered if after Lent?"

Isolde put a trembling hand on her friend's arm. "If we never spoke of it. If it only happened once. If it was like a dream, for I am dreaming of him every night . . ."

Before Ishraq could answer she saw the house gondola turn from the main traffic of the canal. She dragged her friend back into the shadow of the side of the house.

"There's our gondola!" she whispered. "And Luca and Freize and Brother Peter coming home."

They watched the gondola as it pulled up once again in the side canal, at the side steps. "I want to walk," Luca explained, his voice slightly slurred from wine. "I want to walk around."

"You had much better come home and say your prayers and go to bed," Brother Peter said.

"In an hour or so," Luca insisted. "You go in."

"I'll come with you," Freize offered.

"No," Luca insisted. "I want to walk alone and clear my head."

Freize took his arm. "Are you meeting Lady Carintha?" he whispered. "Because I can tell you now, that's nothing but trouble . . ."

Luca pulled himself free, refusing to admit to any assignation, though his heart pounded at the thought of a dark blue dress and mask. "I'll just walk around," he said, and stepped unsteadily ashore.

With a shrug, Brother Peter ordered the gondolier to take him and Freize round by boat to the water gate and left Luca climbing the steps to the quayside.

Isolde and Ishraq shrank back against the wall as Luca got to the top of the steps and turned and looked back over the Grand Canal, a big yellow moon high above, the bright stars shining in the darkness of the sky. He stood for some time, listening to the sounds of distant music and laughter.

"And all in a moment I know that I love her," he said simply, speaking to himself but hearing the words fall into the quietness of the night and mingle with the lapping of the canal on the steps. "It's extraordinary, but I know it. I love her."

He gave a quiet laugh. "I'm a fool," he said. "Half-promised as a priest, fully committed to the Order of Darkness, on a quest, and she is a lady of such high birth that I would not have even seen her if I had stayed as a novice in my monastery."

He fell silent. "But I have seen her," he said steadily. "And she has seen me. And tonight I understand for the first time what people mean by . . . this . . ." He broke off and smiled again. "Love," he said. "What a fool I am! I love her.

I have fallen in love. *Coup de foudre*. In love, in a moment."

He opened the door to the walled garden and let himself in. The girls heard his footsteps crunch the gravel and then silence as he threw himself onto the bench beneath the tree.

On the shadowy quayside, the girls stood in horrified silence.

"Was he speaking of her?" Ishraq said wonderingly. "Of Lady Carintha? Has she done what she said she would do? Seduced him, already, and in only one meeting?"

Isolde turned, and Ishraq could see the shine of tears on her pale cheek beneath the dark blue mask. "He said that he fell in love tonight," she said, her voice low with misery. "Fell in love, *coup de foudre*, all in a moment, tonight. With a lady he would never have seen if he had stayed in the monastery. He's in love with that woman. That painted—" Isolde bit off her words as another gondola edged to the quayside stairs and Lady Carintha, in a cape and hood of deep blue, with an exquisite mask of navy feathers, snapped her fingers for the gondolier to help her step onto the stairs and up to the quayside.

"She's meeting him!" Isolde exclaimed in an anguished whisper as she and Ishraq shrank deeper into the shadows. "She's meeting him in our garden!"

The two young women stood, pressed against the wall, hidden in the shadows while the big spring moon lit the quayside as brightly as day. Lady Carintha, with her back to them, took a tiny looking glass from the gold chain at her waist and scrutinized her dark blue mask, her smiling painted lips, her blue silk hood and cape. Her gaze went past her own reflection and she saw, in the mirror, the two girls, pressed back against the wall and broke into a quiet laugh.

"The pretty virgins!" she said. "Walking the streets. How quaint! And I am meeting a third pretty virgin! What a night for a debauch! Will you come with me?"

Even Ishraq, usually so bold, was stunned into silence at the woman's bawdiness. It was Isolde, with tears hidden by her mask, who stepped forward and said: "You shall not meet him. I forbid it."

"And who are you to forbid or allow a grown man what he shall do?" Lady Carintha asked, her voice filled with care-less scorn. "He wants me. He's waiting for me. And nothing will stop me going to him."

"He wants me too," Isolde said wildly. "He asked me to come to the garden. You can't come in."

"His sister?" Lady Carintha asked. "My! You are a stranger family than I thought."

"She means me," Ishraq intervened. "He asked her to bring me to him."

Lady Carintha put her hands on her hips and looked

at the two younger women. "Well, what are we to do? For I won't share him. And we can't all go in together and let him choose. That would be to spoil him, and besides, I don't take gambles like that. I'm not lining up against you two little lovelies."

"But you like to gamble," Ishraq pointed out. "Why don't we gamble for him?"

Lady Carintha gave a delighted laugh. "My dear, you are wilder than you appear. But I have no dice."

"We have nobles," Ishraq pointed out. "We could toss for him."

"How very appropriate," she said dryly. "Who wins?"

"We each toss a noble until there is an odd one out. That woman wins. She goes into the garden. She has time with Luca—whatever she does nobody ever knows—and we never speak of it," Ishraq ruled. "Do you agree?"

"I agree," Isolde whispered.

"Amen," Lady Carintha said blasphemously. "Why not?"

Ishraq took the borrowed nobles from her pocket and gave Isolde one, and took another for herself. Lady Carintha already had hers in her hand.

"Good luck!" Lady Carintha said, smiling. "One, two three!"

The three golden coins flicked into the air all together, turned and shone in the moonlight, then each woman caught her own as it fell, and slapped it on the back of her hand. They stretched out their hands, each holding a hidden coin under the palm of the other hand. Slowly, one at a time, one after the other, they uncovered them.

"Ship," said one, showing the engraved portrait of the king in his ship on one side of the coin.

"Ship," said another, uncovering her coin.

The two of them turned to the third as she raised her fingers and showed them the shining face of her coin.

"Rose," she said, and without another word, turned to the door in the high wall, turned the heavy ring of the latch and went quietly in.

The light of the moon suddenly dimmed as a cloud crossed the broad yellow face. In the garden, Luca rose to his feet as, very, very quietly, the garden gate opened and a masked figure stood underneath the arch. Luca stared as if she were a vision, summoned up by his own whispered desire. "Is that you?" he asked. "Is it really you?"

Silently, she stretched out her hand to him. Silently, he stepped toward her. Luca drew her into the shade of the tree, pushing the door shut behind them. Gently, he put his hand around her waist and held her to him, she turned up her face to him in the darkness, and he kissed her on the lips.

She made no protest as he led her under the roof of the portico and they sat on the bench in the alcove. Willingly, she sat on his knee and wound her arms around his neck, rested her head on his shoulder and inhaled the warm male scent. Luca drew her closer, heard his own heart beating faster as he unlaced the back of her gown and found her skin, as smooth as a peach beneath the dark-colored silk. Only once did she resist him, when he went to untie her mask and put back the hood of her robe, and then she captured his hand to prevent him from unmasking her, and put it to her lips, which made him kiss her again, on her mouth, on her throat, on the warm hollow of her collarbones until he had spent the whole night in kissing her, the whole night in loving her, in learning every curve of her body, until the first light of dawn made the canal as dark as pewter and the garden as pale as silver and the birds started to sing, and she rose up, gathered her shadowy cloak around her, pulled the hood to hide her hair, shading her face when he would have kept her and kissed her again, stepped silently out of the garden gate and disappeared into the Venice dawn.

The next morning the five of them met for a late breakfast. Luca jumped to his feet to pull out a chair for Isolde and she thanked him with a small smile. He passed her the warm rolls, straight from the kitchen, and she took the bread basket with quiet thanks. Luca was like a man who had been staring at the sun, utterly dazzled, hardly knowing himself. Isolde was very quiet.

Freize raised his eyebrows to Ishraq as if to ask her what was going on, but serenely she ignored him, her eyes turned down to her plate, smiling as if she had a secret joy. Finally, he could contain himself no longer. "So how was your party, last night?" he asked cheerfully. "Did it go merrily?"

Isolde answered smoothly, "We went upstairs to meet Lady Carintha, and we borrowed some gold nobles from her to gamble. I suppose we'll have to return them. The women were a vain, vapid lot. They spoke of nothing but clothes and lovers. Brother Peter is quite right: it is a city empty of anything but sin. We came home about ten o'clock and strolled about for a few minutes and then went to bed."

Luca was staring at his plate, but he looked up just once as she spoke. He stared at her as if he could not understand the simple words. She did not glance at him as he pushed back his chair from the table and went to the window.

"So what are we to do today?" Freize asked.

"As soon as Luca and Ishraq have completed work on the manuscript and returned it to the alchemist and his daughter, then we must report them to the authorities," Brother Peter said firmly. "If you could return it today, we could report them today. I would prefer that. I don't want them coming to our house again. They are criminals and perhaps dabbling in dark arts. They should not visit us. We should not be known as their friends."

"How do we report them?" Ishraq asked. "Who do we tell?"

"We'll denounce them," Brother Peter said. "All around the city and in the walls of the palace of the doge there are big stone letter boxes with gaping mouths. They call them *la bocca di leone*, 'the mouth of the lion.' Venice is the city of the lion: that's the symbol of the apostle, St. Mark. Anyone can write anything about anybody and post it into the *bocca*. All Luca has to do is to name the pair of them as alchemists, Freize and I will sign as witnesses and they will be arrested as soon as the Council reads the letter."

DENONTIE SECRETE
CONTRO CHI OCCVLTERĀ
GRATIE ET OFFICII
O COLLVDERĀ PER
NASCONDER LA VERA
RENDITA Đ ESSI

Isolde blinked at the Venetian way of justice. "When will the Council read the letters of denunciation?"

"The very same day," Brother Peter said grimly. "The boxes are constantly checked and the Council of Ten reads all the letters at once. This is the safest city in Christendom. Every man denounces his neighbor at the first sign of ill-doing."

"But what will happen to Drago and Jacinta?" Freize asked. "When this Council reads your accusation?"

Brother Peter looked uncomfortable. "They will be arrested, I suppose," he said. "Then tried, then punished. That's up to the authorities. They'll get a fair trial. This is a city of lawyers."

"But surely alchemy isn't illegal?" Isolde objected. "There are dozens of alchemists working in the university here, and even more at Padua. People admire their scholarship—how else will anything ever be understood?"

"Alchemy isn't illegal if you have a license, but some applications of alchemy are illegal. And forgery is a most serious crime, of course," Brother Peter explained. "Anyone making gold English noble coins anywhere outside an official mint is a forger, and that is a crime that is very heavily punished."

"Punished how?" Freize interrupted, thinking of the pretty girl and her bright smile.

"The Council will hear the evidence, make a judgment and then decide the punishment," Brother Peter said awkwardly. "But for coining, it would usually be death. They take their currency very seriously, here."

Freize was shocked. "But the lass—the bonny lass—"

"I don't think the doge of Venice makes much exception for how pretty a criminal is," Brother Peter said heavily. "Since the city is filled with beautiful sinners, I doubt that it makes much difference to him."

Freize glanced at Luca, who was still gazing out of the window. "Seems too harsh," he said. "Seems wrong. I know they're forgers, but it seems too great a punishment for the crime. I wouldn't want to turn them in to their deaths."

Luca, hardly listening, glanced up from his silent survey of the canal. "They would be aware of the punishment before they did the crime," he said. "And they will have made a fortune. Didn't Ishraq say they had six sacks of gold on the quayside? And didn't you see the molds for making the gold yourself, and their furnace?"

"I don't say they're innocent, I just think they shouldn't die for it," Freize persisted.

Luca shook his head as if it were a puzzle too great for him. "It's not for us to decide," he ruled. "I just inquire. It's my job to find signs for the end of days, and if I find sin or wrongdoing, I report it to the Church if it is sin or to the authorities if it is a crime. This, clearly, is a crime. Clearly, it has to be reported. However pretty the girl. And these are Milord's orders."

"They're not just forgers," Freize pressed on. "They're inquirers, like you. They study things. They're scholars. They know things."

He reached into the deep pocket of his coat and brought out a little piece of glass. "Look," he said. "They're interested in light, just like you are. I stole this for you. Off Jacinta's writing table."

"Stole!" Brother Peter exclaimed.

"Stole from a forger! Stole from a thief!" Freize retorted. "So hardly stealing at all. But isn't it the sort of thing you're interested in? And she's studying it too. She's an inquirer like you, she's not a common criminal. She might know things you want to know. She shouldn't be arrested."

He put it on the table and uncurled his fingers so slowly, that they could see the little miracle that he had brought from the forger's house. It was a long, triangular-shaped piece of perfectly clear glass. And as Freize put it on the breakfast table between Isolde and Ishraq, the sun, shining through the slats of the shutters, struck its sharp spine and surrounded the piece of glass in a perfect fan of rainbow colors, springing from the point of the glass.

Luca sighed in intense pleasure, like a man seeing a miracle. "The glass turns the sunlight into a rainbow," he said. "Just like in the mausoleum. How does it do that?"

He reached into his pocket and brought out the chipped piece of glass from Ravenna. Both of them, side by side, spread a fan of rainbow colors over the table. Ishraq reached forward and put her finger into the rainbow light. At once they could see the shadow of her finger, and the remnants of rainbow on her hand. She turned her hand over so that the colors spread from her fingers to her palm. "I am holding a rainbow," she said, her voice hushed with wonder. "I am holding a rainbow."

"How can such a thing be?" Luca demanded, coming close and taking the glass piece to the window, looking through it to see it was quite clear. "How can a piece of glass turn sunshine into a rainbow arc? And why do the colors bend from the glass? Why don't they come out straight?"

"Why don't you ask them?" Freize suggested.

"What?"

"Why don't you ask them to show you their work, or tell you about rainbows?" Freize repeated. "He's known as an alchemist, he'll be used to people coming to him with questions. Why don't you ask him about the rainbow in the tomb of Galla Placidia? See what we can learn from them before we report them? Surely, we should know more about them.

Surely, you want to know why she has a glass that makes a rainbow?"

"You're sweet on the girl," Ishraq accused bluntly. "And you're playing for time for them."

Freize turned to her with his comical dignity. "Actually, I have a great interest in the origin of rainbows," he said. "I don't even know what girl you mean."

Isolde laughed, and even Brother Peter raised his head at the clear joy in her voice. "Ah, Freize, admit it! You have fallen in love in this city, where everyone seems to be in love."

"Everyone?" Luca asked her pointedly, but she turned her head away from him with a little color in her cheeks and did not reply.

Freize put his hand over his heart. "I tell no secrets," he said gallantly. "Perhaps she admires me? Perhaps not. I would not say a word to anyone, either way. But I still think you should talk to her and to her father before you hand them over to the doge and his men. We need to know more of what they were doing in that strange secret room of theirs. And why can't we warn them that the game is up and they should pack up their business and go away?"

"They can hardly pack up and go on their way, and nothing more be said!" Brother Peter exclaimed irritably. "They have swindled the merchants of the city of a fortune: making a market, profiteering in the gold nobles. They have cheated the nation of England of thousands of gold coins, perhaps hundreds of thousands, receiving the gold nobles stolen from them. We ourselves have bought gold nobles, giving good money in exchange for bad. This is a serious crime. They must be stopped. And anyway, Milord's orders are clear: we must report them."

"But they're not bad coins," Ishraq insisted. "They're growing in value every day. Everyone is making money. They have made no one poorer. Actually, everyone is getting richer. Us too. The Venetians themselves don't want the coins questioned. We tested the nobles, ourselves, as Milord said that we should. The coins are good, as good as gold. And now they're being exchanged for more than gold. The coins are better than gold."

"I'll visit them," Luca said. "I need to see their work. And we'll ask them about it. And we'll decide what to do."

"Milord has given orders," Brother Peter warned him. "He commanded us to find them and then report them. He didn't say that we should understand why they are doing it, or their other work. His instructions were plain and simple: go to Venice, find the coins, find the suppliers, report them."

"He must be obeyed," Luca agreed. "And I don't question our orders. We will report them as he commands. But not immediately. First, I will go and see them. I'll take Freize and"—he turned to Ishraq—"will you come too? And bring the manuscript page." He hesitated for a moment, clearly wondering if he could ask Isolde to come.

"If Ishraq is to come, she'll have to be masked and hooded and travel from door to door by gondola," Brother Peter ruled. "And, in her absence, Lady Isolde will have to stay at home, or go to church."

"I'll stay at home," Isolde said rapidly, almost as if she wanted to avoid the confessional at church. Almost as if she wanted to avoid Luca. "I'll wait for you to return."

"You'll wait for me?" Luca said, so quietly that only she could hear him.

The glance she directed at him was very cool. "I only meant I would wait for Ishraq to come back with the gondola," she said with a sweet smile that told him nothing.

"In the name of all the saints, what have I done? Have I offended her?" Luca demanded of Ishraq as they sat side by side in the gondola double seat. Freize, with his back to the prow, was in the seat before them.

"No, why?" Ishraq asked blandly.

"Because I thought . . . last night . . . she was so beautiful."

"At the party?" Ishraq prompted him.

"On our way there, yes. I thought that she was so light-hearted and so warm, she smiled at me and wished me good luck as we were in the gondola—and her eyes were shining through her blue mask, and I thought that perhaps after the party we might meet. . . . And then after the party I thought . . . and then today she hardly speaks to me."

"Lasses." Freize leaned forward to make his own contribution to the low-voiced conversation. "Like the little donkey. Easily set on one course, hard to disturb once they have chosen their own willful path."

"Oh nonsense!" Luca said. To Ishraq he said more pressingly: "Has she said nothing about me? Did she say nothing to you about last night?"

"About the party?" Ishraq said again.

"After the party?" Luca hinted tentatively. "After . . . ?"

Ishraq shook her head, her face utterly blank. "She has said nothing, for there is nothing to say. It was an ordinary party and we came home early. We walked for a few minutes, and then we went to bed. We had nothing to say." She paused, lowered her voice and looked directly at Luca. "And you had better say nothing too."

He looked astounded. "I should say nothing?"

She looked at him and nodded her head. "Nothing."

Left in the quiet house, Brother Peter had the breakfast things cleared and put his writing desk on the table to start the long task of preparing the coded report to the lord of the Order, to tell him that the forgers had been discovered, that they would be reported to the authorities at once, and asking for instructions for their next mission. Their work would go on: the lord would command them to go to another town, another city, to discover more signs of the unknown world, of the end of days.

They would go on, Brother Peter thought, a little wearied, on and on until the Second Coming, when they would at last understand all things, instead of as now—glimpsing uncertain truths. The world was going to end, that at least was certain, and it would happen soon: perhaps in this year, perhaps in this very month. A man in Holy Orders must keep watch, be ready, and his companions—his funny, endearing travel companions—must be gathered in, supported, taken with him as they went together on their journey from now to death, from here to the end of everything.

Isolde went up the stairs to the girls' floor and watched the house gondola with Luca, Ishraq and Freize pull out of the palace water gate and join the traffic on the Grand Canal. She put her hands to her lips and sent a kiss after the boat. But she made sure she was far back from the window so that even if Luca looked up, he would not see her.

Her attention was taken by another gondola that seemed

to be coming directly to their house, and she went to the head of the stairs to listen. She could hear the housekeeper send the maid down to the water gate to greet the visitor, and then, looking down the well of the stairs, she saw a slim heavily ringed hand on the bannister coming up the stairs. "Lady Carintha," Isolde said with distaste.

For a moment she wondered if she could say that she was not at home, but the impossibility of getting Brother Peter to condone such a lie, or the housekeeper to make her excuses, convinced her that she would have to face her ladyship. She glanced around their room, straightened a chair, closed the doors to their bedrooms and seated herself, with as much dignity as she could manage, on the window seat.

The door opened. "Lady Carintha!" the housekeeper exclaimed.

Isolde rose to her feet and curtsied. "Your Ladyship!"

"My dear!" the woman replied.

"Please do sit." Isolde indicated the hard chair by the fireside, where a little blaze warmed the room, but Lady Carintha took the window seat, with the bright light behind her, and smiled, showing her sharp white teeth.

"A glass of wine?" Isolde offered, moving toward the sideboard. "Some cakes?"

Her ladyship nodded, and the half nobles in her ears

winked and danced. Isolde noticed that now she had a necklace of big fat nobles wound around her white neck, the gold very bright against her pale skin, the weighty coins hanging heavily on the gold chain. Isolde poured the wine and handed Lady Carintha a plate of little cakes.

"I must repay you for our gambling debts," Isolde said pleasantly. "You were so kind to lend us the money." She went into her bedroom and came out with a purse of gold coins. "I am grateful to you. And thank you so much for inviting us to your lovely party."

"Nobles?" Lady Carintha asked, weighing the purse in her hand.

Isolde was glad that Ishraq had converted the rubies into nobles and that she had these to repay Lady Carintha. "Of course," she said quietly.

"Aha, then I will have made money!" Lady Carintha said gleefully. "For they are worth more this morning than they were last night. I have stolen from you by just lending them to you for a night. You are repaying me with the same coins, but they are of greater value. Isn't it like magic?"

"You're very welcome to your profit," Isolde said through her gritted teeth. "Clearly, you are as skilled as any Venetian banker."

"Actually, you have another treasure that I want," Lady Carintha said sweetly.

Isolde's expression was beautifully blank. "Surely, I can have nothing that Your Ladyship desires! Surely, you have only to ask your husband for anything that takes your fancy."

Her ladyship laughed, throwing her head back and showing her long white throat and the twists of the laden gold chain. "My husband allows me some of my treats, but he can't provide them all," she said meaningfully. "I am sure that you understand me?"

Isolde shook her head. "Alas, Your Ladyship. I have been brought up in the country, I am not accustomed to your city ways. I can't imagine what agreement you have with your husband, except to honor and obey him."

Her ladyship laughed shortly. "Then you are more of a novelty than I even thought!" she said. "I will be plain with you, then, country girl. If you want to walk about Venice as you were walking last night, or meet someone, or be absent from your house for a night, I will help you. You can say that you are visiting me, you can borrow my gondola, you can borrow my cape and my mask, even my gowns. If you concoct a story, you can rely on me to support it. You can say that you spent the night with me, and I will tell everyone that we sat up and played cards. You can lie your pretty head off and I will back you up, no questions asked. Whatever it is that you want to do, however . . . unusual. Do you see?"

"I think I see," Isolde said. "You will cover up lies for me."

"Exactly!" Lady Carintha smiled.

"And if I wanted to lie, and go out of the house in secret, then this would be very useful to me," Isolde said crushingly. "But since I don't, it is largely irrelevant."

"I know what I know," Lady Carintha remarked.

"That would be the very nature and essence of knowledge," Isolde replied smartly. "Everyone knows what they know."

"I know what I saw," her ladyship persisted.

"You saw me, or perhaps Ishraq, go into our garden. Or perhaps we saw you go into our garden. Perhaps we would swear to it. What of it? Your Ladyship, this is meaningless. You had better be plain. What do you want of me?"

"I will tell you simply, then, country girl. Tonight you will open your water gate to my gondola, you will lead me up the stairs to your brother's room, you will let me out again at dawn. And you will say nothing of this to anyone, and even deny it, if you are ever asked." She put a hand on Isolde's knee. "No one will ever ask," she promised. "I am always beautifully discreet."

"But what if my brother does not want you brought to his room?" Isolde was a little breathless. She could feel her temper rising beyond her control. "What if he thinks you too old or too well-worn? What if he does not desire you and wishes you far away?"

Lady Carintha laughed and smoothed her blue gown over her hips as if she were remembering Luca's caress from last night. "He won't be the first young man who has woken up to find me in his bed. He won't be the first young man to be glad of it."

"He is not an ordinary young man," Isolde warned her. "He is not like any other young men that you have met before."

"I agree, he is quite extraordinarily handsome," Lady Carintha said. "And I have a quite extraordinary desire for him. I think I am going to have a quite extraordinary love affair."

Isolde jumped to her feet, as if she could not sit still for a moment longer. "On my honor you will not!" she swore.

"Why should you mind? If I help you in turn? Or if you don't want an alibi for your own love affair, shall I help you meet young men? Or shall I just give you gifts?" Her ladyship put her hand to the dancing coins in her ears. "D'you want these? You can have them! But be very sure that I am going to have your brother. I shall take him as if he were my toy, and I shall leave him besotted with me. That's how it is. I shall leave him like an addict for a drug. He will spend the rest of his life longing for me. I shall teach him everything he needs to know about women, and he will never find a better lover than me. He will spend the rest of his life searching. I will have spoiled him for any ordinary woman."

"No," Isolde said flatly. "He will not long for you. And don't offer me your disgusting money or your repellent cast-offs, for I don't want them. I must ask you to leave. You won't come back."

"Indeed I will come back," the woman swore. "In secret, with or without your help. You can wake in the night and know that he is with me, in the room just below yours. Or he will come to me. D'you think he doesn't want me? D'you think I would be here without his explicit invitation? Last night he asked me to come home with him. Last night after the party. He wanted to meet me in the garden. He is in love with me, there's nothing you can do to stop it."

"He is not!" Isolde's voice quavered as she realized that Lady Carintha was probably speaking the truth and that Luca might well have arranged to meet her. He might have been waiting for her in the garden when the gate opened. "He is not, and I would never let you into his room. Even if I did not—" She broke off, remembering the lie that they must tell. "Even if he were not my brother, I would not condone it. You are an evil, disgusting woman. Never mind Luca, I would not take you to Freize's bedroom, for he is too good for you!"

"Your servant!" the woman half screamed.

"General factotum!" Isolde shouted at her. "He is a general factotum! And worth ten of you! For he is a great general factotum and you are an old whore!"

Lady Carintha launched herself at Isolde, slapped her face and pulled her hair. Isolde, furious, clenched her fist as she had seen Ishraq do when readying for a fight and punched the older woman—*smack*—on the jaw. Lady Carintha reeled back at the blow, fell against the table, recovered and then came forward again, her hands outstretched, her fingernails like claws, aiming for Isolde's eyes. She raked Isolde's cheek with her right hand before Isolde grabbed her arm and twisted it behind her. With Lady Carintha screaming with pain and trying to kick backward with her high-heeled shoes, Isolde pushed her, slowly gaining ground, through the open doorway to the top of the stairs, just as Brother Peter, at his most hospitable and dignified, was mounting the steps and saying: "I was told that Lady Carintha had honored our house with a visit . . . Good God! What is this?"

"She's leaving!" Isolde panted, her cheeks scarlet from rage, her face streaked with blood. "The old whore is on her way out."

Recklessly, she pushed Lady Carintha toward the stairs, and the woman almost fell into Brother Peter's arms, grabbed him to steady herself and then thrust him away and tore down the steps. "A plague on you!" the scream rang up the stairwell. "A plague on you, you prissy girl, and your pretty-boy brother. You will be sorry for insulting me."

Her ladyship paused at the bottom of the well of the stairs and looked back up at them—Isolde with her blonde hair tumbling down where her ladyship had pulled it, her right cheek scratched and bleeding, Brother Peter utterly stunned.

"And who are you, anyway?" Lady Carintha demanded, suddenly swinging from rage to cunning. "For you are like no family that I have ever met before. And why do you keep your brother as closely guarded as a priest? What sister gambles for time with her brother? What game are you playing? Who knows you? What business do you have? Where does your money come from? You'll have to answer to me!"

"Oh! No game! I assure you, Your Ladyship . . ." Brother Peter started down the stairs after her, but she turned and was gone, and then they heard her shouting for her gondolier and the sound of the water gate sliding open as her gondola went quickly away.

In the sudden silence, Brother Peter turned and looked at Isolde. "What on earth is this all about?" he asked. "What were you doing fighting with her like a street urchin? Lady Isolde! Look at you! What were you thinking of?"

Isolde tried for one sentence, tried for another, and then could say nothing but: "I hate her! And I hate Luca too!" and ran into her room and slammed the door.

Luca, Freize and Ishraq waited at the quayside outside the alchemist's house until the bell for Nones rang and they saw Drago Nacari and Jacinta coming toward them from the direction of the Rialto Bridge.

Freize went forward to greet the girl and to bow to her father, and then they came toward the front door, Jacinta producing a giant key from the purse under her outer robe.

"This is a surprise and a pleasure," the alchemist said warily.

Luca nodded. "I wanted to return to you the page of manuscript. I can't see how to make any progress with it. I was hoping that there would be a code that I could understand, but whatever I try, it doesn't come out."

The man nodded. "Would you discover more if you had the entire book?"

"I might," Luca said cautiously. "But I couldn't be sure of it. The more words you had to compare, the more likely to discover their meaning. And some might recur that would tell you they were commonly used words, but I couldn't promise it. I've made no headway, I don't have enough skill—" He broke off as the alchemist opened the door and ushered them inside.

"Come into my study." The alchemist showed them into the large room where the table was heaped with papers. Quickly, Jacinta closed the big double doors to the store-room, but the guests could smell the strange sweet smell of rotting vegetation, and beneath the smell of decay, something more foul like excrement.

"That's the smell of dark matter," the alchemist said, matter-of-factly. "We get used to it; but for strangers it's a disturbing scent."

"You refine dark matter?" Luca asked.

The man nodded. "I have the recipe for refining . . ." He paused. "To the ultimate point. I am guessing that is why you have really come today? You could have sent the page back by a messenger. I am assuming that, really, you wanted to see our work."

The girl stood with her back to the storeroom door as if she would bar them from entering. She looked at her father as if she would stop him from speaking. The alchemist glanced at her and smiled, returning his attention to Luca. "Jacinta is anxious for me, for our safety," he said. "But I too have had a dream about you, and it prompts me to trust you. Shall I tell you what it was?"

Luca nodded. "Tell me."

"I dreamed that you were a babe in arms. You were somehow shining. Your mother brought you to me and told me that she had found you. You were not a child born of man," he said quietly. "Does that make any sense to you?"

Ishraq drew a quick breath and glanced at Freize. Luca's unhappy childhood, when his whole village had called him a changeling, was known only to Freize, and the traveling companions, but they would never speak of it outside the group.

"I have spent my life denying that I was a changeling," Luca said with quiet honesty. "My mother told me that it was only ignorant, frightened people who would say such a thing, and that I should deny it. I have always denied it. I will always deny it, for her sake, for her honor as well as my own."

"Your mother would have her reasons," Drago Nacari said gently. "But in my dream you were faerie-born, and to be faerie-born is a great privilege."

Jacinta stepped forward from the door and put her hand on Luca's arm. "I knew that you could see the cups move," she said gently. "Then you told me that you could calculate where they would stop. No ordinary man can see them move, it's too fast. And nobody could calculate the odds of them stopping in one place or another. You are gifted. Perhaps you are gifted in a way that is not of this world. Dr. Nacari too is a gifted seer. He is speaking a truth from his dream. Perhaps even a truth that cannot be understood in this world."

"Doctor?" Ishraq asked.

Jacinta turned to her. "This is not my real father," she said. "We are partners in this venture. He is a great alchemist, I am his equal. In the world we pass as father and daughter because the world likes to place women in the care of a man, and the world likes a woman to have an owner. But in the real world, the world beyond this one, we are equal seekers after truth, and we have come together to work together."

"Not his daughter?" Freize said bluntly, grasping the one fact he could be certain of in this talk of one world and another.

She smiled at him. "And not a young woman either," she said. "I am sorry to have deceived you. Dr. Nacari and I have worked together for many, many years, and we have discovered many things together. Among them, an elixir that prolongs life itself. I am an old, old soul in a young body. You, Freize, make this heart beat faster; but it's only fair that I should tell you that it is a very old heart. I'm an old woman behind this young face."

Freize glanced at Luca and raised his shoulders. "This is beyond me, Sparrow," he said. "Someone is mad here, it might be me or them."

But it was Ishraq who spoke next. "It's about the gold," she said frankly. "We have come about the gold. We have come to warn you."

The alchemist smiled. "Was it you who broke into our house, Daughter?"

Freize shook his head in instant denial, but Ishraq met the older man's eyes fearlessly, and nodded. "I am sorry. We are commanded to find the source of the gold nobles. Our master demanded that we pretend to be a wealthy young family and investigate. We followed Israel, the money changer, and he came to your door. So we knew you had a store of gold nobles."

"We knew as soon as we came home, that someone had been into the inner room. And the things . . . the dark matter, the mouse in the jar, the coins in the fire—they were all disturbed, just a little, by your presence. Things are not the same when they are watched. Something changes when it has been seen."

"You knew we had been in the room?" Freize asked skeptically.

Luca stirred at the suggestion that an object might sense an observer, but Ishraq simply answered: "Yes, I thought you might know. And we took a print of the Duke of Bedford's seal and a piece of glass from the writing table."

"The rainbow glass," Luca said. "The glass that makes a rainbow when the light falls on it. I have been interested in rainbows since I saw the mosaic at Ravenna. Do you know how they are made in the sky? How does the glass do it on the earth?"

"The glass splits the light into its true colors," the alchemist told Luca, understanding his longing for knowledge. "Everyone thinks that light is the color of sunshine. But it is not. It is made of many colors. You can see this when it goes through the glass."

"Is it always the same colors?" Luca asked him. "I saw a mosaic of a rainbow, an ancient mosaic, centuries old, and it was the same colors that we see today. The ancients must have somehow known that light made a rainbow."

"Always the same colors," Jacinta confirmed. "And always following the same order. Light appears as clear brightness when all the colors flow together, but if you allow a beam of light to fall on a piece of glass, cut in the right way, it will split the light into its colors and you can see them. Put another piece of glass on the rainbow and you can make them meld together again and become invisible once more. One piece of glass can split the light, and then another makes it whole again."

"So what makes a rainbow in the sky?" Ishraq asked.

Jacinta turned to her. "I believe that the drops of water of the rain split the light, just like the glass splits it. You often see the rainbow against rain clouds, or against mist."

Luca nodded. "That's true, you do."

"But the interesting question to me . . ." Jacinta went on. "The interesting question is: why is it curved?"

"Curved?" Freize asked, utterly baffled, but wanting to join in.

The alchemist smiled at him. "Why would the bow of the rainbow be curved?" he asked. "Why would it not run straight across the sky?"

Freize shook his head, and even Luca was blank.

"Because it follows the line of the earth. It proves that the earth is not flat but shaped like a ball. And the great length of the rainbow proves that the ball is far greater than philosophers think, and round, not humped. It tells us that the earth is round but bigger than we thought. Much bigger than we thought."

Freize put his hands down and held on to the table as if to steady himself. "Why would you think such a thing?" he said, complaining of their imaginations, which made the ground heave beneath his feet. "Why would you repeat such a disturbing thing? And obviously untrue. Why would you say such a thing, even if you are mad enough to think it? It makes my head spin."

Jacinta put her small hand over his as he gripped the table. "Because we consider all possibilities," she answered. "And it is true about the world being round. But, of course, people don't like to think about it." She looked up and smiled at Luca. "Keep the glass piece," she said. "And see what light shines through it. Who knows what you will discover?"

"And what about you?" Ishraq asked. "You know, you can't stay here, counterfeiting coins. This has to stop."

"You call us counterfeiters?" The alchemist drew himself up to his full height. "You think I am a common criminal?"

For the first time Ishraq felt uneasy. She looked from Jacinta to the man who had passed as her father and remembered that she, Luca and Freize were three, against the two of them. But there was something about these two that made her wonder if they were safe, even with those odds. "I didn't mean to offend you, Dr. Nacari, but what else am I to think?" she said carefully.

"We saw the silver *piccoli* in the hearth," Freize said bluntly. "We saw the sacks of gold at your water gate. We know that you supply Israel, the money changer, with his gold coins. We assume that you supply others. You've got the seal of the Duke of Bedford—we know it's his seal. Altogether, it looks very bad." He turned to Jacinta. "It looks as if you are counterfeiting gold. You may be as old as my great-grandmother and the world may be round— though I have to tell you that I doubt it—but I would not have any harm come to a lass with a smile like yours."

At once she beamed, as radiant as a girl. "Ah Freize,"

she said intimately, "you have a true heart. I can see that as clearly as I can see anything."

The alchemist sighed. "Come in here," he said. He opened the door to what had once been the storeroom in the house, and the warm rotting smell intensified. He led the way into the inner room, and Luca looked around in amazement from the vat of rotting garbage to the bubbling, dripping glass vessels.

"I won't deny that we have started to make gold," the alchemist said to Freize. "There are the molds for pouring the gold. Here . . ." He pointed to a great round crock sealed and thrust into the deep heat of the fire. "Do you know what they call that?"

Freize dumbly shook his head.

"The philosopher's egg," he said, and smiled. "It absorbs an unbearable heat, and inside it the metals, pure and impure, melt and blend. When we pour the molten mix into the molds, we make gold nobles."

"Pure gold?" Luca confirmed, hardly able to believe it. "Because we tested some coins when we first arrived in Venice."

"Those would have been the first we ever had, from our patron. We didn't make them. Those were real gold nobles, from the Calais mint. We sowed the market with them. At first we just sold the coins he provided, creating an interest in the market, watching the price rise, and then we started to make our own. We have only just started making our own, from mixed metals. They pass as gold, they are just one step away from being pure gold, they are close, very close to perfect. I need only a little time to make them pure. I have to work on them some more. One last stage of refinement."

"We can't do it here, anymore," Jacinta reminded him. "Freize is good to warn us. We'll have to move on."

"Yes, I see we must be on our travels again. We will have to tell our patron that we have to find a new home."

Ishraq saw the young woman turn from the alchemist with regret, saw her glance at a bell jar on the table. Where the little brown mouse had been on their last visit, there was now another creature, a little like a lizard. Ishraq could not see more than the hairless back and the little outspread legs as the creature slept on its tiny belly at the bottom of the jar.

"Who is your patron?" Luca asked.

The alchemist smiled at him. "He works in secret," he said. "He works in darkness. But we have done what he wanted us to do. He commanded us to come here and put the coins that he gave us into the marketplace and then make our own, and now we are only one step from pure gold, only one step from eternal life."

"Wait a moment, you brought gold coins here?" Freize asked. "You didn't make them all here?"

"Our first task was only to trade gold coins." Jacinta

moved to the table and tossed, nonchalantly, a cloth over the bell jar. The little thing inside moved as the cloth fell down, hiding it from sight, and then lay still. "We found a trader we could trust—Israel, the man that you know—and then we put the gold nobles out into the market. We watched the traders bid for them and drive up the price. Everyone wanted them. We created a fashion for them, and we supplied them in thousands from our store. Our second task, once people were calling out for the coins, was to take enough silver to make our own gold. To refine it and work on it, according to the recipe. You saw us collecting silver in the market square, with the cups-and-ball game. You saw the coins heating up in the forge. Then, when we had converted it into gold, we sold our alchemical gold into the market we had created for the real gold nobles. But you have seen all this. You know how we do it?"

Freize shook his head. "We were in a hurry," he said, looking slightly embarrassed. "We visited, as it were, like burglars."

The alchemist turned to Luca. "If I could have gone on here with my work, I would have changed this vat of dirt into gold itself. Imagine it. The purest metal from the basest filth. But as it is, we have made a start, transforming the *piccoli*. We collected purses of silver and copper. Jacinta won it for us every day."

"But where did those first gold coins come from?" Freize asked, clinging to the few facts that he thought he might be able to understand. "Your master's gold that he gave you? The first gold that you didn't make, but only sold on. Where did your master get it?"

Jacinta lifted some of the glass jars off the table and put them up high, on the shelves. Ishraq glimpsed the desiccated bodies of a couple of mice, and one splayed specimen, pinned on a board, which looked like a dead cat. The young woman tidied them out of sight and then turned to answer Freize.

"They were true gold nobles," she said. "We cannot be accused of forging them, they were the real thing. Gold nobles created and stored by John, Duke of Bedford. A great alchemist. A great adept. They came in his caskets for us to use, under his own seal."

"From the mint at Calais? He had them made from real gold and stored to pay the English troops? When he was regent?" Luca asked.

She laughed and wagged a finger at him as if it was a great joke. "Ah, don't ask me!" she said. "He commanded the mint, so they may be English gold. They might be the real thing. But he also owned the manuscript book that we showed you. He was translating it when he died. His is the recipe that we are using to turn dark matter into gold. He spent his life and his fortune trying to make the philosopher's stone. Who knows whether the gold came from mines or from his alchemical forge? Who knows? Who cares? As long as it is good coin?"

"Because if it's alchemy gold, then he had found the secret of life, and you have it, even if you can't read it yet!" Ishraq exclaimed. "You are working toward it. In the pages of the manuscript, in your forge here, in your still, you have the secret of how to make gold from nothing, how to make eternal life!"

Jacinta smiled. "Of course we do. But if we had stolen the gold and all that we have made is a clever forgery, then we are counterfeiters and we will confess it to no one," Jacinta replied steadily. "So don't ask me which it is. Because I won't say."

Freize sat down heavily on one of the stools. "It's beyond me," he said. "But I know one thing . . ."

There was silence in the room but for the gurgle in the vat of first matter and the drip of a distilling pipe.

"No, I know two things," Freize said, thinking furiously. "The world is flat, of course, for if not, how could hell be below and heaven above? And that I was taught in the monastery and they even had a picture of it on the wall of the church that I saw several times a day and many times on Sunday so I am sure of that at least: hell below, earth in the middle and heaven above.

"And the other thing is something that I know, but you

do not. Something that you should know and be warned. Our master, that is to say, Luca's master, Milord, has ordered that we find the counterfeiters and report them. Our traveling companion, Brother Peter, will obey him, whether we agree or not. If you want to save your skins, you had better pack and go. It doesn't matter if you confess to alchemy or confess to counterfeiting, or deny them both, for Brother Peter will report you; and I, for one, would rather not see the doge's men come here and take you off to boil you in oil."

"They boil forgers?" the girl asked with a horrified shudder.

"God knows what they do to them," Freize said to her. "But, sweetheart, you don't want to find out."

Solemnly, the alchemist nodded. "You are right to remind us that we are in danger. We will take the most precious things and leave tomorrow, at dawn."

"Better go tonight," Freize prompted him.

"I am sorry for it," Luca said. "I see that you have been doing great work here. I should have loved to work with you. I should have been honored to see the transformation from first matter to gold."

The man shrugged. "We will have to start again. But this time we start with a proven recipe. Making gold is for the greedy criminals of this world. We wanted to make life itself. That is the point of alchemy, translation from the lesser to the greater till the purest point of all. Gold is nothing, life is the great secret."

Luca shook his head at the waste of them packing their treasures and leaving when they were on the brink of discovery. "I wish to God you could tell me all that you know," he said.

"Then we are equal, for I wish to God that you could tell me what you know, for I think you have it in you to be a great adept," the alchemist said gently. "Mortal born or changeling boy, you have the third eye."

"What?" Freize asked. "What do you say he has got?"

Drago Nacari put his forefinger to the center of his own forehead, between his eyebrows, and then pointed to Luca's forehead. Luca flinched as if at a touch. "The third eye," Drago said. "The gaze that can see the unseen things. I think you are indeed of faerie blood. You are a changeling."

"We've got to go," Freize decided, disturbed by this talk about his friend. He got to his feet and took Jacinta's hand and kissed it. "We'll do what we can to prevent Brother Peter reporting you at once. But don't you wait upon your going— pack up and go at once, for your own safety."

She took his hand and put it to her cheek in a brief, warm gesture. "Thank you," she said. "I will remember you as the sweetest thing in this extraordinary city. Truer than true gold itself, a finer thing than we could refine."

He flushed like a boy and turned to the alchemist and gave him an awkward nod. "Sorry," he said. "About the breaking and entering. Work, you understand."

Drago Nacari nodded in return. "Sorry about the false coins," he said. "Work, you understand."

Luca went to the doorway and bowed to them both. "I wish you the very best," he said. "And we will not report you till tomorrow, after dawn, at the earliest. You will have till then to get away."

The young woman came after them and slipped her slim hand into Freize's pocket.

"What's this?" he asked, pausing.

"Your penny," she said softly. "I promised I would return it to you. It is as true as you." She raised her face to his and Freize bent down and kissed her warm lips. "Good luck follow you," she said. "Blessings be." She went back to stand beside Drago Nacari, beside their bench, in the noisome laboratory among the bubbling stills.

Freize looked back, to get a last sight of her, and thought that they were like a lost couple heroically going down on a little boat, sunk by their own determination, then he caught up with Ishraq and Luca as they went quietly out of the front door and closed it behind them.

The waves lapped at the stone quays as their gondola went quietly down the small canals. "Drop me here," Luca said suddenly. "I want to see if Father Pietro is still at the Rialto Bridge."

"We'll wait for you," Ishraq decided. The gondola took Luca to a set of stairs in the quayside, and he ran lightly up and then crossed the square to where Father Pietro was seated, in his usual place, with his little table before him and his tragic roll of names unfurled.

"Father Pietro, do you have news?"

The priest leaped to his feet and came to Luca with his hands held out. "Praise God!" he said. "Praise God, I have news. My messenger saw Bayeed and was able to take a passage on a fast ship back to me with the greatest of news."

"My father? Guilliam Vero?"

"He is found. He is found, my son!"

A great darkness clouded Luca's vision, and he felt his head swirl. Out of the mist he felt the priest grab his arm, tap his cheek. "Luca? Luca Vero?"

"I'm all right," Luca gasped. "I could not hear. I cannot believe what I heard! My father is alive? And can we ransom him?"

The priest beamed at him. "I didn't know you had friends in high places. You should have told me that you had a great friend."

"I don't," Luca stammered. "I have no great friend. I am all but friendless. Until this moment I was all but an orphan. I don't know what you mean."

"A very great man had already sent a message to Bayeed, asking him if he had a Guilliam Vero on board, telling him that he must release him to his son, Luca, if requested. You know who did that?"

Luca started to shake his head. "I know no one except . . . the man who told me of you, he went by the name of Radu Bey."

Father Pietro laughed delightedly. "Because that is his name. And a great name among the infidel. If you have his friendship then you are favored by one of the greatest men in the Empire."

"I had no idea. . . . I met him only once. I asked about my father and one of his slaves said he was with Bayeed. I had no idea he would think of me again. He showed no interest in me or my father, he didn't seem to care at all. And he is the mortal enemy of my lord."

"Well, you are wrong. He's no enemy of yours. He took an interest, and to great effect. Bayeed was ready for your request, he regarded it as a request from the sultan, Mehmet II himself, and he sends me this reply." The priest showed Luca a small piece of paper with a scrawl of black ink and a roughly stamped seal.

Guilliam Vero, galley slave   Five English nobles

Father Pietro frowned a little. "He's kept his price at five English nobles, though their value has risen, and is still rising. That'll cost you twelve ducats now. Last week it would have been ten."

"It's all right," Luca said, still breathless with the news. "I have funds, I have nobles." He shook his head again. "I am stunned. I am dazzled." He drew a breath. "What do we do now? Do I go to fetch him?"

Father Pietro shook his head. "No, certainly not. You give me the money and I send it by my emissary to Bayeed. He will leave tonight, pay over the money and receive the slave, your father. He'll take him to an inn and get him a wash and some food, and some clean clothes. I find that all the men want to take a moment to return to life." He smiled. "It's a shock you know, the rolling back of the rock from the tomb. A man needs to take a moment to come back to life. He has to learn what has happened during the passing of the years, he has to prepare himself for the world he left so long ago. How long has your father been gone?"

"Four years," Luca said. "That's why I want to fetch him myself, at once."

"You only have to wait a little longer, my son. My messenger will bring your father to you."

"How long?" Luca demanded impatiently.

"If you give me the money, my agent can sail for Trieste, he'll be there by tomorrow evening or at worst the next day, a day to ransom him, and get him fed and clothed, then two days' journey home." The priest had been counting on his rosary beads as an abacus. "Say five days in all. You will see him within the week."

"I'll fetch the money at once," Luca swore, all thought of the alchemists driven from his mind. "I've got my gondola here. I'll fetch the money from home and come back to you."

"Come before sundown. I will be here until dusk."

"At once! At once!"

Father Pietro nodded. "One moment, my son," he said gently. "I would bless you."

Luca curbed his impatience and dropped to his knees. With great gentleness, the priest put his hand on the young man's bowed head. *"In nomine Patris et Filii et Spiritus Sancti."*

"Amen," Luca replied fervently.

The priest kept his hand on Luca's warm head, he imagined that he could almost feel the whirling thoughts swirling beneath his fingers. "Prepare yourself," he said gently. "You will find him much changed."

Luca rose to his feet. "I will love him, and honor him, however he is," he promised.

The priest nodded. "He will have led a life of brutal

cruelty, he will be scarred by it, outwardly on the skin of his back, in the brand on his face, and perhaps inwardly too. You must expect him to be different."

"But I am changed too," Luca explained. "He last saw me as a boy, a novice hoping to be a priest. Now I am a man. I have loved a woman, I have kept my love for her as a secret, I have seen some terrible things and looked at them and made a judgment. I am in the world and I am worldly. We will both see a great difference in each other. But I have never stopped loving him, and I know he would never have stopped loving me."

The priest nodded. "So be it," he said gently. "And I shall pray that the love of a father for his son and the love of God helps you both in your reunion."

"Where shall I meet him?" Luca demanded.

"Come to me here at the Rialto, at Sext, in five days' time, for news, and then you can come every day till he arrives," Father Pietro said.

"I'll be here," Luca promised. "Five days from now."

Dazed, he walked away from the busy bridge and found his way to the waiting gondola. He shook his head to the questions of Ishraq and Freize. "My father is found," is all he said. "I am to send the money. He is to come home to me."

Back at the house Brother Peter was waiting for them at the water gate stairs.

"I have no idea what is going on," he complained. "That woman came, and she and Isolde had some kind of quarrel, a terrible fight, and now Isolde is locked in her room and won't come out, nor speak to me, and she says she will never ever speak to Luca as long as she lives." He turned to Luca. "What have you done?"

The rush of crimson that rose from his white collar to his black hat would have convicted anyone. "Nothing," he said, glancing guiltily at Ishraq. "I've done nothing."

Ishraq stepped out of the gondola and went up the stone stairs, past the men's floor to the top story, into the big room where the reflection of the water made rippled light on the ceiling, and tapped on the door to Isolde's bedroom. She turned to see that Luca had followed her, his hat twisted in his hands, his young face wretched.

"Isolde?" she called. "Are you there?"

"Yes," came the muffled monosyllable from inside.

"What's the matter?"

"That woman was here and I punched her and she scratched my face, she pulled my hair and I pulled hers, and we were like fishwives in the Rialto. I was not better than her. I was like a jealous . . . *puttana*. I demeaned myself!"

"Why?" Ishraq was finding it hard not to laugh.

"Because she said . . . she said . . ." Isolde choked on a sob.

"Ah." Ishraq was moved at once. "Don't cry. It doesn't matter what she said."

"It *does* matter. She says that Luca made an assignation with her and that was why she came to the house last night, that he was going to lie with her in the garden. They had agreed to meet. He wanted her. And she ordered me to let her into the house tonight. She says that he wants her. She says that she will make him desire her. She says that she can drive him mad for her, that he will be her toy."

"I never!" Luca exclaimed unconvincingly. He stepped toward the door and rested his forehead lightly against the panel as if he would feel Isolde's cool hands on his face. "I never invited her," he said. "Not at all! Or at any rate, not exactly."

"Are you there too?" Isolde exclaimed from the other side of the door, her voice muffled by the wood as if she were leaning her lips to the panel, to be as close to him as she could.

"I'm here. I'm here."

"Why? Why are you there?"

"Because I cannot bear the thought of you being unhappy. And never because of me. Because I would do anything in the world to make you happy. I would give everything I own to prevent your distress. There is only one woman for me. There has only ever been one woman for me. There only ever will be one woman who I love."

"She said you were ready to fall in love with her."

"She lied."

"She said that she can make you fall in love with her."

"She cannot, I swear that she cannot."

"She said that you had agreed to lie with her after the party, that you had agreed to meet."

He stammered. "I did agree. I was a fool, and she said . . . it doesn't matter. But then in the garden I thought it was not her, but another. . . . Isolde . . . I don't know what happened. I thought . . . I hoped . . . I was certain it was . . ."

"Luca, I think she is a bad woman, a vile woman."

"Isolde, I am a man, I felt desire, I touched, I kissed . . . but it was dark, I didn't know. . . . All along I thought it was . . . I didn't know it was her, I was half-drunk, I was thinking of . . ."

"Don't say. Don't think. Don't say what you thought. You can never say what you thought. You can never say who you thought you were with."

"I'll say nothing," he swore, his hands flat against the door, his forehead pressed to the wood, his lips whispering so that only she could hear him.

"No one will ever say who went into the garden last night," Ishraq said to him quietly.

Luca turned to her and saw her dark gaze on him. He gasped as a thought struck him as powerful as a bolt of desire. "Ishraq? Was it you?"

"We won't even think about it," she said.

Silently, she gave him a little smile, turned away and crept down the stairs.

"Ishraq?" Isolde whispered.

"She's gone. She said nothing," Luca replied. "But I must know! Beloved . . ."

"What? What did you call me?"

"I called you beloved, for that is what you are to me. If you insist then I shall never speak of the night in the garden and the stranger who came to me. If you tell me it was a terrible mistake, then it was a terrible mistake. If you tell me it was a moment of love, out of time and out of place, never to be mentioned again, then I will believe that. If you tell me that it was a gift from another girl who I love almost as much as I love you, then I will keep that secret too. But if you tell me it was a dream, the most wonderful dream that I could have, then I will believe that. I am yours to command. It is a secret, even if I don't know it. But I know that I love only you. Only you."

There was a long silence from the other side of the door, and then he heard the key turn in the lock, and Isolde stood there, her hair tumbled down, her eyes red from crying.

"Can you keep the secret and never even ask? Never know for sure? Can you never ask and live not knowing?"

"I don't know," Luca said honestly. "I dreamed I was

with you, I longed to be with you, I had taken too much wine, I am so much in love with you that I thought I was with you. Can you tell me? Was I mistaken? Terribly mistaken? Or was I the happiest man in all of Venice?"

Slowly, she shook her head. "I can never tell you," she said. "You will have to live with never knowing for sure."

Strangely, he did not press her for an answer. It was as if he understood. Simply, he opened his arms to her and she stepped toward him and laid her head on his shoulder and her hot face against his shirt.

"I will never ask," he said. "It was like a dream. A most wonderful dream of something that I did not dare to dream. It can stay as a dream. If you order it: I just had a most wonderful dream."

Brother Peter and the two young women were waiting for Luca and Freize to come home in the gondola from the Rialto Bridge. Luca had dashed out of the house with a purse of gold nobles, a hurried kiss on Isolde's hand, desperate to get the money to Father Pietro at once.

"It is money that Milord gave us to support our lie that we are traders," Brother Peter said anxiously, standing at the window and looking down at the busy canal. "It's not for Luca to use to ransom his father."

"Milord must have known that Luca would use the money to save his father. And Luca might be lucky and earn it back with trades and gambling. Aren't the nobles worth more today than when we first bought them?"

"Usury," Brother Peter said depressingly. "He should not be making money by trading in a currency."

"He's supposed to!" Ishraq said impatiently. "Milord commanded it. He's supposed to trade. And if he makes a profit on his cargo, he can surely spend it as he likes!"

Brother Peter shook his head. "A good and careful servant would make the profit for the glory of God," he said. "And then give it all back to Milord. That is good stewardship. Think of the parable of the talents."

"But when Luca's father comes home, that will be to the glory of God," Isolde remarked. "And the greatest joy that Luca could have. Surely, we must be glad for him?"

"I cannot help but fear what he is becoming, when he rides around in a gondola like a young merchant prince." He glanced down at her. "I can't help but fear for you too. Fighting with that woman like a fishwife. Your father did not raise you to behave like this, Lady Isolde."

She nodded. "I'm ashamed of how I behaved," she said. "I am ashamed of more than you know, Brother Peter."

"Have you confessed?" he asked her very quietly. Ishraq

tactfully stepped to the back of the room and left Isolde to answer.

She shook her head. "I am too ashamed to confess."

"You were born and bred to be a lady," Brother Peter reminded her. "A lady with duties and obligations. It is your part in life to show self-control, good manners, self-discipline. You cannot be ruled by your heart in love, or by your temper and start fighting. You are meant to be better than this. Your father raised you for a great place in the world, not to be a silly girl with love affairs and fights."

She looked up at him. "I know this," she said. "But I am not in a world where I can behave well and people around me behave well. I am in a world of temptation and even anger. I want to be able to fight for myself. I want to be able to feel desire and act. I want to be able to defend myself against attack."

"A lady will find her defenders. The men around you will speak for you if need be," Brother Peter assured her, not realizing that he was recommending a view of women that had kept them powerless for centuries and would lead them to be victims of male anger and male power forever.

She bowed her head. "I will try," she said.

At the back of the room, Ishraq, who disagreed with everything that Brother Peter had said, shook her head and could not stop herself making a little "tut" noise of annoyance.

"There they are now," Brother Peter remarked, seeing the boat swerve through the busy traffic on the canal.

They heard Giuseppe call: "Gondola! Gondola! Gondola!" in his bubbling cry as he turned the gondola across the bows of the other boats and steered it neatly into the house, and then they heard Luca and Freize, talking quietly as they came up the stairs and entered the dining room.

"Is everything all right?" Isolde asked Luca, going straight to his side as she saw his slight frown.

He nodded. "We sent seven nobles in case he asked for more. It ought to be all right. It's just that the nobles are soaring against every other sort of coin. The slaver will not know what their value is in Venice when he sells my father in Trieste. It's going up so fast you have to be at the money changer's table to see it change. It's even going up against gold."

"How can a coin be more valuable than its ingredient?" Ishraq asked. "How can a gold coin be more valuable than gold itself?"

"Because people trust the gold noble even more than gold," Freize answered her. "There was a long queue before Israel, the money changer. People were changing solid gold into nobles because you can pay with a noble anywhere, and now it is worth more than its own weight. People are taking their gold jewelry, their wives' necklaces, and exchanging them by weight for a gold noble and then adding more to buy the coin. Buy a gold bar and it could be lead with a gold skin. You don't know—you have to get it tested. Buy a gold necklace and you don't know what you're getting. But all the gold nobles are always good, and they're all worth more today than they were yesterday."

The travelers exchanged an uncomfortable glance.

"This is getting more and more serious," Brother Peter said. "People will be speculating in gold nobles, but only we know where they came from. Only we know that some of them are not pure gold and have been made by alchemy!"

He crossed the room and checked that no one was listening at the door and then gestured that they should all sit around the table. "We have to decide what to do. This situation is getting worse and worse. I know you feel tenderness toward the alchemist and his daughter, but we are bound to report them at once."

Luca paused for a moment, almost as if he was reminding himself that he was on a mission, and that he was the inquirer. Slowly, he took the chair at the head of the table. For the first time it was as if he was consulting Brother Peter as his clerk—but not as his mentor. "Wait. We have to think this through," he ruled. "Some things are clear. We can report to Milord that we have completed our inquiries and we know what has happened here. The alchemist pair came with gold that they had obtained from their patron to trade on the market of Venice. They admit that they released many gold English nobles, but will not say whether this was alchemical gold from the great master John, Duke of Bedford, or whether it was true gold, earthly gold, from the mint that he controlled at Calais."

"Agreed," Brother Peter said. "And I have prepared the report in code, saying just this. It is ready to go once you have signed it."

"They also said that the world was round," Freize pointed out. "And the pretty girl said that she was an old lady. So it might be that they are just mad, poor things."

"Peace!" Luca commanded him. "Most scholars believe that the world is round."

"They do?" Freize was scandalized. "What about the other side?"

"What other side?"

"The underneath. If the world is round, then what about the underneath? The underneath of the ball? What's it sitting on? That's the question. Never mind rainbows! And what happens when you go round the middle? If you traveled to the underneath, you would fall off." He put both hands to his head and gently pulled his own ears. "You would be upside down! It makes me dizzy just thinking about it."

"Never mind all that. They were talking about something else entirely different."

"Why were they talking about the world being round at all?" Isolde asked, distracted from the most important issue by Freize's confusion. She leaned forward and gently took his hands from his ears. "Hush, Freize. Be calm. It's no worse than thinking that if the world were flat, you could travel to the edge and fall off it."

"Fall off it?" he repeated, horrified. "There is an edge?"

"We were talking about rainbows," Luca explained briefly to Isolde.

"Actually, that's no comfort," Freize said quietly to Isolde. "Actually, it's worse. Falling off the edge? Saints save us!"

"But to our business with them," Luca said, interrupting the digression. "They say that after some weeks of trading the Bedford gold, they started to make gold nobles of their own, with the Duke of Bedford's own recipe. And then they released these gold nobles on the market with the others. So we can be sure that there is already a mixture of good English gold nobles and alchemy gold nobles coming into the market together."

"Can you tell one from another?" Brother Peter asked. "Or are they all equally good?"

"I think people may be able to do so," Ishraq replied, worried. "They seemed to suggest that their own gold, made from silver and base metal, needed another stage of refining. They said they needed more time."

"Lady Carintha had new gold nobles in a necklace," Isolde offered. "They looked as good as the others. If they were alchemy gold, you couldn't tell by looking."

"But their main work, their greatest work, was not the gold, they said, but life," Freize said. "They said that. Didn't they?"

"They did," Luca confirmed. "They were very clear that the making of gold was a lesser art, one for greedy men. Their principal ambition was to make not the philosopher's stone that can make everything into gold, but the philosopher's elixir—to make life itself."

"They have a powerful number of dead animals," Freize pointed out. "In all those jars. And for people making life they have a terrible stink of death in their storeroom."

"The young woman said that she was an old woman," Ishraq told Brother Peter. "She said she was not as she seemed. She said that she was an old woman in a young woman's body and that she and the man she calls her father had worked together for many, many years."

There was a little silence.

"But they said many things that cannot be true," Freize reminded them. "I don't even want to think about it."

"We have to report them," Brother Peter said heavily. "I see that they are philosophers, and their work is perhaps valuable, but Milord was clear that we had to find the counterfeiters, and this pair have admitted to making coins. He said that we must report them—and we have to do so."

"Give them the rest of today to pack up and go, and we will report them after dawn tomorrow," Luca ruled.

"Milord said . . ."

"Milord wanted Radu Bey dead," Ishraq cut in scornfully. "He accused him of being an assassin. Milord only told Luca that it was possible to buy his father's freedom months after he first met him. He said nothing before Luca knew it already. He could have told Luca how to free his father when they first met, but he did not bother to do so. Milord gives orders, but they are not always to our good. Milord can wait a day."

There was a sharp indrawn breath from Brother Peter. "You are disrespectful," he reproved her. "Milord never ceases in the work of the Order. Night and day he serves God and the Holy Father. He fights the powers of darkness and the infidel in this world and the other. I am sworn to the Order and so is Luca Vero. Milord is the commander of our

Order and we have to obey him. We are sworn to him."

"But I am not!" Ishraq insisted. "Don't look so shocked, I am not suggesting that we disobey him. I don't oppose him. Brother Peter, I don't oppose your mission, I don't even argue with you about how you think women should behave, and I have served you well over the last few days. All I say is that we should do as Luca thinks and report the alchemists tomorrow at dawn. It's what we promised them."

"I think so too," Isolde agreed, exchanging a quick hidden glance with Luca as if they had made a promise and would always be a partnership. "Tomorrow, as Luca says."

"Tomorrow," Freize said. "That's fair enough."

Brother Peter looked from one determined young face to another. "Very well," he said with a sigh. "So be it. But tomorrow at dawn."

He rose from the table and walked to the door, stiffly dignified, when there was a sudden tolling of the bell in the water gate and a sound of men, a whole brigade of men, running up the marble stairs, their boots hammering on the stone. The door banged open, was held open by the fore-runners of the doge's guard, who poured into the room, followed by an officer, beautifully dressed, holding a silver handgun, cocked and ready to fire. "You're under arrest," he said abruptly.

Luca's chair crashed to the floor as he pushed it back and jumped before Isolde to shield her. "What charge?"

"We've done nothing!" Brother Peter exclaimed, falling back from the door as the men rushed into the room.

Behind the men, the ashen face of the housekeeper peered in, and behind her, gleaming with triumph, came Lady Carintha, dressed in scarlet, with her husband in tow.

"This is a private matter," Luca said as soon as he saw her. He turned to the officer. "Commander, there is nothing to investigate, no crime here. There has been a misunderstanding between myself and the lady, an unfortunate quarrel between neighbors." He crossed the room at once, and bowed low and took her hand. "I am sorry if I offended you," he said. "I meant no insult." He bowed to her husband. "An honor to meet you again, sir."

"He's no trader," she said bluntly to the doge's officer, completely ignoring Luca. "And I doubt that they are brothers. She is certainly not his sister, and God knows who the Arab slave is. Is she their dancing girl? Is she in his harem? Is she their household witch?"

Amazingly, Ishraq did not fire up to defend herself against the insults, but meekly bowed her head and went quietly to the door. "Excuse me," she said.

"Where's she going?" Lady Carintha snapped.

"To my room," Ishraq said, her eyes modestly turned down. "I am kept in seclusion. I cannot be in this roomful of men."

"Oh, of course." The officer waved her away as she drew the veil of her headdress across her face and the soldiers stepped back to let her go past.

"That's a lie!" Lady Carintha exclaimed. "She's not in seclusion at all, she's a bold-faced slut. If you let her go, she'll be running away!"

"No one to leave the house!" the officer ordered Ishraq. "You may only go to your room."

Ishraq bowed very humbly and went up the stairs to her room.

"Put a man on the door," the officer ordered, and one of the soldiers followed her at a respectful distance.

"My dear," Lady Carintha's husband said quietly. "We can leave the officer to make his inquiry. Now that you have done such good work of denouncing them."

"They're forgers," Lady Carintha said to the officer. "Look what she gave me."

She threw on to the table the purse that Isolde had given her to repay the gambling debts. "False gold," Lady Carintha accused. "Counterfeit coins. Counterfeit English nobles as well, which is worse. Arrest them."

Isolde was ready to brazen it out. "There's nothing wrong with the gold," she claimed. "And if there is, I had it in good faith. I bought these nobles in Venice, thinking they were good. I would not have paid someone like you in a false coin. I would not have done anything that might cause you to return here!"

"I don't come for pleasure, be sure of that!" the woman snapped. She turned to her husband. "See how she speaks to me! Who would ever be fooled into thinking she was raised as a young lady? She's as fake as the coins in the purse."

"Lady Carintha . . ." Luca said quietly. "Let us discuss this as friends, there is no need for ill feeling."

"We are honest merchants, a family of honest merchants." Brother Peter repeated the lie with so little conviction that it was as bad as confession.

"Arrest them!" Lady Carintha demanded.

"Shall I fetch our traveling papers?" Freize asked the officer. "Our letters of introduction? You will see we have a sponsor, a very important man."

The guardsman nodded. Freize went to the door.

"Look at the coins!" Lady Carintha shouted. "Never mind his letters. He can forge letters as well as coins, I daresay." She thrust her hand into the purse, and they saw her beautiful face change, the anger was suddenly wiped from her features as she froze, and then her face contorted with a sort of horror.

She pulled her hand out of the purse, and they saw her fingers were sticky with some red liquid, almost like blood. "My God," she exclaimed in disgust. "Look at my hand! The coins are bleeding. They are so false, they are bleeding like the wounds of murdered men."

She turned to show her hand to her husband, and he recoiled from her—she was so horrific with her fingers reddened as if she had dipped them in an open wound. Every man in the room flinched from her as if she were oozing blood like a murdered corpse.

She felt a strange sensation on her neck, like a crawling insect, and put her clean hand to her ear. The gold noble earrings were dripping blood onto her neck. The gold noble necklace was making a trail of red at her throat as if someone had taken a knife and sliced into her.

"Clean me!" she said, her voice shaking. "Get it off me."

Nobody could bear to step toward her, nobody could bring themselves to touch her. They could only watch in terrified fascination as the gold noble earrings drip-dripped blood down her white neck and into the low-cut lace at the top of her gown.

"Get it off me!" she screamed, her fingers slipping at the intricate clasp of the necklace, unable to grip for the red liquid. "It's burning me! It's scalding my skin! Get it off me!"

Her husband forced himself to step forward to help, gritting his teeth against his distaste. The officer drew his dagger and put the blade of his stiletto under the clasp of the necklace, careful not to touch the oozing coins.

"Cut it off!" Lady Carintha screamed. "It doesn't matter that it's gold. Get it off me! It's bleeding on me! It's burning! It's burning my skin!"

Her husband held the necklace away from the nape of her neck as the young officer pulled upward and away with his knife. The blade was as red as if he had stabbed her in the heart, and the necklace pulled against her neck and made her shriek before it clattered to the ground, smearing scarlet on the marble floors as if a murder had been done in the horrified room.

There was a sudden black flash of something going past the window, but only Luca, facing in that direction, saw that it was Ishraq, pointed like a spear in a long fearless swallow dive, from her high bedroom window into the canal.

"What the hell was that?" demanded the officer of the guard, pushing past Lady Carintha to look out of the window. "I saw something go by. . . ."

"Nothing," Luca said at once. "A cormorant, perhaps." Luca looked down with him. In the canal they could see a circle of bubbles but nothing else.

"A murdered body bleeds when the murderer comes near!" Lady Carintha declaimed, pushing herself forward, scrubbing with a cloth at her reddened neck. "These coins are bleeding because they are in the house of the counterfeiters!"

"I'm going to have to search your property," the officer said, turning from the window to Brother Peter.

Luca was still looking out at the Grand Canal. After what felt like a long, long time he saw Ishraq's dark head, wet as a seal, emerging from the water. Someone pulled her on board a rowing boat, and she crouched in the prow, but they did not return to the house. The boatman leaned over his oars and rowed as hard as he could down the canal, before anyone from the palazzo could raise the alarm or come after them. They were out of sight in a moment. Luca guessed Freize was at the oars and Ishraq was urging him on to warn the alchemists.

"What was that?" The officer returned to look out with Luca. "Looked like something was thrown from an upper window."

"I'll go and see," Isolde volunteered. "My slave may have dropped something."

"You'd better not have thrown away any evidence," the officer warned. "We can drag the canal, you know."

"Of course not!" Isolde said.

Before anyone could stop her, she pushed past Lady Carintha and ran up the stairs to her room. They heard her slam the door and turn the key in the lock as Lady Carintha poked the bleeding necklace with the toe of her satin shoes and said, her voice shaking: "False coins, false hearts. Bleeding coins are a sign of guilt. These are wicked people. You must arrest them all. Especially the young women. They must be put to the question. They must be taken to the doge's palace and held in his prisons."

"Where did you get this purse from?" The officer spilled the bloodstained coins onto the dinner table, and they smeared their sticky redness in a pool.

Brother Peter exchanged one brief look with Luca.

"I can find out," the officer said. "I only have to ask in the Rialto and someone will tell me. But it would be better for you if you were to answer me now."

Luca nodded. Clearly, they would have to tell the truth. "We got our nobles from the money changer Israel," he said. "But I am certain that he thought that they were good. We certainly thought they were good. It was a simple transaction between two honest parties."

The officer turned his head and spoke briefly to one of his men. At once he left the room and they could hear him running down the stairs.

"I am arresting you on suspicion," the officer said.

"Of what?" Luca said. "We may have received forged nobles, but so has Lady Carintha. Where did she get her necklace from? It was not from us! We are buyers of coins, not counterfeiters. You can search the house."

"We know Lady Carintha, she is a Venetian born and

bred, and her husband is a great trader in this city, his name is in the Gold Book. He is on the Council. You, on the other hand, have just arrived and everything about you is strange. Lady Carintha says you are not what you seem, you have been arranging to buy a fortune in gold from one money changer, you speak of a ship that has yet to come in, you are often seen with Father Pietro and you seem to be favored by one of the greatest enemies of Christendom."

Luca raised his eyebrows at the extent of the officer's knowledge. "You have been watching me?"

"Of course. We watch all strangers. Venice is filled with spies. There is a *bocca di leone* for denouncing the guilty in every square. And you have great wealth and dubious friends. You have been under suspicion from the moment you arrived."

"He is not a dubious friend. Radu Bey was a chance acquaintance, who chose to help me trace my father who was captured as a slave of the Ottomans. The city of Venice itself trades with the Ottoman Empire. The doge himself trades with Radu Bey."

"But the doge does not use counterfeit coins," the man returned.

"He does," Lady Carintha said spitefully, pulling her earrings out of her ears and throwing them down on the table with a shudder. They sat in a little pool of redness, oozing wetly. "He almost certainly does. His hands will be bloody too."

"What?"

"Since this family arrived, everyone in Venice has gone mad for the English gold. Ask my husband. The price has soared. No doubt the doge has bought them, no doubt he has sold them on. Perhaps his hands are dirty too. Perhaps we are all going to be ruined." She rubbed her stained hands against the skirts of her gown and shuddered. "What *is* this?"

"It looks like a sort of rust," Luca said. "Perhaps the metals are breaking down and rusting away."

She looked at him and her beautiful face was twisted with jealousy and spite. "Rusting gold?" she said. "Against the laws of nature. You and that sister of yours? Unnatural too. As unnatural as forgery. As false as counterfeit coin."

"What are you suggesting?" the officer asked her. "Are you saying they are sinners as well as criminals?"

"God knows what they are guilty of," Lady Carintha swore. "You should take them in at once. He is false as the most beautiful gold coin, and she passes for a lady but fights like a cat. Who knows what they have done together?"

"My dear . . ." her husband interpolated.

"I want to go home." Lady Carintha suddenly became soft and tearful. She turned to her husband. "We have done our duty here. I can't bear it here with these bloodstained coins in this house of wicked strangers."

Solemnly, he nodded. "Do your duty for the doge and the Republic," he said pompously to the officer. "The survival of the greatest city in the world depends on our wealth and our trustworthiness. This family—if they are truly a family and not a counterfeiting ring in disguise—have challenged both. They must be destroyed before they destroy us! Arrest them at once and take them before the Council of Ten!"

The two of them were too powerful to be denied. The officer looked from Luca to the stained gold nobles scattered over the table. "I am arresting you on suspicion of counterfeiting coins, trading in false gold with a Jew, and incestuous relations with your sister," he said. "You will have to come with me. In fact, I am arresting you all."

Brother Peter put his hand over his eyes and made a little noise like a low sigh, but at that moment, the door opened and Isolde came into the room. She was transformed. She was wearing her blonde hair piled high on her head and a tall scarlet pointed headdress on top of it that made her look six feet tall. She was wearing one of her most beautiful Venetian-made gowns in a deep crimson, the slashed sleeves showing white silk underneath. She stood very tall and very proudly. Beside her Lady Carintha looked old and tawdry with her dirty neck and her bloodstained ears.

"This has gone far enough," Isolde ruled. "It must stop now." At her tone of command the officer hesitated, and Lady Carintha's husband made a half-bow, halted by a sharp hidden pinch from his wife.

"I am Lady Isolde of Lucretili," Isolde said directly to the officer. "This is my mother's signet ring. You can see our family crest. I am traveling with my servant and companion Ishraq, and with this escort: my tutor Brother Peter, a man of unquestioned probity, his scholar Luca Vero and our man-servant and general factotum. We decided to pass as a noble family interested in trade in order to travel without being known and for my personal safety."

"Why would you do that?" the officer queried. Lady Carintha stood dumb, clearly overwhelmed by Isolde's gran-deur.

Isolde answered the officer, completely ignoring the woman. "My brother has usurped my place at the castle," she said. "He is passing himself off as the new Lord of Lucretili. I don't want him to know that I am going to seek help against him from my godfather's son. That is why we are traveling through Venice. That is why we assumed differ-ent names."

"And who is your godfather's son, Milady?" the officer asked deferentially.

"He is Count Vlad Tepes the Third, of Wallachia," Isolde said proudly.

The officer and all the guards pulled off their hats at the mention of one of the greatest commanders on the frontiers of Christendom, a man who had conquered his country of Wallachia from the unstoppable Ottoman army, been driven out, and would, without a doubt, conquer it again. "You are the great count's goddaughter?" the officer confirmed.

"I am," Isolde said. "So you see, I am a woman of some importance." She took another step into the center of the room and looked Lady Carintha up and down with an expression of utter contempt. "This woman is a bawd," she said simply. "She keeps a disorderly house where there is gambling and prostitutes. She boasts of her own immorality and she quarreled with me only when I refused to join in her lascivious ways."

Slowly, Lady Carintha's husband detached himself from her gripping hand and turned to look at her.

"I imagine it is well known to everyone but you, sir," Isolde said gently to him. "Your wife is little more than a common whore. She has quarreled with me because I would not let her into this house at night and lead her to the room of this young man of my household, whose spiritual well-being is my responsibility. She wanted to lie with him, she offered to buy time with him by giving me jewelry or an alibi for my own absences, or introduce me to a lover. She said she would make him into her toy, she would have him for *Carnevale* and then give him up for Lent."

Brother Peter crossed himself at the description of sin.

Luca could not take his eyes off Isolde, fighting for their safety.

"She's lying," Lady Carintha spat.

"When I treated these offers with contempt, this woman attacked me," Isolde said steadily.

Lady Carintha crossed the room and stood, her hands on her hips, glaring at Isolde. "I will slap your face again," she said. "Shut up. Or you will be sorry."

"I am sorry that I have to speak like this at all," Isolde said glacially, one glance at Brother Peter as if she was remembering his claim that a lady should not fight for herself. "A lady does not tell such shameful secrets, a lady does not soil her mouth with such words. But sometimes, a lady has to defend herself, and her reputation. I will not be bullied by this old streetwalker. I will not be scratched and pinched by such a she-wolf." She smoothed back the veil that flowed from her headdress and showed the officer the scratch marks on her cheeks. "This is what she did to me this very afternoon for refusing her disgusting offers. I will not be assaulted in my own home. And you should not work at her bidding. Any denunciation from such as her means nothing."

"Absolutely not!" he said, quite convinced. "My lord?" He turned to Lady Carintha's husband. "Will you take the woman home? We cannot accept her denunciation of this family when she clearly has a private quarrel with them.

And this lady"—he bowed toward Isolde, who stood like a queen—"this lady is above question."

"And she receives forged coins," Isolde added quietly. "And gambles with them."

"We'll go," Lady Carintha's husband decided. To Isolde he bowed very low. "I am very sorry that such a misunderstanding should have come about," he said. "Just a misunderstanding. No need to take it further? I would not want our name mentioned to the count, your kinsman. I would not have such a great man thinking badly of me. I am so sorry that we have offended, inadvertently offended . . ."

Isolde inclined her head very grandly. "You may go."

The officer turned to Brother Peter and Luca. "I apologize," he said. "Of course, no arrest. You are free to come and go as you please."

He bowed very low to Isolde, who stood very still while he ordered the men from the room, and they waited until they heard the clatter of their boots on the stairs and then the bang of the outer door.

There was a sudden total silence. Isolde turned and looked at Brother Peter as if she expected him to criticize her for being too bold. Brother Peter was silent, amazed at this newly powerful version of the girl he had seen before as a victim of her circumstances: clinging to a roof in a flood or weeping for the loss of her father.

"I will defend myself," she said flatly. "Against her, or against anyone. From now on, I am going to fight for my rights."

Freize rowed in determined silence, heaving the little boat through the water, until Ishraq, hunched in the prow, shivering a little in her dripping gown, looked behind and said: "Nobody's following."

He paused then, and stripped off his thick fustian jacket. "Here," he said. "Put this round your shoulders."

Almost she refused, but then she took it and hugged it to her.

"You look like a drowned rat," Freize said with a smile, and set to the oars again.

She made no reply.

"A sodden vole," Freize offered.

She turned her head away.

"It was a hell of a dive," he said honestly. "Brave."

Ishraq, like a champion of the games receiving the laurel crown, bent her head, just a little. "I'm cold," she admitted, "and I hit the water with a terrible blow. I knocked the air out of myself."

"You hurt?" he asked.

He saw her indomitable smile. "Not too bad."

They found their way through the network of little canals toward the Jewish quarter of the city, and rowed slowly along the outside of the steep ghetto wall, until Ishraq said: "That must be it. That must be their water gate. It's on the corner."

The alchemists had no gondola, and their gate was closed, the two halves of wrought metal bolted together. Ishraq was about to pull the bell chain that hung beside the gates when Freize raised his hand for her to wait, and said: "Listen!"

They could hear the noise of someone pounding on the outer door to the street, they could hear someone shout: "Open in the name of the law! In the name of the doge: open this door!"

"We're too late," Freize said shortly. "They must have got to the money changer, and he must have told them that he got the coins from here."

Ishraq listened to the loud hammering. "The guard isn't in yet," she said. "We might be able to get them away. . . ."

Without another word, Freize rowed the boat toward the gate and Ishraq leaned over the prow and struggled to push the heavy bolt upward. But whenever she pushed against the gate, the boat bobbed away. Finally, in frustration, she stepped out of the boat altogether and, clinging to the wrought iron of the gate, her bare feet flexed on the trelliswork, she used all her strength to push the bolt upward. Stretching between the stationary gate and the one that was opening, she kicked off from the anchored gate and swung, slowly inward, dangling over the cold waters.

Freize brought the boat up against the slowly opening gate and Ishraq stepped back into the prow and then turned as he took the little boat against the internal quay. She jumped ashore and took the rope, tying it to the ring in the wall.

Now they could hear the noise more clearly, the hammering on the door echoing through the stone storeroom and through the wooden hatch to where they stood on the quay.

"Sounds like a raid," Freize said. "Ten men? Maybe eight?"

Cautiously, he tried the hatch that led from the quay to the storeroom. It opened a crack, and Freize looked in.

"They've bolted the door to the street," he said. "But I can hear the doge's men breaking it down now." Freize pulled the hatch from its housing and jumped upward, getting his chest and belly over the ledge, and wriggled through the low gap. There was a crash from inside the house as he got to his feet, and Freize whirled around to see Jacinta running through the door, her father behind her, their arms filled with rolls of manuscript, a chest of papers in her hand.

She recoiled for a moment, as she saw Freize's broad

frame and the open hatch, and then she recognized him. "Thank God it's you!" she exclaimed. She thrust the papers at him. "They can't have these," she said. "No one can see these. They're secret."

"Get in the boat," Freize said shortly, throwing the papers through the hatch. "We've got one in your water gate, waiting."

"I have to fetch . . ."

They could hear a steady violent thud at the front door as the men took a ram to it and started to break it in. Drago Nacari was gathering up small glass jars in his haste, passing them through the hatch to Ishraq, who stacked them pell-mell into the bottom of the boat.

"Come!" Freize shouted at the pretty girl, who was piling small spice boxes one on top of another to carry away. "That door won't hold! Come now or you will lose everything!"

She raced toward the hatch and handed the boxes to Ishraq on the waterside. Drago Nacari was through the hatch already and at the oars of the boat. "Come!" he commanded her.

"The baby!" she shouted.

"Baby?" Freize repeated, horrified.

There was a crash as the outer door to the street yielded to the battering ram, and then shouts as the guard came up against the locked storeroom door. Jacinta dragged a stool across the stone floor and jumped up on it so that she could reach the highest shelf. She stretched out her hands for the bell jar where Freize and Ishraq had first seen a little brown mouse beside a flickering candle, and then, on their later visit, seen the naked lizardlike thing.

"This . . ." she said as the kitchen door burst open and a band of the doge's guards hurled themselves into the store-room. One man threw himself at her, grabbing her around the knees and bringing her down.

The bell jar flew from her hands and smashed on the floor. The young woman screamed, struggled in the man's grip, writhing like a serpent as her cap fell off and her rich russet hair tumbled down around her shoulders. Freize took hold of the guardsman in a strong grip from behind, pulling him off her, so he was facing Jacinta as she wormed out of the man's grip. Freize saw her, saw her transformed: her long straggling locks of completely white hair, her face gnarled and old, her merry brown eyes pouched under drooping eyelids and her wrinkled lips stretched over toothless gums as she gave a croaky scream.

For one second they were all frozen still with horror, and then the guardsman released her with a bellow of shock, pushed her away from him, thrusting her away like a man in terror. In that moment she was out of his arms, and through the hatch, wriggling like a white-headed snake through the gap, down to the quay, and into the boat, and Drago and Jacinta were gone.

"Good God!" the man said. "Did you see? Did you see that?"

Freize did not reply, so shocked that he could not catch his breath. Then he saw the contents of the bell jar that Jacinta had tried so hard to save. Amid the broken shards of the glass bell jar there was a little creature. At first he thought it was a lizard, only pale and pink. Then he thought it was a kitten that they had obscenely skinned and left to bleed. Then he saw the thing more clearly. The little being rose up on its hind legs and held up its arms to him, and he heard a tiny piping voice say: "Help me! Help me!"

The other guardsmen were pouring into the storeroom and kicking in the wooden frame of the hatch that led to the quay. Among the turmoil of the broken glass and the stamping of leather boots the little thing called again to Freize: "Help me!"

Compassion overcame his disgust and with a horrified shudder Freize bent down toward the tiny animal that stood no taller than six inches, like a perfectly formed naked man, but with a grimace of fear on its miniature bare face, and a word written in silver across its forehead: *EMET*.

Freize could not bring himself to touch it, but he pulled the cap from his head and laid it down. The little thing took a bold leap and landed in the cap like a fish in a net. Freize shook his head in horror and bafflement. "What am I to do with you?" he whispered.

He heard the breath of a whispered reply: "The canal."

The guardsmen had kicked out the old wooden hatch that closed off the quay and now they saw Ishraq's pale frightened face in the opening.

"There's a girl here!" someone shouted. "Get her!"

One man bent down and tried to slide through the opening feetfirst as Freize made a mighty dive, hands first, getting in before him, blocking the gap with his shoulders. "Ishraq!" he yelled, and thrust the cap toward her.

She caught the cap in her hands. "What?" She recoiled at the little being, curled up inside. "What's this? My God, Freize! What is it?"

The soldiers fell on Freize's legs and dragged him backward from the hatch. "Get it in the canal!" Freize shouted to her. "Get it in the water." Someone trod on his outstretched hands in their haste to get through the hatch to capture Ishraq. "Let it go!" Freize yelled. "Set it free!"

He saw her duck away from the hatch toward the canal, but then someone kicked him in the head and something fell beside him with a loud clatter, and then everything was dark.

Quietly dripping, Ishraq approached the garden gate of the palazzo on the Grand Canal, and tried the latch. It yielded and she stepped into the garden. It was dusk, and the waning spring moon was rising over the shadow of the wall. She was still wet, and her hair was in rat's tails down her back, her costly gown torn from hem to hip and tied out of the way. She stepped warily into the enclosed space and looked up at the house.

Everything seemed quiet. Ishraq tiptoed barefoot to one of the windows and listened. There was silence; she cupped her hand over her eyes and peered in. The room was empty. Carefully, Ishraq went under the shade of the portico to the garden door and pushed it open. There was a slight creak, but in a moment she was in the stone-flagged back hall, and then picking up her damp skirts, she crossed the hall and mounted the stairs, past the main room and up to the floor that she shared with Isolde.

The door to their rooms was locked. Ishraq tapped the rhythm that they had used from childhood

and at once the door opened and Isolde pulled her in.

"I have been waiting and waiting for you. You're freezing! Are you safe? You're soaked! Did you get to them in time?"

Isolde ran to her room and fetched a linen sheet and started to towel Ishraq's hair, while the girl pulled off her wet torn clothes.

"I got to them before the doge's men came, and they got away. Their equipment was broken and Freize is arrested."

"No! We must tell Luca!"

Ishraq took a blanket and wrapped it around her bare shoulders. "Has the guard all gone?"

"They left only one man behind, at the water gate. That's why I stayed locked in, up here, though they have gone. They didn't see you go, so they think you're locked in here with me. Change your clothes and nobody will ever know you were out of the house. There's nothing to connect us with the alchemists. Hurry—we have to tell Luca and Brother Peter about Freize."

Ishraq rubbed her hair dry, pulled on a dress and tied her hair back. "Let's go," she said.

The two young women hurried down the stairs and into the main room. Brother Peter and Luca were at the window, looking down to the darkening canal, as the door behind them opened and they turned around and saw Ishraq.

"Thank God you're safe!" Luca exclaimed. "What a

dive you made! Ishraq, what a risk you took!" He crossed the room and hugged her to him. "You're still wet!" he said.

Brother Peter was shaking his head. "I suppose you went to warn them," he said. "Were you seen?"

"Worse," Ishraq said briefly. "I am sorry, Brother Peter. They saw me, but I got away, and they arrested Freize."

"Freize!"

"We rowed there together. We went in by their water gate. We could hear the doge's men at the front door. The alchemist and Jacinta were trying to get their things, the books and the manuscripts and some herbs and things from their workroom. They got into our boat . . ." Ishraq broke off at the memory of the horror of the young woman with the old, old face and straggling white hair who had rushed past her to get into the boat. "Anyway. They got away in our boat. But the men charged in, and they got Freize. I swam for it."

She stopped again. Somewhere in the water, not far from her as she had dived off the quay, had been the little thing, something like a baby, something like a lizard, something like a frog. She had held the cap toward the water's edge and seen it jump into the water, seen it dive, the soft skin of its back gleaming palely as it went deep down into the canal.

"What happened?" Isolde asked, seeing the expression of blank horror on her friend's face.

Ishraq shook her head. "I don't know what they were

doing there," she said. "I don't know what they had done. I don't know what they had made, in that bell jar of theirs. I don't know what sort of thing it was."

"What sort of thing?" Luca repeated, taking her hand.

She met his honest brown eyes with a deep sense of relief, as if Luca was the only person that she would be able to tell.

"Luca," she whispered. "I want to tell you." She hesitated. "But I am afraid to even speak. It was horrific—and pitiful. I want to tell you. I can't."

Without thinking, he put his arm around her shoulders and walked her away from the other two. When their heads were close together and his arm was tight around her waist, he felt her lean toward him and relax against him, as if he were warm, as if he were safety for her.

"You can tell me," he said. "Whatever it was."

She turned her face to his neck and then raised her mouth to whisper in his ear. She could smell the light warm scent of his hair; he smelled of the real world, of normality, of a young man. She felt desire as if it were the only real thing in a dangerous world filled with mysteries. It was as if the only thing that was real, the only thing that she could trust, was Luca. "I think they had made a homunculus," she breathed.

He froze at the word and turned to face her. "Would that

be what they meant by saying they were making life?"

Her eyes dark with fear, she nodded. "Perhaps. I don't know."

"What was it like?"

"Like a tiny man, like a horrible tiny man. I thought it was a lizard, but it was a person, a tiny, tiny person. It was in the bell jar. I think they had made it in the jar. Jacinta was trying to get it away, but when the bell jar broke, Freize took it up and passed it through the hatch to me."

"Why? Why did Freize save it?"

A ghost of a smile touched her lips. "Because that's what he's like, because he's Freize," she said. "If it called out to him, he would have to answer. It wanted to be in the canal. Freize had put it in his cap. I held the cap to the edge of the canal and it jumped out." She shivered. "I didn't throw it in," she said quickly. "I wasn't trying to drown it. He told me to set it free. It jumped in, and then it dived down, like a fish, and then it was gone." She gave a deep shudder.

"What?" Luca asked.

"Luca, it wasn't like a fish, it was just like a child. I saw its face as it bobbed in the canal. It took a breath and then dived down. I saw its rump and its feet as it went down. Like a child but tiny, as small as a rat, but swimming like a man. Horrible."

He held her closer as she trembled. "And then?"

She raised her head and spoke so that the others could hear her. "I dived into the water and I swam round to the side canal beside the Nacari house. I waited in the water. I kept down low. I saw the doge's guards bring Freize out in manacles. He was walking all right, he was not hurt, but he looked dazed. They put him into their galley, the guards' galley with a wooden prison at the back, and I ducked down below the water to let them go past me into the Grand Canal, then I swam out too. I swam for a long time until a fisherman picked me up and brought me back here."

She turned her face to Luca's shoulder. "It was terrible," she said with a little moan of fear. "It was really terrible, Luca, being in the water and knowing that the little thing was in the water too. I was afraid he would come on the fishing boat with me. I was watching the oars in case he climbed on board. I was afraid he would follow me home."

She gave a shaky sob. "I kept waiting for the touch of his little hand in my hair," she whispered. "I thought he would hold on to me and make me bring him home."

He tightened his grip on her. He held her close, her face against his neck, so that she could not see the horror on his own face, the fear of the unknown, the ancient fear of the creature that is not of earth or air, which is not beast, fish or fowl.

"What if it's a golem?" she breathed.

He composed himself and faced her. "There is no such thing," he said staunchly. "It's not like you to frighten yourself with imaginary fears, Ishraq! It was a lizard, or a plucked bird, or something like that, and Freize must have imagined that it cried out. It won't come after you. It can't have swum. It will have drowned in the canal. It's nothing. You're safe."

He turned from her, as if the matter was closed, and to Brother Peter he said: "We'll have to go and get Freize out. We'll probably have to say who we are to clear our names. We'll have to take our papers from Milord. Will you come with me?"

Brother Peter nodded, appalled at the whole situation. "I'll get my cape. The young ladies should go to their rooms, and stay there." He looked severely at them both. "If anyone comes at all, don't admit them. Don't say anything, and don't show yourselves. The doge's guard will stay at the water gate but don't speak to him." He scowled at Ishraq. "Don't you go diving out of the window," he said crossly. "Just wait here till we get back, and try not to cause more trouble."

The guard at the water gate had been reinforced by a second man, and they had clearly been told to take anyone from the household if they wanted to see the city magistrates.

"Do you think they were waiting for us to confess?" Luca asked Brother Peter quietly as the two guardsmen took their seats in the gondola at prow and stern.

"Yes," Brother Peter replied shortly.

"They were waiting for us to ask to go to the palace?"

"They would perhaps have ordered us to attend later, after midnight. They mostly work at night. They usually arrest people at night."

Luca nodded, hiding his growing fear. "Do you think that they didn't believe Isolde is the Lady of Lucretili?"

"They believed her. But they would still want to question us if they know you have been working with the forgers."

"They can't know that," Luca argued, denying his own doubt.

"They probably do," Brother Peter said dourly.

There was no sound for a moment but the slap of water against the gondola's single oar, and another boatman crying: "Gondola, gondola, gondola!" as he made a blind turn into a small tributary canal.

"They will release Freize to us, won't they?" Luca confirmed.

"It depends on three things," Brother Peter said dryly. "It depends on what he has done. It depends on what they think he has done. It depends on what they think that we have done."

Giuseppe rowed the gondola just a little way up the Grand Canal and then drew up between the forest of black mooring poles in the canal at the imposing white carved front of the doge's palace.

"What's that?" Giuseppe suddenly demanded, startled, looking down at the glassy waters of the canal.

"What?" Brother Peter asked irritably.

He shook his head. "I thought I saw something," he said. "Something like a frog, swimming beside us. Odd."

"Help me out," Brother Peter said crossly. "I have no time for this."

Flanked by the guardsmen, Luca and Brother Peter went up the shallow steps to the quay, where the waves were slapping like a gabble of denunciations, and then the two men and the guards waited before the great palace doors, where a row of burning torches showed their pale faces to the sentries.

"I need to consult the Council of Ten," Luca said with more confidence than he felt. "We are on business for the Pope."

Boyishly, he feared that the man would simply ignore him, but the sentry saluted and pushed open a low door cut inside the great ceremonial gate, and Luca and Brother Peter ducked their heads and went through.

At once they caught their breaths. They were in a massive courtyard, big enough to house an army, as broad and wide as a square of the city: the heart of the doge's palace. On their left was a great wall of red brick pierced by white windows, newly built and all but completed. Ahead of them was a white stone façade, and behind that the towering bulk of the doge's own chapel, the massive church of San Marco. On their right was a wall as high as a white cliff, studded with windows. It was the doge's palace, the heart of government, and all the offices. Most of the windows showed a light—the Republic never slept, business was always pressing, and spying and justice were done best at night. The whole courtyard was ringed by a square colonnade studded with huge white towers. Above the colonnade rose a series of narrow windows, placed one set on top of the other in the three tall stories. It was as if all four walls of the palace were staring down at them with blank accusing eyes.

Two guards came toward them and guided them to the building on their right, and led the way up the stone staircase. Luca found he was growing more and more apprehensive with every step he took. At the top of the stairs, the guard tapped on the huge wooden door, and a smaller door swung open. A man dressed in the black robes of a clerk, seated on a small plain chair at a wooden desk, beckoned them in.

"I am Brother Peter, I serve the Order of Darkness under the command of the Holy Father. We are ordered to inquire into the end of days and all heresies and signs of the end of the world. This is Luca Vero, one of the inquirers." Brother Peter was breathless by the end of his introduction. It made him sound nervous and guilty.

"I know who you are," the clerk said shortly. To the guards before and behind them, he said simply: "Take them to the inquiry room. They're expected."

One guard led the way through the narrow passage, the other followed behind. Luca was certain that they were being observed, that the latticework in the wood paneling in the walls served as a window for another room and that an inquisitor was watching them walk by and judging their anxious faces. Luca tried to smile and stride confidently, but then thought he must appear as if he were playing a part, as if he had something to hide.

The corridor twisted round and round; clearly, they were threading between secret rooms, their footsteps muffled on the uneven wooden floors. As they walked, dozens of half-wild cats scattered before them, as if these tunnels were their home. Then they stopped before a great door, where a silent sentry stood. The man nodded and stood aside, opened the door only to reveal a second closed door behind. He tapped, it swung open and Luca and Brother Peter went into the room where three magistrates, wearing dark robes, were seated behind a great polished table. To the side, four clerks were seated around a smaller table. There was a fire in the fireplace for the comfort of the magistrates, but it did not heat the room, which was miserably cold.

The double doors swung shut, first the inner one with a sharp bang, then the outer door with a dull thud, making the room soundproof, almost airtight. Luca and Brother Peter stood before the table in complete silence.

At last, the magistrate in the central seat looked up at them. "Can I help you, my lords?" he asked politely. "You want to give evidence to us?"

Luca swallowed. "I am Luca Vero, an inquirer for the Order of Darkness, sanctioned by the Holy Father himself to investigate the rise of heresy, the danger of the infidel and the threats to Christendom. This is my clerk and advisor, Brother Peter."

Blandly, the three regarded Luca. Moving as one, they turned their heads to look at Brother Peter and then back again.

"My servant was in the course of making an inquiry for me at the house of an alchemist, Drago Nacari," Luca went on. "He was arrested by the Venetian guard. He has done nothing wrong. I have come to request his release."

The magistrate glanced at his two colleagues. "We were expecting you," he said ominously. "We have been watching you for some days."

Luca and Brother Peter exchanged one aghast look, but said nothing.

"Your papers? To prove your identity?" One of the clerks rose up from the table and held out his hand.

Brother Peter produced the papers from his satchel and the clerk glanced at them. "All in order," he said briefly to the silent men at the table. He offered to pass them over the table, but they waved them away. Clearly, they were too important to bother with letters of authority.

"Authorized by the Holy Father himself," Brother Peter repeated.

The clerk nodded, unimpressed by the status of the Church. Uniquely in all of Christendom, all the administrators of Venice were laymen; they had not been recruited and trained by the Church. They served the Republic before they served Rome. Luca and Brother Peter had the misfortune of being in the only city in Europe where their papers would not command immediate respect and help.

"So you are not, as you claimed, servants in the household of the Lady Isolde of Lucretili," the clerk observed.

"No," Luca said shortly.

The clerk made a small note as if to record Isolde's lie.

"And what was your business with Drago Nacari, the counterfeiter?" the magistrate seated in the center of the table asked quietly.

"We didn't know that he was a counterfeiter at first," Luca said honestly. "As you see from our instructions, we were on a mission to find the source of the gold nobles. The lord of our Order had told us to come here, to pass as merchant traders, to find whether the nobles were good or fake, and if they were fake, where they had come from."

"Did you not think to inform us?" was the question from the magistrate on the left.

"We were going to inform you," Luca replied carefully. "As you see from our orders, we were commanded to inform you as soon as we had evidence to give to you. Indeed, we were on our way to inform you when our own palazzo was raided and we were put under house arrest. Then we agreed that we should come and talk with you at dawn. But when our own servant was arrested by you this night, we had to come and disturb you—even though it was so late."

"Considerate," the third man said shortly. "Did you not think to inform us before you began your inquiry? When you arrived in our city looking for counterfeit gold? When you started questioning our merchants and deceiving our bankers? When you started buying counterfeit gold, trading in it, and profiting from the deception? Withholding information that would have affected the price?"

"Of course not," Brother Peter said smoothly. "We were obeying the orders of the lord of our Order. We did not know what we might find. If we had found nothing, we would have been very wrong to disturb the confidence of your traders."

"They are disturbed now," the magistrate observed.

"Unfortunately, yes."

"And what was your relationship with Drago Nacari the alchemist?" the second magistrate asked. "For we know he was an alchemist as well as a coiner."

"He consulted me about a manuscript that he had," Luca admitted. "He brought it to my house for me to read, and I returned it to him."

"And what did it say?"

"I was not able to translate it. Not at all."

"And what was your impression of his work? When you went to his house?"

"I did not see enough to be sure," Luca said. "He certainly had a lot of equipment, he had a number of pieces of work in progress. He had a forge and a vat of rotting matter. He said that it was his life's work, and he spoke of the philosopher's stone. But I saw nothing of such importance that I would report to my lord or to you."

"Everyone speaks of the philosopher's stone," the Council leader said dismissively.

Another nodded. "It is irrelevant. He had no license to practice here so he was a criminal on that count alone." He paused. "Was he trying to create a living thing?"

Luca stifled a gasp with a little choke.

Brother Peter stepped into the awkward silence. "How could he? Only God can give life."

Luca nodded. "Excuse me. No. I saw nothing but some dead and dried animals and insects."

The clerk took a meticulous note.

"So to the most important accusation: that he was coining," the first magistrate moved on. "Did you see any evidence of his coining?"

Luca nodded. "He, himself, showed me the molds for the coins. He told me that the first coins had come from John, Duke of Bedford, that he had known him long ago in Paris. First he had the duke's true coins, and then here in Venice he made a batch of coins according to the duke's recipe, and planned to pass them off as good, using the duke's seal."

"And yet still, you did not report this to us?" one of the men queried, his voice like ice. "Counterfeiting is a crime that strikes against the very heart of the Republic. Do you know what a run on a currency can do to traders in Venice?"

Luca shook his head, thinking it wiser to stay silent.

"Ruin them. Ruin us. Ruin the greatest city in the world. And you did not think to report it at once? This criminal confessed to you and you stood in his house and saw the evidence and you did not tell us?"

"We were on our way," Luca said. "We were coming to you tomorrow morning. At dawn."

There was a terrible silence. Finally, the man at the center of the three spoke. "Did he tell you how many chests of good coins he had released?"

Luca said: "No."

"Did he tell you how many forged coins? The bleeding coins, the weeping coins? They are going bad all over the city tonight. People will be hammering on the shutters of the bankers' houses, demanding their money back as soon as it is light. Nobody wants bloodstained coins. Nobody wants forgeries. How many are out there?"

Brother Peter cleared his throat. "We were coming to you with the evidence against the forgers at dawn tomorrow. Of course we were going to report all that we knew as soon as we had evidence. We were prevented by the charges laid by Lady Carintha. But we don't know how many coins."

"But you were able to send your servant out of the house though you were under arrest?" one of the men said silkily. "In that gravest moment, you did not send him to us to warn us that the coins were melting and bleeding. In that crucial moment you sent him to them—to the alchemists. Why did you do that?"

Luca opened his mouth to speak, found he had nothing to say and closed it again.

"Your own officer saw the coins bleed," Brother Peter said feebly. "He must have reported to you? He must have sent men to arrest the money changer and the counterfeiter?"

The door to the right of them opened, and Freize stood in the opening. His clothes were torn, and he had a black eye and a bruise on his forehead. Someone pushed him from behind, and he took a stumbling step into the room. Luca exclaimed and would have gone forward, but the clerk put a firm hand on Luca's shoulder and held him back.

"Freize!" Luca exclaimed.

"I'm all right," he said. "Took a bit of a kicking, that's all."

"He resisted arrest," the clerk said to the gentlemen at the table. "He's nothing more than bruised. He has been held in the inquiry room since his arrest. He hasn't been harmed."

"Did you send him, this servant of yours, to warn the

forger? So that they could get away before our men arrested them?" the head of the Council asked Luca directly, and at once all the clerks paused, their pens poised, ready to write the incriminating confession.

"No! Of course not!" Luca said quickly. He tried to smile reassuringly at Freize but found his mouth was too strained.

"What did you send him for, then? Why did he go?"

"I went," Freize said suddenly. "I went of my own accord, to see the pretty lass."

All three heads of the magistrates turned to Freize. "You went to warn her?" one of them asked him.

Luca could see the trap that Freize was walking toward. "No!" he said anxiously. "No, he didn't!"

"I went to see her," Freize said. "My lord didn't send me. I went of my own accord. I didn't know they were going to be arrested, I didn't know they had done anything wrong. I didn't know anything about them at all, really. All I knew was that I had taken a fancy to her. I thought I'd make a visit." Freize scrunched his battered face into an ingratiating grin.

One of the clerks raised his head and remarked quietly to the leader of the magistrates, "He got out of the house after the guards had gone in. He must have known they would be arrested. He took a rowing boat and went straight to the alchemist."

"They got away in the boat that you rowed to them," the second Council man said. "You helped them escape, even if you did not go to warn them."

"Oh for heaven's sake! I asked him to go," Brother Peter said suddenly, very clearly and as if he were wearied beyond bearing. "He went at my request to collect some potion for me. I wanted the medicine before they were arrested. Nobody knew about it but me and the alchemist and then this . . . this dolt. If he had any sense, when he had seen your guards at the door he would have come away, but he pressed on, to get me my . . . er . . . potion. And so got himself arrested, injured and exposed us to this difficulty and me to this terrible embarrassment."

Everyone looked from Brother Peter's scarlet face to Freize, who kept his eyes on the floor and said nothing.

"And now he's lying to try to protect me from my embarrassment," Brother Peter said, torn between fury and shame. "Of course, it only makes it worse. Fool that he is. The alchemist had promised me a—er—a potion. For my—er—affliction."

"I didn't know you were ill?" Luca exclaimed.

"I didn't want anybody to know anything!" Brother Peter exclaimed, a man at the end of his patience. "I must have been mad to trust Freize with such a delicate mission. It was a matter of urgency for me. . . . I should have gone myself . . .

and now . . . Now I wish I had never consulted the alchemist at all."

"What potion?" one of the magistrates asked.

"I would rather not say," Brother Peter replied, his gaze on the floor, his ears burning red.

"This is an inquiry into a counterfeiting forge that has had more impact on the safety of the Republic than anything else in a decade!" The magistrate at the end of the table slammed his hand down and swore. "I think you had better say at once!"

The color drained from Brother Peter's face. "I am ashamed to say," he said in little more than a whisper. "It reflects so badly on me, on my vows, and on my Order."

His misery was completely convincing. The leader of the three leaned forward and said to the clerks: "You will not record this." To Brother Peter he said: "You may speak in confidence. If I decide, nothing will go beyond these walls. But you must tell us everything. What potion did you order from the alchemist?"

Brother Peter turned his face from Freize and Luca.

"Shall I order them from the room?"

"They can stay. I am shamed. This is my punishment. They will think me a fool, an old fool."

"Tell us what you ordered, then."

"A love potion," Brother Peter said, his voice very low.

"A love potion?" the man repeated, astounded.

"Yes."

"A man in your position? In Holy Orders? On a papal mission? Advising an inquirer of the Holy Father?"

"Yes. I had fallen into sin and folly. This is why I am so ashamed. This is why this fool is trying to hide his mission. To save me from this shame."

"Why did you want a love potion?"

Brother Peter's head was bowed so low that his chin was almost on his chest. The bald spot of his tonsure shone in the candlelight. He was completely wretched. "I was very attracted by Lady Carintha," he said quietly. "But I have no . . ." He broke off and struggled to find the words. "I have no . . . manly abilities. I have no . . . vigor."

The three magistrates were leaning forward, the clerks frozen, their pens held above the paper.

"I thought Drago Nacari could make me a potion so that she would be drawn to me, despite herself. And if she were disposed to be kind to me—she is such a high-spirited lady—I would want to be man enough for her." He glanced briefly at the table of gentlemen. "You can ask her if I was not attracted by her, dazzled by her. She knew it. She knows well enough what she can do to a man. My fear was that I would be unable to respond."

Two of the magistrates nodded as if they had experienced

Lady Carintha's high spirits for themselves and sympathized with Brother Peter's fears.

"I have little experience with women," Brother Peter said, his voice a thread, his eyes on the floor. "Almost none. But I imagined she would want a man who could . . . who would . . . I feared that if she were to look kindly on me, I would not be man enough for her."

One of the magistrates cleared his throat. "Understandable," he said shortly.

"I was a fool," Brother Peter admitted. "And a sinful fool. But God spared me the worst of it, for the foolish servant I sent to get the love potion was caught while he was carrying out my sinful errand. And besides, Lady Carintha has turned against all of us. She'll never look at me again."

"But you knew they were coiners?" one man persisted.

Brother Peter dropped to one knee and rested his forehead against the table. "That's the worst of it. That's why I sent Freize then. I knew they were the coiners of the false coins and that once you had found the money changer Israel you would find them. I wanted my love potion before they were arrested. That's why I ordered Freize to go at once, although I knew it was dangerous for him to be found with them. I put him at risk for my own selfish . . . lust."

The gentleman rounded on Freize. "Is that what you were doing there?"

Freize gulped. "Yes, just as my lord says."

"Why didn't you tell us at once?"

"Discreet," Freize said. "Lamentably discreet. Against my own interests sometimes."

The three magistrates put their heads together in a swift exchange of words. "Release him," the leader of the Council said. "No charge."

He rose to his feet. "If we catch Drago Nacari and his accomplice, the young woman, then they will be charged as coiners and counterfeiters and you will have to give evidence against them," he ruled.

"We will," Brother Peter promised.

"In the meantime, we have serious work to do. We are going to have to release reserves of gold to the banks. Everyone is selling gold nobles and everyone wants pure gold instead. The price of nobles is falling to that of *piccoli*. Our citizens and our traders will lose fortunes in the first hour that they open for business. And now the Ottoman Empire is refusing to take any English coins at all—good as well as bad. We are having to make good what those wicked coiners have done. It will cost us a fortune."

"I am very sorry that we did not catch them earlier," Luca said. "It was our intention, it was our mission."

The Council nodded. "Then you have miserably failed in your mission," the leader said icily. "You can tell the lord of your Order that you are incompetent and a danger to yourselves and others. And you"—he turned to Brother Peter—"you failed in your vows. You will no doubt confess and serve a hard penance. You seem to be shamed and you should be ashamed. We are very displeased with all three of you, but there are no legal charges as yet. It seems that you are fools but not criminals. You are incompetent idiots but not wicked."

"Thank you," Luca muttered. Brother Peter was too shamed to speak.

"Go then," the Council leader said, and Luca, Brother Peter and Freize bowed in the contemptuous silence and turned and filed from the room.

Not a word passed between them as they crossed the broad quay from the front door of the ducal palace and got into the rocking gondola. Freize gripped Luca's hand as Luca helped him into the boat, but the two young men said nothing.

Brother Peter drew up the hood of his robe and sat hunched, in the prow of the boat, his back to the other men as they paddled swiftly down the canal, turned in the palazzo water gate and Giuseppe brought the gondola to the quayside.

The guard had already gone from the water gate and there was no soldier on the street door. Luca called up to the girls' level: "Isolde! Ishraq! We're back!" and heard the girls cross the floor above and come down the stairs as they went into the dining room.

The two girls came in and looked at the three silent men, at Freize's bruised face and Brother Peter's dark expression. Isolde closed the door behind them. "What has happened?" she asked fearfully.

Luca shook his head. "I swear that I don't know," he said. He glanced uncertainly at Brother Peter. "Perhaps we should never speak of it," he said carefully.

Brother Peter rounded on him, exploding with rage. "Fool!" he said. "Call yourself an inquirer? And you could not see a lie as wide as that damned canal and twice as deep?"

Isolde recoiled in shock at Brother Peter's rage, but Freize went toward him and bowed, with his hand on his heart. "I thank you," he said. "It was the last thing that I expected you to say. I could do nothing but stare like a dolt."

"Indeed, I was certain that you would play the part of a dolt very well," Brother Peter said nastily.

Isolde took Freize's hand and turned him toward the candlelight to look at his damaged face. "They hurt you?" she said quietly. Gently, she touched his cheek. "Oh Freize! Did they beat you?"

"Not much," Freize said. "But Brother Peter here saved me from hanging."

"Saved you?" Luca asked, still shaken by Brother Peter's abuse.

"Of course," Brother Peter said roundly. "Did you really think that I was in the least attracted to that well-hung limb of Satan? Did you really think that I would send an idiot like Freize to a crook like Drago Nacari for a love potion? Do you think that I am a fool like Freize? Like you? To lose my head for a pretty face? And that one not so pretty anyway?"

Luca shook his head, slowly understanding. "I believed you when you spoke before the Council," he said. "Call me a fool, but I believed every word that you said."

"Then you had better learn the skill to look into men's hearts even when they are lying," Brother Peter said. "For you cannot be an inquirer if you can be fooled by a charade like that."

"You lied to save Freize?" Isolde asked, grasping the main essential. "You pretended that you had sent him to the Nacaris for a love potion?" Her voice quavered on a laugh, and she tried to keep her face straight but failed. "You confessed to lust, Brother Peter? And to needing a love potion?"

Brother Peter would not speak while Ishraq collapsed into giggles. Isolde started to laugh too and Luca gritted his teeth to stop himself from joining them. But Brother Peter and Freize were still grave.

"You laid down your reputation for my safety," Freize said to him. "I thank you. I owe you my life."

Brother Peter nodded.

"You made a great sacrifice for Freize," Isolde said, recovering from her laughter as she understood the importance of what Brother Peter had done. "You made yourself look like a fool for him. That's a great thing for you, Brother Peter. That is a great gift you have given for Freize."

"And you told a lie," Ishraq wondered.

"I was not on oath, they did not ask me in the name of God," Brother Peter specified. "And they were quick to believe that a thin old clerk would dabble in such rubbish for lust of a well-used Venetian matron. I would have hoped that Luca might have thought better of me—but apparently not."

"I am sorry," Luca apologized awkwardly. "I should have guessed at once, but I was overwhelmed . . . and I couldn't think."

Brother Peter sighed as if they were all of them, equally unbearable. "We'll say no more about it," he said stiffly, and left the room.

"He is remarkable," Isolde said as the door closed on him.

"Saints witness it—he was impressive," Luca agreed with her. "He was completely convincing."

"He admires me," Freize said confidentially to Ishraq.

"He finds it hard to admit, being a man who thinks very highly of himself—but he thinks very highly of me. This is the proof of it." He paused. "And I think very well of him," he said with the air of a man giving credit where it was due.

Venice was seized with panic the next day as soon as the banks opened their doors and the traders set up their stalls. Ishraq and Isolde walked to San Marco, with their purse of gold nobles, hoping that they might find someone who would change it into ducats, even into silver, but found all the money changers closed. The church itself was crowded with people on their knees, praying for their fortunes, terrified of poverty, terrified that they would be stuck with the worthless gold nobles. The gold coins were sticky with a red rust like blood in every other purse.

Luca, Freize and Brother Peter went to the Rialto by gondola and found the shops were closed and shuttered and the money changers were absent from their stalls. Nobody wanted anything but true-tested gold, and there was no gold to be had.

The great banking houses on San Giacomo Square had only one shutter open at each entrance and they were changing gold for a limited number of coins, so much for each customer, refusing anything that was stained or wet, desperately afraid that their own reserves would run out.

"I have gold, I have plenty of gold," Luca heard one of the clerks say at the window. "There is no need to fear. My lord has gone to fetch more from his country estate. He will be back tomorrow. The bank is good. You need not change all your nobles now. You can change them tomorrow. There is no need to press, there is no need to panic."

"Tomorrow the value of the English nobles will be as nothing!" the man shouted back at him, and the crowd behind him elbowed each other out of the way and shouted for their turn. "Even worse than now!"

"I will pay tomorrow," the clerk insisted. "You don't have to change them today."

"Now!" the people shouted. "Now! Take the English nobles! You were quick enough to sell them! Now buy them back."

A band of the doge's guards came swiftly in a galley, trumpet blowing, and marched up the steps into the square. The officer unfurled a proclamation.

"Citizens! You are to disperse!" he shouted. "The doge himself promises that there is enough gold. He himself will lend gold to the bankers. Your coins will be exchanged for gold. We will bring the gold from the doge's treasure stores this afternoon. Disperse now, and go back to your homes. This unrest is bad for everyone."

"The rate!" someone yelled at him. "It's no good to me that the banks have gold tomorrow if they won't buy the nobles at today's rate. What's the rate?"

The officer swallowed. "The rate has been set," he said. "The rate has been set."

"At what?" someone shouted.

He showed them the sealed proclamation, holding it high above his head so that it fluttered in the light spring wind. "The doge himself has set the rate that he will pay to all Venetian citizens. He will pay a third of a ducat for every English noble, and so will all the Venetian banks," he said.

The crowd was suddenly silent as if at news of a death. Then there was a long slow groan as if everyone was suddenly sick to the belly. It was a moan as everyone in the crowd realized that the fortune they had made in speculating in the English nobles was gone, had gone overnight. Each English noble was now valued at a third of a ducat, though it had been three ducats only yesterday. The merchants who had bought hundreds of English nobles, trading in good gold, other currencies and even goods, were staring at ruin.

"So they think that between the good nobles and the bad only a ninth of the coins will be found to be real gold?" Luca whispered to Brother Peter.

"They have to buy back the English nobles one way or another, they have to set a rate or nobody will trade at all.

The people will bring down the banks with their demands for gold. This crowd isn't far from riot."

"This is terrible," Luca said.

Brother Peter looked at him. "This is the value of reputation," he said. "You saw Lady Isolde defend her reputation. You saw me devalue my reputation yesterday." He looked at the crowd, which was dwindling as the merchants went into their houses, slamming the doors, and the smaller traders walked to stand beside the canal, stunned with shock, trying to face their own ruin in the sparkling surface of the bright waters. "This is how the market works," he said. "Great gains always mean great losses later and then probably gains again. This is usury. This is why a good man does not play the market. It always brings wealth to a few but poverty to many."

He grabbed Luca's shoulder and turned him to face the deserted square and a man sobbing with his mouth open wide, drooling with grief and horror. "Look and understand. This is not what happens when the market goes wrong: this is what happens when the market works. Sudden profit followed by sudden ruin: this is what is supposed to happen. This is the real world. The days when a noble doubled in price overnight were the chimera."

Luca nodded, then his face suddenly clouded. "The ransom!" he gasped. He turned on his heel and hurried to the Rialto Bridge, where Father Pietro usually set up his stall. The low post that he used as a stool was empty; half the stalls on the Rialto Bridge were closed. It was as if everyone was afraid to spend money in any currency.

"Have you seen Father Pietro today?" Luca asked a woman as she was passing by.

Silently, she shook her head and went on.

"Have you seen Father Pietro?" Luca asked a merchant.

He ducked away from the question as if an answer would be too costly.

"We'll come back later," Brother Peter ruled. "See if he is here later."

"It's the ransom for my father," Luca said, trying to escape the feeling of growing dread. "They wanted to be paid in English nobles. We sent the money in English nobles as they asked."

"When did the messenger leave?" Brother Peter asked.

"Yesterday," Luca said blankly. "Before dusk."

"Then perhaps he has kept ahead of the news and is even now paying the slave owner and your father is safe in his keeping. Certainly, they won't hear that the currency has failed till hours from now. The news has to get from Venice. They might have done the trade already and your father might be safe right now."

"I should send pure gold, in case the nobles bleed." Luca

took a step forward to the bank and then fell back, realizing that he could not even obtain gold—the banks did not have it—and that he had nothing to buy gold but the dishonored English nobles.

His young face was gaunt with shock. "Brother Peter, we put all of Milord's fortune into the nobles. We are ruined too. We have lost all of Milord's money and I cannot buy gold to free my father!"

Brother Peter's face was sternly grave. "We gambled, and we have lost," he said. "We pretended we were wealthy and now we are poor."

"I'll have to wait," Luca said aloud to himself. "I'll have to wait. I can't see what else to do. I swore I would free my father and now . . . I'll have to wait. Perhaps . . . but I'll have to wait. There's nothing else to do."

"Pray," Brother Peter advised him.

They got home to find Freize and the girls sitting before a simple meal of soup and bread. "The market is almost closed," Isolde said. "The stallholders will only accept silver and the price of silver is sky-high."

Ishraq looked ill with shock. "They won't take English nobles, not even if you weigh them against gold in front of them, on the spice scales," she said. "Even if they can see that the nobles are solid gold, they won't trade with them. You can't even buy vegetables with them. They say that nobody knows what they are worth, and now they are saying they are unlucky coins. Nobody can tell a coin that bleeds from one that is good. Nobody wants anything. I sold Isolde's mother's rubies for dross."

Isolde put her hand on Ishraq's shoulder. "Don't blame yourself," she said quietly. "We're no worse off than everyone else in Venice."

"Everyone else who was greedy enough to try to trade in coins," Ishraq said bitterly. "I kept those jewels safe through a flood, through a robbery and through the criminals of the nunnery. And then I robbed you myself."

"Enough," Brother Peter said quietly. "You have done no worse than the great men of business. We'll see what gold you can get for the coins tomorrow, when the doge releases his treasure. You can go out early. Freize can take you to the money changers."

Ishraq nodded, her face still downcast. "We know what we'll get," she said miserably. "One ducat to three nobles. And I sold the rubies when it was almost the other way round."

"We have work to do," Brother Peter said to Luca.

"What?" Luca said. He found he was exhausted, sick with worry about the ransom for his father. He could not even bring himself to remind Ishraq that he shared her failure. Actually, he had been more foolish than her, trading in Milord's fortune for English nobles, trying to buy his father's freedom in forged currency, ruining himself and betraying his father.

"We have to write to Milord," Brother Peter ruled. "We'll have to tell him what has happened here. And I will have to put it into code before you sign it. We should get the report sent today. Better that he hears from us than from someone else in Venice."

"Who reports to him from Venice?" Freize asked, looking up from his bowl of soup.

"I don't know," Brother Peter replied. "But someone will."

Luca sat at the table and drew the ink and pen and paper close. "I hardly know where to begin," he said.

"From the end of the last report. We had told him that we had located the forgers and were going to report them," Brother Peter reminded him. "He is bound to be very displeased that we did not report them."

"We found the counterfeiters, but we let them go." Luca listed their mistakes. "We put all of Milord's fortune into English nobles and they are now worth only a tiny part of their former price. We have lost him a fortune."

"And by letting the counterfeiters go and the money fail we have ruined many good men and destroyed confidence in

Venice," Brother Peter added. "I have never been involved in such a disastrous inquiry before."

"What does he do when he is displeased?" Luca asked nervously.

Brother Peter shrugged. "I don't know. I've never failed so badly. I've never been with an inquirer who failed to report a crime, who associated with the criminals and who disobeyed orders."

There was a terrible silence. "I am sorry," Luca said awkwardly. "I am sorry for failing the Order, and him, and you."

To his surprise, Brother Peter raised his head and gave Luca one of his rare smiles. "You need not apologize to me," he said. "You pursued the truth as you always do— steadily and persistently, with flashes of quite remarkable insight. But the truth is that speculation and profiteering and trade is a rotten business, and it falls in on itself like a rotten apple, eaten out by maggots. Milord knows this as well as you and I. He sent us into a city of vanities and we have seen its ugly side. We have done nothing wrong ourselves, but we have followed his orders in a sinful world. If we had reported the coiners earlier, they still might have got away. It was Ishraq and Freize who helped them escape—not us who belong to the Order. And even if we could have stopped them earlier, we would have been too late—they had already released the bad coins into the market by the time we knew."

"I thank you," Luca said awkwardly. "You are generous to overlook my mistakes. You wanted to report the forgers earlier, and you were right. We should have done that. And I thank you for saving Freize."

Brother Peter turned his head away. "We won't talk of that," he said. "We won't put that in the report."

The next day Isolde was waiting for Luca in the dining room when he came down to breakfast. "I couldn't sleep for thinking about your father," she said. "I have been praying that they ransomed him before they had the news about the nobles."

Luca's handsome young face was drawn. "I couldn't sleep either," he said. "And we will have to wait until Sext to see Father Pietro, if he comes today. He may not come at all."

"Let's go to church and pray," she said. "And then we could walk to the Rialto. May I come with you?"

Luca shrugged. "Since nobody cares who we are anymore, I don't see why you shouldn't come with me."

"I want to come with you," she said.

"We'll all go," he said, his mind on his father.

Tentatively, she reached out to him, but he had already turned away to call up the stairs for Freize. His back was turned to her. He did not even feel her touch when she gently kissed the fingers of her hand and pressed the kiss to the cuff of his sleeve.

The moment that the five of them stepped out of the house it was apparent that some fresh disaster had hit the city. People were gathered on street corners, their faces grave. Everyone was whispering as if there had been a death in the city. The gondoliers were not singing, the boats were busy on the canal, but there were no cries of people selling their goods. Everyone had laid aside their bright costumes, there was no spirit of carnival in the ruined city: Lent had come early to Venice this spring, early and cold.

"What now?" Luca demanded anxiously.

All five of them went quickly to Piazza San Marco and found that many of the merchants were assembled in the square already, and many of the foreign traders, their costumes bright, their slaves around them, were waiting on the quayside before the doge's palace. The balcony before the doge's window was draped with flags and standards. "Looks like he is going to speak to the people," Brother Peter said. "We'd better wait and hear what he is going to say."

Freize and Luca put the two young women between them, anxious about the push and sway of the growing crowd. "What d'you think is happening?" Isolde said quietly to Luca.

He shook his head.

"Will it be about the gold nobles?"

"Surely not. Since the doge has already set the price, what more is there to say?"

There was the bright shout of a trumpet fanfare, and the doge stepped out from the windows onto the balcony and raised his hand to acknowledge the crowd. Slowly, he took off his distinctive hat and bowed.

"He is a citizen of Venice, just as they all are," Brother Peter explained. "It's a most extraordinary system. He's not a king or a lord. He is one of the citizens, they choose him for the post. So he shows that he is in their service. He goes bareheaded to them."

In reply, the crowd took off their hats. Isolde and Ishraq made a little curtsy and stood still.

"I am sorry that I have bad news for us all," the doge said, his voice so loud and steady that even the men at the farthest edge of the crowd could hear him.

"As you know, the gold nobles that were being made in

this city, without our knowledge or consent, have failed us. The bleeding nobles can be exchanged for three gold nobles to a ducat. At no more than thirty nobles per man today."

There was a little whisper that ran through the crowd, but most people had heard the proclamation yesterday. This was old bad news.

"I have today had a public complaint from the ambassador of the Ottoman Empire," the doge went on. At once a complete silence fell on the square. Someone at the back moaned and was still. The Ottoman Empire was the greatest power in the world. The uneasy peace between the Ottoman Empire and Venice was essential if the city were to survive. The Ottomans commanded the Mediterranean Sea and the Black Sea. Their armies had occupied the lands to the east of Venice. If the Ottoman ambassador was unhappy then the city was on the brink of terrible danger.

"It seems that the Christian countries that pay tribute to the Ottoman Empire have this year all paid their debt in gold nobles," the doge said. "Alas . . ." He paused. "Alas," he said again. There was a low groan from the crowd.

"Alas for us. The Ottomans believe that we have knowingly given them worthless dross. So they say that we have failed to pay them the proper tribute as agreed. They say that we agreed to pay in gold nobles, but we have sent them rust."

There was a low gasp from every man in the crowd.

Failure to pay tribute to the Ottomans would call down an immediate and powerful punishment on all the tribute states. It could cause a renewed war and thousands would die before the unstoppable Ottoman armies.

"Therefore the Council and I have decided that we will redeem the failed English nobles from the Ottomans also, and that we will pay them the same as we pay to you: a third of a ducat for each noble. They will only get a small portion of tribute this year, and we hope that they will understand that this is all we can do."

There was a moan like a breeze blowing through Piazza San Marco. Someone started crying in fear, and a man walked blankly away from the rear of the crowd, knowing that his homeland would be seized, his family taken into slavery, and his life destroyed, and that there was nothing he could do to prevent it.

"We are therefore raising a tax on every house in Venice, to help us meet these great debts," the doge said steadily. "I, and every member of the Council, will pay, and will loan the city more gold from our own fortunes. I urge you all to pay in full, pay in gold, for the sake of our city and great republic. If you have to use your wife's jewelry then do so, if you have to take the gold leaf from your furniture then do so, if you have to cut off the handles from your gold gates then do so. I shall take my wife's jewelry, my mother's jewelry. I shall take the gold leaf from my throne. I shall take the gold handles from my doors and sell the masterpieces from my walls. We must all surrender our most beloved treasures. This is our time of need; you must answer. God bless you and God save Venice."

"Amen," the crowd said with one low voice, and the doge turned on his heel and went bareheaded, back inside the palace.

Isolde turned to Luca and saw that he was white with shock.

"Come," Brother Peter said shortly, and led the way back to the palazzo.

"I must go to the Rialto and see Father Pietro . . ." Luca protested.

"No! We have to do something first."

"Brother Peter?"

"Come!"

"What?" Ishraq trotted beside him, trying to keep up with his long strides. "What's so important?"

"Milord gave me some orders that I was to open the moment that I learned that the territories were going to default on their tribute."

"He knew this was going to happen?" Ishraq suddenly stopped. "Milord knew that the territories would use bad coin?"

"He can't have known that." Brother Peter strode on,

unhesitating. "How could anyone know that? But he was prepared for it. He was prepared for anything on this mission. In the event of there being a default he gave me some orders to open. We have to open them now."

Isolde and Luca were half running to keep up with Brother Peter's great strides. Luca caught at Isolde's hand, and kept pace with him. Freize came swiftly behind them.

"How does he know such things?" Freize demanded of himself. "Those sealed orders? How does he write them ahead of time. Just to torment me?"

Brother Peter pushed through the crowd and paced ahead of them to get to the side entrance and enter the palazzo.

He went without hesitating, upstairs to his bedroom and brought the sealed orders out to the rest of them in the dining room. Luca pulled out chairs for Isolde and Ishraq and then seated himself at the head of the table. Freize dropped onto a stool near to the door. "The sealed orders," he said irritably. "Always. Out they come. Always bad news."

Brother Peter took no notice of anyone. He broke the seal and spread the paper on the table. He frowned and pushed it over to Luca. "You read," he said. "You can translate the code much quicker than I."

Luca took the paper, scowled for a moment, and then read aloud.

*"In the event of the territories failing to pay tribute to the
Ottoman overlords, you are to take this note to the Hungarian
ambassador, show him the seal and authorize them to buy the
false coins with the gold that they have in store. You are to take
this note to the Comarino family and authorize them to use their
private gold store to buy the false coins. You yourself are to use
whatever coins and whatever gold you have to buy the English
nobles at the lowest price you can pay for them. You will not sell
any English gold nobles that you have. If the ship comes in after
you have read these orders, you will use all the cargo to buy the
devalued English gold nobles at the lowest price possible."*

Luca stopped reading and put down the paper. "Has he
gone mad?"

"But everyone else is selling gold nobles, for far less than
their value," Isolde said. "Everyone is selling, not buying."

"They have no value," Ishraq pointed out.

"What do we do?" Luca asked.

"As he orders," Brother Peter said wearily. He rose up
from the table and held out his hand for the letter for the
Hungarian ambassador and for the Comarino bank. "Shall I

take these? And you buy the nobles with our remaining gold? And go to a bank and promise them that we will take their nobles in exchange for the cargo, when the ship comes in?"

"But why?" Ishraq asked. "Why would Milord want us to spend good money on bad?"

Brother Peter's face was as dark as when he had confessed his pretended shame. "I don't know," he said. "I don't need to know. I am to obey Milord's commands and do the work of God though it leads me into the deepest sin. I have to trust him. I have to trust his judgment. I have to obey his orders." He glanced up. "Will you come with me, Freize?"

"Of course," Freize said with his quick sympathy. He glanced at Luca. "If I may?"

"Go," Luca said absently. "I'll go through the treasure chest and take what gold we have left to the money changers. There's not much, but they'll be glad to take it in return for the worthless nobles, I don't doubt."

"But why?" Ishraq demanded again. "Why would Milord want you to buy the bleeding nobles? When everyone knows they are no good?"

"I don't ask why," Brother Peter answered her.

"We'll help," Isolde spoke for her and Ishraq.

"But I do! I ask why!" Ishraq exclaimed.

"I'll send the gondola back for you," Brother Peter said

heavily, and they heard him and Freize go down the stairs together to the water gate and call for Giuseppe.

Luca went into his bedroom and drew a great wooden chest out from beneath his bed. The girls followed him and watched as he opened the lid.

"You have a small fortune here," Ishraq whispered as she saw the gold nobles in the little purses.

"I *had* a small fortune," he corrected her. "Now it is almost worthless."

He moved the purses of the gold nobles and found beneath them a single gold bar and three gold rings.

"I'll buy your bleeding nobles from you," Luca offered, "if you will take the low price that Venice has set. At least I can take them off your hands."

"No," Ishraq said, forestalling Isolde, who was eager to accept. She turned to her friend. "It was my mistake to try to make money on this market, but if we sell the nobles at this rate then we have lost your mother's rubies forever. Let's hold on to them, bad as they are, and see what happens. Luca's lord must be planning something. He must have some reason to want to buy nobles."

"Nothing can happen!" Isolde said irritably. "You traded my mother's jewels for fools' gold. We have to pay the price."

"But Milord is doing something else," Ishraq said cautiously. "He's buying false coins."

"But you don't know what for? You don't know why?"

"I don't," Ishraq said. "But I know he's no fool. I'll keep our English nobles until he sells his."

"When we could have gold instead?" Isolde said regretfully, gesturing to Luca's handful of gold rings.

"If you won't take this then I have to go to the Rialto and buy dross," Luca said. "I wish we could write to Milord to make sure it is what he wants. I wish we knew what he plans. For this is madness: throwing good money after bad."

When the gondola came back for Luca and the two young women, they were ready to go to the Rialto, with their gold and silver coins in their purses and pockets, and the rings on their fingers. The bridge was busy again—the news that the exchange rate for the gold nobles had been fixed by the doge himself had made people confident enough to open their shops. Only the money changers were still missing, and where Israel had sat there was an obscene scrawl on his board and, in spiky thick letters, the word:

Arrestare

Luca went at once to the mooring post at the foot of the bridge and started forward when he saw the priest, bending over his little writing table. "Father Pietro!"

Slowly, the old priest turned to look at the young man and,

at the sorrow in his lined face, Luca did not need to ask more.

"The nobles failed," the priest said quietly. "Bayeed is not in Trieste; he came to Venice yesterday for repairs to his ship and moored near to the Arsenale. My messenger found him there. So he knew all about the failure of the coins as soon as we did. The nobles bled when he tipped them out of the purse, and then he heard the doge announce that the whole Ottoman Empire believes that it has been cheated. He thinks that Venice tried to cheat his empire and that you tried to cheat him. He called me a cheat also. I am sorry, my son."

"He is here?" Luca could hardly believe that his father was in the same city, just one mile away, in the dockyard where the galleys were built. "Then I can go to him. I have some gold, I can promise more . . . I can explain!"

Father Pietro nodded. "We will try again, in a month or so. When Bayeed's anger has abated."

"But he cannot be angry with us. . . . We have all been cheated!"

Father Pietro shook his head, tears filling his eyes, turning his head away from Luca.

"What is it?" asked Ishraq quietly, coming up behind Luca and sensing the older man's distress. "What is it, Father?"

Blindly, he reached out to her, and she took his hand on her shoulder as if to support him. "Wait a moment," she said to Luca, who was breathlessly impatient. "Wait, let the Father speak."

The old man raised his head. "Forgive me. This has been a blow. This has been a terrible blow. Last year the Ottoman Empire took tribute and traded in pure gold and the best of coins. As they always do. Sometimes they take goods, of course, always they take young boys to serve in their armies. This is how it is. This is how the Christian lands suffer for their defeat by the infidel. This is how the Christian rulers pay for peace: they have to pay tribute in gold and in children. This is our suffering, this is our Stations of the Cross." He paused.

"This year, before tribute time, they let it be known that they would take gold or the English nobles. Then, as the English nobles went up in value, they said they would only take the coins. Everyone works to pay the tribute, the whole country has to pay the tax to give to the Ottoman overlords. They took goods also, and the young men, but this year they only wanted the gold coins. They loved the gold coins, the English nobles."

"And what happened?" Luca asked, unable to contain himself any longer. "When did they find out?"

"The coins bled," the old man said simply. "Bled like the wounds of Our Lord. Bled into the hands of the murderous infidel. And they swore that they had been cheated. They think they have been cheated by us. They think we gave them false coins on purpose, that we thought the coins would not break down and bleed until they had taken the tribute home and spread them throughout their country, destroying trust in every village market throughout their infidel empire. And so they are angry—beyond anger—and they are sending back the bleeding coins and demanding gold. Every country that has to pay tribute has to find the money all over again, and this time, send gold, only solid gold. It is a terrible burden. It is a terrible price to pay."

He bowed his head and wiped his eyes on the sleeve of his gown. "We cannot pay it," he said simply. "And so they will take the children. Our children. When we cannot pay the money they will take many, many children into slavery to serve as their soldiers. We will lose our children from their nurseries and their souls from salvation. God help us," he whispered. "God help us all. People will starve to death to get this tax together. Half of Greece will be ruined, and hundreds, thousands, of innocent children will be taken from their mothers and into slavery. All the Christian lands conquered by the infidel will be crucified all over again."

"And my father?" Luca breathed.

Father Pietro rubbed his face with his hands. "He will remain enslaved," he said shortly. "Along with the half dozen other men who expected their freedom today or tomorrow. Yours was not the only ransom we paid. Bayeed has sent back the false coins and will set sail tonight cursing us for cheats. He accuses us of double dealing, my reputation as an agent for enslaved men is destroyed. My years of service are made worthless. My name is shamed."

He took a breath, trying to steady himself "We will try again, my son, we will try again. We will find our courage, and I will rebuild my reputation and we will try again. But your father will not be free this month, nor the next."

"But I sent the money." Luca could hardly speak. "I sent the money in good faith."

"And Bayeed would have released your father in good faith. But you sent counterfeit coins, my son. You sent fools' gold, and Bayeed is no fool."

Luca turned away like a man stunned as Brother Peter and Freize came up to the little group. "Give me the purse," Brother Peter said shortly. "There is a bank here that will give me counterfeit coins for Milord's gold or silver. They will even take coppers—whatever we have."

Wordlessly, Luca held out the purse.

"You are buying the counterfeit coins?" the priest asked in utter amazement. "The bleeding nobles?"

Brother Peter hushed him, and nodded. "I should not have spoken aloud. I beg you not to repeat it."

"But why, my son?" Father Pietro said quietly, putting a hand on Brother Peter's arm as he took the purse from Luca and the girls pulled the rings off their fingers. "Why would you buy false coins?"

"Because I am ordered to do so," Brother Peter said shortly. "God knows, I take no pleasure in it and it makes no sense to me."

Father Pietro turned to Luca, but the young man was silent and stood as if he were dreaming. Ishraq and Isolde stood on either side of him, and when he did not move, took his arms and guided him, like a fever patient, back to the gondola. They helped him down the steps and waited with him in the boat until Brother Peter and Freize joined them.

"They will keep the coins at the bank for me until we are ready to leave this accursed city," Brother Peter said. "We will have sacks and sacks of dross to carry." He turned to Freize. "You'll have to buy us another donkey to carry nothing but rust."

Dully, Luca shook his head. Isolde and Ishraq exchanged a worried glance behind his back. Giuseppe guided the gondola into the center of the canal. "Home?" he asked monosyllabically.

Nobody replied until Freize said: "Home," and they all thought how cheerless the word seemed today.

"My father will never come home," Luca said quietly.

"We'll try again," Isolde assured him. "We know where he is now, and we know how to get a message to Bayeed. We'll try again. And we know where your mother may be. We can try again, Luca. We can hope. We can save money and make them an offer. We can try again."

He sighed wearily, as if he were tired of hoping, and then he rested his chin in his hands and stared across the water as if he wished he were somewhere else and not in the most beautiful city in Christendom.

They had a quiet cheerless dinner. Brother Peter said nothing but a few words for grace over the dishes, Luca was completely silent, Freize tried a few remarks and then gave up and concentrated on eating. Isolde and Ishraq watched Luca, ate a little, and said a few words to one another. After dinner, Brother Peter rose up, gave thanks, said a quiet goodnight to them and went into his room and closed the door.

"I will go to him," Luca said suddenly. "Bayeed the slaver. I will go and see him." Suddenly decisive, he rose up from the table. "They could sail at any moment. I'll go now."

"What for?" Ishraq asked. "We have nothing to buy your father's freedom with."

"I know he won't trade," Luca said. "But I want to try to

see my father. Just to see him. To tell him that I tried and I
will try again."

"Can I come with you?" Isolde asked quietly.

"No," Luca said shortly. "Stay here. I have to go at once.
I can't think. . . ." He broke off and bent his head and kissed
her hand. "Forgive me. I can't think of you now. I have to go
to my father and tell him I will find him again, wherever that
monster takes him, and I will free him. If not now, then soon,
as soon as I can."

Freize cleared his throat. "Better take Ishraq," he said.
"For the language." He turned to her. "Can you wear your
Arabic clothing?" he asked.

She nodded and ran to change out of her gown.

"And money," Freize said. "To bribe the guard, there's
bound to be a guard."

Luca rounded on him. "I have no money!" he shouted.
"Thanks to your pretty girlfriend and her father, I have no
money to buy my father's freedom!"

"I'll give you something," Isolde interrupted. "Don't
blame Freize. It's not his fault. I've got something. A little
gold ring."

"I can't take your mother's jewelry."

"You can," she said. "Please, Luca. I want to help."

She ran from the room to fetch it and came back with
two thin rings in her hand.

"I'll get Giuseppe," Freize said, and went downstairs, leaving Luca alone with Isolde. She took his hand and pressed the rings into his palm. "It's worth it," she said. "For you to see your father, to bring him some hope."

"Thank you," he said awkwardly. "I am grateful. I really am."

"Please let me come with you," she whispered.

He shook his head, and she thought he had not really heard her, he did not even see her stretch out her hand to him as he went from the room, and then she heard him run swiftly down the stairs to the waiting gondola.

Giuseppe, standing tall in the stern of the gondola, worked the single oar, rowing the narrow black boat down the Grand Canal in silence broken only by the splash of the waves. The light from the lantern in the prow bobbed and danced, reflecting in the dark water, the waning moon traced a silvery path before them. Ishraq sat with her back to the gondolier. The two young men sat facing her, Luca constantly turning to look toward their destination over the glossy darkness of the moving tide.

Even at night, even on the water, even during carnival they could see that the city had been hit by loss. There were far fewer people in costume, there were far fewer assignations. One or two determined lovers were being slowly rowed around, the door of the cabin tightly shut, but Venice was in mourning for money, quietly at home, turning over bleeding gold nobles, trying to settle up the accounts.

Luca was taut with nerves, staring ahead into the darkness as if he would see the towers of the Arsenale looming up before them. They went past the square of San Marco, where the lights burning in the high windows of the doge's palace showed that surveillance was unsleeping. Freize nudged Luca.

"They held me in a room like a wooden box," he said. "And from the little window of the box I could see a rope, two ropes, hanging from the high ceiling, and a set of stairs to climb up to them."

"Do they hang men indoors?" Luca asked without interest.

"Not by the neck. They hang them by their wrists till they give information," Freize said. "I was glad to be most ignorant. Nobody would waste their time hanging me, if they wanted information. You would have to hang me by my heels to shake a thought out of my head." He had hoped to make Luca smile, but the young man only nodded briefly and carried on staring into the darkness.

There was a cold wind coming across the water, and it blew raveled strips of dark cloud across the stars. There was a waning moon, which helped the gondolier to see the bank. It was a long way. Ishraq wrapped her cloak tightly around her and pulled her veil over her mouth for warmth as well as modesty.

"Here," Giuseppe said finally. "Here is where the galleys are moored overnight when they wait for repair."

Luca stood up and the gondola rocked perilously.

"Sit down," Giuseppe said. "What is the name of the captain?"

Ishraq turned to tell him: "Bayeed."

"From Istanbul?"

"Yes."

Giuseppe pointed to a long low building. "The galley crews sleep in there," he said. "The master goes into town. He will come at dawn, perhaps."

"In there?" Luca looked with horror at the building, the barred windows, the bolted doors.

"Sentry on the door," Freize remarked quietly. "Sword in his belt, probably a handgun too. What d'you want to do?"

"I just want to see him," Luca said passionately. "I can't be so near him and not see him!"

"Why don't we try bribing the sentry?" Ishraq suggested. "Perhaps Signor Vero could come to the window?"

"I'll go," Freize said.

"I'll go," Ishraq overruled them. "He won't draw his sword on a woman. You can watch out for me."

Luca fumbled in his pocket and found Isolde's two rings. "Here."

Ishraq took them, recognized them at once. "She gave you her mother's rings?"

"Yes, yes." Distracted, Luca dismissed the importance of the gift. "Go to him, Ishraq. See what you can do."

Giuseppe brought the gondola to the quayside. Ishraq went up the steps and walked toward the sentry, careful to keep in the middle of the quay so that he could see her slow progress toward him, spreading her hands so that he could see she was carrying no weapon.

"*Masaa Elkheir,*" she called from a distance, speaking Arabic.

He put his hand to his sword. "Keep back," he said. "You're a long way from home, girl."

"You too, warrior," she said deferentially. "But I would have words with you. My master wants to speak with one of the galley slaves. He will pay you, if you allow such a thing, for your kindness. He is a *faranj*, a foreigner and a Christian, and it is his father who is enslaved. He longs to see the face of his father. It would be a kindness to let them speak together through the window. It would be a good deed. And you would be well rewarded."

"How well rewarded?" the man asked. "And I want none of the English nobles. I know they are as precious as sand. Don't try to cheat me."

In answer she held up a golden ring. "This to let him come to the window," she said. "The same again as we sail away safely."

"He must come alone," the man stipulated.

"Whatever you say," Ishraq said obediently.

"You give me the ring and go back to your gondola and send him. The gondolier and everyone else are to stay on board. He can have a few minutes, no more."

"I agree," Ishraq said. She made a gesture to show that she would throw the ring, and he snapped his fingers to show that he was ready. Carefully, she threw it into his catch, and then went back to the gondola.

"You have a few moments, and he has to have the other ring at the end of your talk," she said. "But you can go to the window. You can talk for only a few minutes."

Luca leaped out of the gondola and was up the steps in a moment. He gave a nod to the sentry and went quickly to the window. It was set high in the wall, but there was a barrel nearby. Luca rolled it under the grille and jumped up on it. Dimly, he could see a dark room, filled with sleeping men, and he could smell the stench of exhaustion and illness.

"Guilliam Vero!" he said in a hoarse whisper. "Guilliam Vero, are you in there?"

"Who wants him?" came a muffled reply, and Luca recognized, with a gasp, the accent of his home village, his father's beloved voice.

"Father, it's me!" he cried. "Father! It is me, your son, Luca."

There was a silence and then a scuffling noise, and the sound of a man cursing as Guilliam made his way, stumbling over the sleeping men, to the window. Luca, looking in and downward, could see the pale face of his father looking up from the sunken floor below.

"It's you," Luca said breathlessly. "Father!" He tightened his grip on the bars over the window as he felt his knees weaken beneath him at the sight of his father. "Father! It's me! Luca! Your son!"

The old man, his skin scorched into leather by the burning sun on the slave galley's deck, his face scored with deep lines of pain, peered up at the window where Luca peered in.

"I was trying to ransom you," Luca said breathlessly. "Bayeed refused the coins. But I will get pure gold. I will buy your freedom. I will come for you."

"Do you know where your mother is?" His voice was husky. He rarely spoke these days. When they slaved over the oars, obedient to the beat of the pace-drum, they never spoke. In the evening when they were released to eat, there was nothing to say. After the first year he had ceased to weep, after the second year he had stopped praying.

"I am looking for her," Luca promised. "I swear I will find her and ransom her too."

There was a silence. Incredulously, Luca realized that he was within speaking distance of his long-lost father and he had so much to say that he could not find words.

"Are you in pain?" he asked.

"Always," came the grim reply.

"I have missed you and my mother," Luca said quietly.

The man choked on his sore throat and spat. "You must think of me as dead to you," was all he said. "I believe I am dead and gone to hell."

"I won't think of you as dead," Luca exclaimed passionately. "I will ransom you and return you to our farm. You will live again, as you used to live. We will be happy."

"I can't think of it," his father flatly refused. "I would go mad if I thought of it. Go, son, leave me in hell. I cannot dream of freedom."

"But I—"

"No," came the stern reply.

"Father!"

"Don't call me Father," he said chillingly. "You have no Father. I am dead to you and you to me. I cannot think of your world and your hopes and your plans. I can only think about every day and every night, and then the next one. The only hope that I have is that I will die tonight if possible, and this will end."

He turned to go back into the darkness of the prison, Luca saw the scars from the whip on his back. "Father! Don't go! Of course I will call you Father, of course I will ransom you. You can hope! I will never leave you. I will never stop looking for you. I am your son!"

"You're a changeling." Guilliam Vero rounded on Luca. "No son of mine. You said you would ransom me, but you have not done so. You say you will come again, but I cannot bear to hope. Do you understand that, stranger? I cannot bear to hope. I don't want to think of my farm and my son and my wife. I will go mad if I think of such things and live like this—in hell. I have no son. You are a stranger. You are a changeling. You have no reason to ransom me. Go away and forget all about me. I am a dead stranger to you, and you are a changeling boy to me."

Luca shook with emotion. "Father?" he whispered. "Don't speak so to me . . . you know I am . . ."

Guilliam Vero stepped away from the light of the grille, and all Luca could see was darkness.

"Enough!" the sentry said flatly. He gestured to Luca to get down from the barrel and go away. When Luca hesitated he put his right hand on the hilt of his long curved scimitar, and felt for the handgun strapped to his belt with the other.

Ishraq stepped off the gondola and, holding the ring high above her head, came slowly across the quay. "Come, Luca!" she said gently.

He stumbled down from the barrel and grabbed hold of it to support himself as his knees buckled beneath him.

"Come on," Ishraq beckoned to him. She saw his face was contorted with shock. "Luca!" she said urgently. "Pick yourself up, get back to the gondola. We have to leave."

"He denied me!" he gasped. He levered himself to his feet, using the barrel, but she saw he could not walk.

"Be a man!" she said harshly. "You are putting Freize and me in danger here. Now we must go. Find your feet! Walk!"

The sentry stepped closer and drew the wicked blade from the scabbard, and it shone in the moonlight. Ishraq knew that he could behead Luca with one blow, and would think nothing of it.

"Get up, fool!" she said, and the anger in her voice cut through Luca's grief. "Get up and be a man."

Slowly, Luca straightened up and hobbled, awkwardly, toward her. As soon as he was within reach she grabbed his arm and put it over her shoulders so that she could take his weight. "Now walk," she spat. "Or I will stab you myself."

"We thank you," Ishraq called toward the sentry, her voice sweet and untroubled. She sent the gold ring spinning through the air to him. She put her arm around Luca's waist and helped him, as if he were mortally wounded, walk slowly and painfully to the gondola, step heavily on board and sit in silence as Giuseppe cast off, spun the gondola round and headed back toward the palazzo.

Isolde was waiting up for them, but Luca went past her without a word, into his bedroom and closed the door. She looked to Ishraq for an explanation.

"I don't know it all," Ishraq said quietly, scowling with worry. "We couldn't hear what his father said, but Luca went white as if he was sick and his legs went from under him. We only just got him back to the gondola, and since then he has said nothing to either of us."

"Did his father blame Luca for the ransom failing?"

Ishraq shook her head. "Luca said nothing, I don't know. He must have said something terrible; it just felled him."

"Did you comfort him?" Isolde asked. "Couldn't you talk to him?"

Ishraq gave her a crooked little smile. "I was not tender to him," she said. "I was hard on him."

"I'm for my bed," Freize said. "I was glad to get away

from that quayside." He nodded at Ishraq. "You did well to get him walking. Perhaps he'll talk to us in the morning." He yawned and turned to the door.

"You must be worried for him," Isolde said, putting her hand on his arm.

Freize looked down at her. "I am worried for us all," he said. "It feels as if we are all bleeding in this city, not just the false nobles. Trying to make money in speculation and not in honest work has cost us all, very dear. I don't think we even know how much."

At dawn there was a sudden hammering on one of the bedroom doors. "Get up!" they could all hear Luca shouting. "Get up!"

Ishraq and Isolde lighted their candles from the dying embers of the fire in their room and pattered down the stairs, pulling shawls around their nightgowns. Freize was already on the shadowy stairs, his club in his hand, ready for an attack. Luca was hammering on Brother Peter's bedroom door.

"Let me see that letter! Show me that letter!"

Brother Peter unlocked the door and came out, long-legged as a stork in his nightgown. He gave one reproachful look at the young women, turned his gaze from their bare feet and said: "What is it? What is this uproar? What's happened now?"

"The orders! The orders! The sealed orders that you opened yesterday! Let me see them."

"You read them yourself!" Brother Peter protested. "Why do you need to see them again?"

"Because I have to understand," Luca said passionately. "Always! You know what I'm like. I have to understand. And I don't understand this. I was so distressed at the loss of my father that I couldn't think. I lay down to sleep and in the darkness all I could see before my eyes was the letter from Milord: the orders. Show them to me!"

Ishraq's brown eyes were shining. "I ask why!" she repeated to herself.

Brother Peter sighed and went back into his room. He came out pulling on his robe over his nightshirt, with the letter in his hand. He gave it to Luca and sat down at the dining table with the air of a man tried beyond endurance. The others pulled out their chairs and took their places around the table in silence, while Luca read it and reread it. Only Ishraq looked delighted.

"What are we to do when we have bought up the false nobles with all the gold that Milord provided?" Luca asked, hardly glancing up from the page.

"We are to store it at the bank and open the orders with our next destination," Brother Peter said.

"We are not to test the nobles? To separate the bad from the good?"

Brother Peter shook his head.

"So Milord does not care if there are good nobles among the bad," Luca muttered to himself. "Why would that be? Can he know already?" To Brother Peter he said: "And he told you to open the instructions to buy the counterfeit coins as soon as you learned that the Ottomans had accused the occupied countries of trying to cheat?"

"As I did," Brother Peter said patiently. "As I told you."

There was a silence. "What are you thinking, Luca?" Ishraq said quietly.

Luca looked across the table at her with a hard intensity. "What are *you* thinking?" he countered. "For you have been suspicious of Milord from the moment that you met him. And yet you did not sell your nobles once you knew he was buying. You refused to sell your bleeding nobles to me for gold. Isolde wanted to—but you refused."

"I don't trust him," she confessed. "I think he did you no favor with the ransoming of your father. First, he didn't tell you about Father Pietro at all—it was Radu Bey, an Ottoman commander and your lord's especial enemy, who did that.

351

Then if your lord had any reason to believe that the coins would fail, he could have told you, to make sure that you paid the ransom in pure gold, or paid early. Then the coins would have failed, but you would still have got your father back."

"Yes," Luca conceded. His mouth turned in a bitter twist for a young man. "This I know."

"Your lord allowed the failure of the ransom," Ishraq accused. "He let you try when he knew that the bad coins would be discovered."

"Milord's doings should not be questioned!" Brother Peter said hotly. "His calling is to command us, not to answer to us."

"Yes, but I question everything," Luca explained. "Like Ishraq. And what she says is true: he did not think of me, nor of my father, when he planned that we should come here. We have suffered, all of us, and so have many others: the alchemists, Israel the money changer, the people who have been left with worthless coins, the territories who will be punished for failing to pay a tribute, the city itself. There are many who will curse the day that Milord ordered us to trace forged gold nobles. All we did was expose the forgeries and break the market."

"Surely, all that he planned here was to find the counterfeiters," Brother Peter reasoned. "We were told to find them and report them to the authorities. We were told to stop them from making false coins. We were here to inquire and then enforce the law. There was nothing wrong in that. There was much good. Our failure was that we did not find them and stop them quickly enough."

In answer, Luca silently raised the letter that commanded them to buy the false coins.

"No, I don't know why he wanted us to buy," Brother Peter admitted.

"But I have an idea," Luca said slowly. "What if Milord knew all along that there were counterfeit nobles being made by Drago Nacari and Jacinta? What if he knew from the very beginning that they had great chests of gold nobles from the Duke of Bedford, which they were putting onto the market, and that they also had a recipe to make more? What if he sent us here too late on purpose?"

Ishraq nodded. "But he would have known that sooner or later you would find them. He knew that you would not stop until you found them. So he must have wanted them to be exposed, he wanted them to put the false nobles out into the marketplace, and only then be arrested."

"I find them, they escape—but that is by the way, for the main thing is that they are unveiled. My task was to expose the forgery. My task was to be so blunderingly clumsy, so obvious, that all of Venice would know that there were counterfeit coins and a massive forgery had taken place."

Luca's face was white and bitter. "He knew that I would go after the scent like a stupid hound—showing everyone where I was going, a hue and cry all on my own."

"The coins bled," Ishraq pointed out. "That exposed the Nacaris, not us."

"We were going to expose them," Freize said. "Brother Peter insisted on it. Those were the orders. The coins bled the night before we would have reported them. We had all agreed to obey Milord's orders. They would have been exposed one way or another."

Luca nodded. "The bleeding coins made no real difference," he said. "They were the flaw in the Nacaris' work. But the Nacaris would have been unveiled by us and reported."

"And then the price of the nobles collapses." Ishraq was thinking aloud with Luca. "As soon as everyone knows they are forged. As soon as we are arrested."

"And everyone wants to sell, and the doge sets a tiny price, a price for scrap metal."

"And everyone sells, but Milord commands us to buy," Ishraq said. She tapped her hand on the table as she suddenly realized what she was saying. "Because he must know that some of the nobles are good. Some of them will be old coins from England, they will be good. We tested them, we know that they are good. Perhaps all the coins that came from the Calais mint were good. And if we buy up all of them, good and bad together, then some of them will be worth six times the price that we pay for them."

"And we will have made Milord a small fortune," Luca breathed.

Brother Peter bowed his head. "The Church," he said. "We will have made a small fortune for the Church. We must be glad of it. It is holy work to make a fortune for the Church. These have been dark days, but perhaps we have done the right thing."

"But the Ottomans . . ." Ishraq said slowly.

Luca switched his gaze to her. "What about them?"

"They are sending back the bleeding nobles, and they are accepting a reduced tribute. They believe that they were paid in worthless coins. They have been cheated of their tribute, they have been hugely cheated of the fee they draw from the conquered lands. They are settling for a reduced fee this year."

"They should not have it, they should not collect it in the first place!" Brother Peter burst out. "They deserve to be cheated. It is God's work to cheat them!"

Ishraq ignored him, and she looked at Luca. "Milord has struck a powerful blow at the very heart of the Ottoman Empire," she said. "If this is his crusade, he has had a powerful victory, thanks to you They may have won Constantinople, but this year they are much the poorer."

Luca nodded. "Bayeed is poorer too," he said. "He rejected the ransom, but some of the coins must have been good." He paused. "And my father suffers for it," he said. "My father suffers for this brilliant trick, and so do so many others." He shook his head. "So many, many others."

Freize looked from one to another. "So what do we do now?" he asked into the silence.

Nobody spoke, and then slowly the four young people realized that there would be orders. One by one they looked toward Brother Peter. "I know that when our work here is successfully concluded, we have to ride north," Brother Peter volunteered. "I am to open the orders later, but we are to set out northerly."

"And what's in the orders, then?" Freize asked bitterly. "For I don't think we can bear to succeed again like this. Luca has lost his father, Isolde has lost her fortune, and we have sickened ourselves of Venice."

Ishraq rose from the table and opened the shutters. A cold morning light came into the room, making the candles look tawdry. Isolde blew them out.

"We have completed our work here?" Luca looked older in the gray light from the windows. "Another successful mission?" he asked bitterly. "Our enemies cheated of their money, some people made bankrupt, my father still enslaved, his heart broken and I am disowned by him. He denied me.

He called me a changeling and dishonored my mother and me. We have accomplished all that Milord wanted? We can leave? Our work is done? We should be happy?"

"Often, it is hard," Brother Peter said quietly to the younger man. "You are walking a solitary path in hard country. Often a victory does not feel like victory. There is a great work of which we are only a small part. We cannot tell what part we play. We have to trust that there is a great cause that we serve in our own small way."

Luca bowed his head over his clasped hands and closed his eyes as if he were praying for courage.

"And I wonder where the alchemists have gone," Isolde said, speaking for the first time since Luca had called them all into the room. Luca raised his head and looked at her. "I wonder where they have been ordered to go," Isolde said. "For they have their patron, who gives them orders, just as we have Milord."

There was a silence as Isolde, and then all the others, realized what she had said.

"They have a patron who they don't know," she went on wonderingly. "He commanded them to come here and to make the counterfeit coins, he commanded them to make the alchemy coins. He ordered that they should find the secret of life. He sent them here, and then Milord sent us after them."

Slowly, Luca rose to his feet and went to the windows.

There was a little paler strip of cloud to the east where dawn was beginning to break.

"They said they had a patron who was no friend," Ishraq supplemented. "They never saw his face, but he sent them orders and gave them the recipe for the false nobles. He gave them the chests of the good nobles too. He told them to make a market for the coins and then swell it with forgeries."

"Do you think that it was perhaps Milord who commanded them?" Luca asked, speaking almost idly, not turning back to the room but staring out of the window at the silvery canal and the black cormorants sitting on the water and then suddenly folding their wings and plunging below for fish. "Do you think that Milord ordered both the counterfeiters and those that were to unveil them? Did he command both the hind and the hounds. Do you think he played both sides at once?"

"Perhaps to him it is a game." Isolde came and stood beside him and put her hand on his shoulder. "Like the cups and ball that Jacinta played. Perhaps Milord has quick hands too, and nobody can see what he is doing till the end of the game. Perhaps he has cheated us all."

They rode out of Venice heading north, the warm spring sun on their right-hand side. Brother Peter led the way with Luca behind him, Isolde at his side. Behind them came Freize and Ishraq, and the little donkey heavily laden followed Freize's big cob Rufino. Another donkey came behind the first, also carrying sacks of gold nobles. Some of them were rusting away inside the leather purses, but in every rusting coin there was a heart of solid gold. Milord's great gamble would pay off.

Everyone was happy to be leaving the city behind them. Brother Peter was glad to be in his robes again and not living a lie, Ishraq was reveling in the freedom of being on the road and not cooped up as a Venetian lady companion, Isolde was setting off to her godfather's son with renewed determination and Luca was heading for his next inquiry with a sense that the world was filled with mystery—even his own mission puzzled him.

"Are you glad to leave Venice?" he asked Isolde.

"It is the most beautiful city I have ever seen," she said. "But it has a darker side. Do you know I saw the strangest thing as we were going in the ferry to fetch the horses?"

"What did you see?" he asked, eager to be distracted from his own sense of failure and loss.

"I thought I saw a child," she said seriously. "Swimming in the water, after our boat. I nearly called out for us to stop. A little child coming after us, but then I saw it was tiny, no bigger than a little fish, but swimming and keeping up with the ship."

Luca felt himself freeze. "What d'you think it was?" he asked, trying to sound careless. "That's odd."

She looked at him. "I assumed I had seen a pale-colored fish and made a mistake. There could be nothing in the lagoon like a tiny person?"

He contained his own shiver of superstition and leaned toward her to put his hand over hers. "I won't let anything hurt you," he promised her. "Nothing can come after us. And there couldn't be anything like that in the waters."

Trustingly she let his hand rest on hers, slowly she smiled at him. "I feel safe with you," she said. "And at least Venice taught me to stand up for myself."

He laughed. "Will you protect me, Isolde?"

She was radiant. "I will," she promised.

"And did you learn to choose the one you love?" he asked her very quietly.

"Did you?" she whispered. "Do you even know who you chose?"

Luca gasped at her teasing and laughed aloud, glancing back to see that no one was in earshot.

Behind them, completely deaf to their low-voiced conversation, Freize was wordlessly delighted to be reunited with his horse. Gently, he pulled Rufino's thick mane, patted his neck and sometimes leaned forward to stroke his ears. "You would not believe it," he remarked to the horse. "No roads! No fields! No forage nor meadows, not even a grass verge for you to have a quiet graze. "What sort of a city do you call this?" I asked them. They could not answer me. For sure, a city that has no room for horses cannot thrive. You must have missed me. Indeed, I missed you."

The donkey behind him was dawdling. Freize turned in the saddle and gave it a little admonitory whistle.

"The dross of the coins is rusting away," Ishraq observed, riding alongside him. "It is dripping from the bags as we go. At this rate we will be left with saddlebags of gold."

Freize was distracted from his conversation with Rufino. "He's a clever man, that Milord," he said. "What an engine to set in motion! Devious."

"He's made himself a fortune, but I think his main aim was to cheat the Ottomans." Ishraq observed. "And in this round of the battle between him and Radu Bey, I think he has won."

"Because they were forced to accept only a third of the tribute?"

"Yes," she said slowly. "But best of all for him would be—don't you think?—that he made fools of them. He tricked them into sending back good gold. He made them think it was all bad. He tricked us, he tricked Venice, but really he tricked them. That is what will infuriate them worse than the reduced tribute. He tricked them into sending back good gold. He destroyed the reputation of the coins, and then we bought them. He made fools of them. It really is fools' gold."

Freize shook his head at the mendacity of the man. "He is a cunning man," he said. "Deep. But I know that I'd like to ask him one thing."

"Only one thing? I'd like to ask him lots of things," she agreed. "What would you ask?"

"About this world," Freize said thoughtfully. "A man like him with so much knowledge? I'd ask him whether he truly thinks that it might be round, as the pretty girl said."

She nodded, without a glimmer of a smile, as thoughtful as he was. "Freize, you do know that the sun stays in the same place all the time, night and day, and the world goes round it, don't you?" she asked.

"What?" he exclaimed so loudly that Rufino threw up his head in alarm, and Freize soothed him with a touch. He looked at her more closely and saw her smile. "Ah, you are joking," Freize decided. "But you don't fool me." He pointed to the comforting sun, slowly rising up in the sky toward the midday height and shining down on him as it had always done. "East to west, every day of my life," he said. "Never failed. Course it goes round me."

Ahead of them, Brother Peter started to sing a psalm, and the other four joined in, their voices blending in a harmony in the cool air as tuneful as a choir. Freize put his hand in his pocket, seeking his little whistle to play a descant, and suddenly checked.

"I had forgotten! I had quite forgotten!" he exclaimed.

"What?" Ishraq asked, glancing over to him.

In answer he drew a coin from his pocket. "My lucky penny," he said. "The lass, Jacinta, the gambling girl, put it back in my pocket the last time I saw her and wished me luck with it. I had quite forgotten it. But here it is again. I shall be lucky, don't you think? After all that has passed, to have it returned to me as a gift from her must make it more lucky than ever."

"Why did she have it?" Ishraq asked. "Did you give it to her?"

"She took it from me and then returned it as a keepsake," Freize said. "Gave me a kiss for it." Without looking at it closely, he passed it over to her. Ishraq took it and then pulled her horse to a standstill. "I should think you are very lucky," she said oddly. "Very lucky indeed. Look at it."

Isolde glanced back and, seeing that they had stopped, called to Brother Peter and halted her own horse. The older man rode back, and they all gathered round as Freize took his lucky penny from Ishraq and examined it.

"You know, it does look very like gold," he said quietly.

"But it is the one I gave to her, I swear it. I would know it anywhere. It is my own lucky penny, I recognize the mint and the date, it is mine without a doubt. Just as I gave it to her. But now it looks like gold."

"Enameled with gold," Brother Peter said. "She put a skin of gold on it for you. Another pretty trick."

Without a word, Freize handed it to Luca, who took a knife from his belt and made the tiniest of nicks in the side of it. "No," he said. "The same color all the way through. We can test it properly when we get to an inn, but it looks like gold. It looks like solid gold."

There was a silence as they each absorbed what this meant.

"You are certain it is your lucky penny and not another gold coin that she gave you?" Isolde asked.

Mutely, Freize passed it to her. "The penny. My lucky penny. Minted in the Vatican in the year of my birth. She would not have such another. She *could* not have such another. It must be mine. But now it is as heavy as gold, and soft as gold, and golden as gold."

"Did they do it, then?" Ishraq wondered. "They really did it? They found the philosopher's stone that can change everything to gold, and they turned Freize's penny to gold?" She nodded to Luca. "D'you remember they said that they had one more step to take and they would be able to refine any matter to gold? Perhaps they did it, on this one coin, and we were in the room where they did it. They made true gold from dross. They really did."

"And the Venetians drove them away," Isolde said. "Sent them into exile with the secret of how to make gold in their pocket."

"We gave them the boat!" Freize exclaimed, his voice cracking on a laugh. "We helped them to run away with the secret of a fortune, the secret that alchemists have never yet found."

"And not just that. They had the secret of life itself," Ishraq reminded her. "The philosopher's stone, which makes gold, leads to the philosopher's elixir, the elixir of life that cures death itself."

"And we lost them," Luca said, staring at the coin in his friend's hand. "We were standing by the forge where they had made the secret of life itself, and we let them go, and then we ran away. We have been fools indeed. We have been the greatest fools of all."

Freize tossed the coin high in the air, and they watched it turn and glint in the bright sunshine and fall heavily, as a solid gold coin will fall. He caught it with a slap of his hand, shook his head in wonderment, and put the coin back in his pocket. "Fools' gold," he said. "Fools indeed."

Ishraq smiled at him. "Do you still think you're lucky?" she asked. "Is it still a lucky penny? Since a woman with the secret of eternal life and the secret of how to make gold gave it to you, and then she went away forever? With her secrets safely with her?"

"Said I had a true heart and then turned into my grandmother," Freize reminded her. "Gave a little monster into my keeping, which frightened me to death. Strangest girl I have ever kissed. But am I lucky? I would say so."

Luca clapped him on the shoulder with sudden brotherly affection. "Still lucky," he said. "Always lucky. Not hanged for alchemy, not drowned in the flood. The sun going round him, his feet on a flat earth. A golden penny in his pocket. Freize is born lucky. Always lucky!"

"Born to be hanged," Brother Peter said, but he smiled at Freize. "No fool."

AUTHOR'S NOTE

I hope you enjoyed *Fools' Gold* and that you go on to explore anything that struck you as odd or interesting in the story. Some of it is based on historical truth, some of it is based on old beliefs, and some of it is made up.

Luca, Isolde, Freize, Ishraq and Brother Peter are fictional characters—as are all the other characters they meet in this novel—but the world they inhabit is very like the medieval world of 1454, and some of that wonderful world survives today. You can go to Ravenna and see the rainbow mosaics in the tomb of Galla Placida or you can look for the images online. They are still there, perhaps sunk a little more deeply into the damp soil of Ravenna than at the time of Luca's visit.

The Venice that Luca and his friends discover is still there too, of course. Though the modern day Venice is served by a railway and an airport, and the islands are built-up and merged one with another, the gardens for which medieval

Venice was famous are now squares and quays and pavements, but you can still see the medieval paths and canals and you can visit the doge's palace, which they were building when Luca was there and is now completed. You can even take a tour through the winding wooden corridors where Luca was led for questioning, and you can see the double soundproofed door into the secret rooms, and the cell where Freize was held prisoner.

I am going to write more about the lives of Jews in the medieval world but the experience of Israel as a money changer was typical of the lives of many of the Jews of Venice. They had to live in a designated closed area known as the "ghetto," meaning "workplace," and they suffered persecution—blame for when things went wrong, and exploitation during good years. The villain of Shakespeare's play *The Merchant of Venice* would recognize the difficulties that Israel expressed in getting Christians to pay their legitimate debts to him and surviving in a hostile world. But at least Venice was tolerant enough to allow anyone to live and work in their city. In a few decades' time from the date of this novel, the Jews would be expelled from Spain and banned from many other European countries.

The description of the alchemists in this story is based on the history of the times, and you can find out more about alchemy from my website. Alchemy was a sort of medieval chemistry—it gave its name to the science—and many of the earliest experiments of what we would now call science were done by brilliant thinkers who would have called themselves philosophers or alchemists. Some of them believed that they had discovered the philosopher's stone, and have left persuasive accounts of their work. The Voynich Manuscript, which Drago brings to Luca, is a real document—it has still not been translated or understood. I chose not to try to explain away some of these unsolved riddles. I wanted to leave Jacinta and Drago and their work as something of a mystery. And some things are still unknown. And here I have to thank Mr. Mark Robinson and Mr. Mark Edwards of the Physics Department at St. Peter's School in York, who helped me understand gold density.

At the heart of this book is the dangerous and erratic market for gold nobles. This is a fictional story, but the history of capital has included many enthusiasms and scares that have made and lost fortunes. In the western world we are in the middle of a slump that followed a boom right now, and in some ways the bundling of paper debt and the selling of it at an unreal price is like the other events in history that economic writers call "a bubble"—because it always goes pop. I have written before about the great excitement around the tulip market (*Earthly Joys*, 1998) and here I am writing a fiction about a market for gold nobles created and destroyed by Luca's mysterious boss, Milord.

You can read more about him, and about our four young adventurers, Brother Peter and even the horse Rufino in the next Order of Darkness book, which I hope to write and publish in 2014. You can find out the title and when it is due and all about my other books on my website, PhilippaGregory.com.

Philippa Gregory

PHILIPPA GREGORY